Kingdom of Secrets

Fae Touched

Claire Leggett

BANTILLY
PUBLISHING

First published by Bantilly Publishing in 2022

Kingdom of Secrets: Fae Touched

EPUB format: 978-1-925696-91-2
Print: 978-1-925696-92-9
Large Print: 978-1-925696-93-6

Cover design by Get Covers
Edited by Ann Harth
Proofread by Teena Raffa-Mulligan

About the Author

Claire Leggett has loved dragons, magic and everything fantastical since she read The Enchanted Wood by Enid Blyton. As a child she used to sneak to the bottom of the garden in the hope of finding fairies. Alas she never found any, so she brought them alive in her own imagination. Her stories are full of magic, adventure and escape.

When Claire's not writing she can be found creating her own handmade journals, swinging on a sidecar, or in the garden attempting to grow something other than weeds.

Claire lives in Western Australia with her husband, who loves even her most annoying quirks, and is currently learning how to crochet.

You can connect with Claire by joining her reader group.

(http://www.claireleggett.com/reader-group/).

Also by Claire Leggett

Part 1
Tartalan

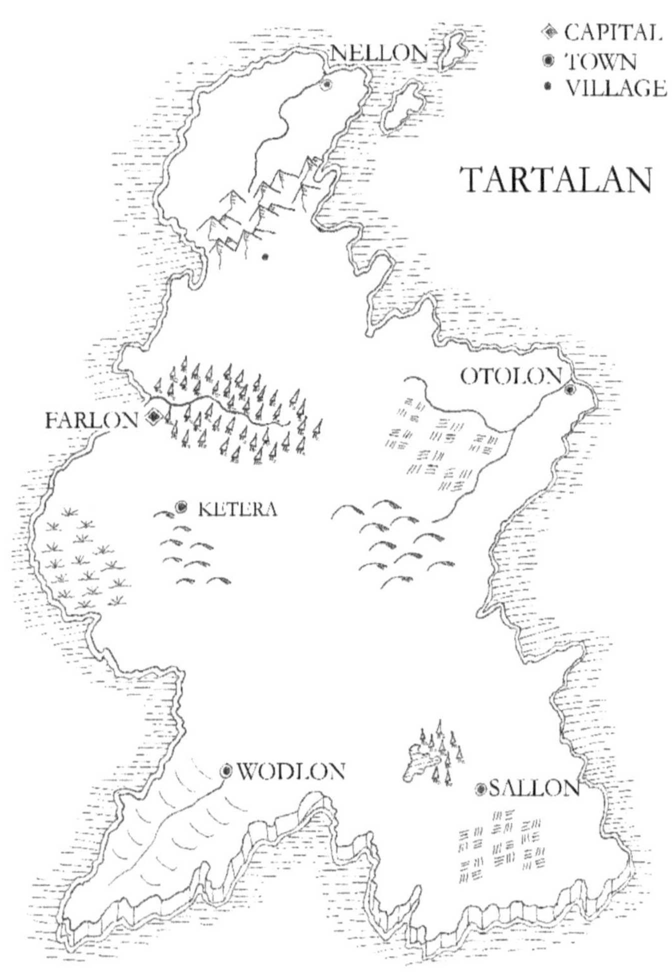

CAPITAL
TOWN
VILLAGE
NELLON
TARTALAN
OTOLON
FARLON
KETERA
WODLON
SALLON

Chapter 1

The door crashed open, jerking Prince Darrien from his sleep. He groaned as sunlight hit his eyes, and the pain from last night's drinking session pierced him.

"Darrien, you're going to be late," Hadden called.

Darrien would revoke his friend's privileges in the castle for waking him so abruptly, especially after the night he'd had. "Late for what?" he groaned. "Can't you see I'm suffering?"

"Late for the court trials." Hadden threw back the curtains.

Nerves clashed with the nausea already swirling in his stomach, and he felt a violent urge to vomit. He had hoped his drinking binge the night before would have somehow magically prevented him from having to sentence these people. People he didn't know, people whose crimes seemed insignificant. "Can't Captain Pelham preside?" He pulled the blankets over his head.

"It's Freedom Day," Hadden pointed out. "Only a member of the royal family can pardon people."

Darrien groaned again and wished the bed could swallow him. It was his nightmare brought to life. Everything he'd done up until now had been to avoid having to pass sentence on one of his subjects. And on today of all days, he'd be stuck inside a dark hall listening to the arguments of criminals who wanted to be free, instead of enjoying the celebrations and perusing the market stalls.

Frantically he thought of alternatives. "Can't Kerwin do it then?" His younger brother was the only other royal left on the island—his babysitter, while the rest of his family were in Sylta celebrating his aunt, the Queen of Sylta's, fiftieth birthday. If he could convince Kerwin, Darrien could defend his title as reigning champion of the mock final battle and be as far away from judging these people as possible.

"He's at the harbour overseeing the celebrations there," Hadden replied.

The covers jerked back, and Darrien stared at the slight disdain on his friend's face. Guilt and embarrassment joined the nausea, and he fought the urge not to squirm as he sat up. "Got any nastin plant?" The magic elixir cured most common ailments, but the fae controlled its distribution carefully.

"Here." Hadden handed him a mug.

Darrien swallowed the bitter, lumpy contents in three gulps and grimaced. Nasty stuff, but at least it worked. The thumping in his head faded immediately. If only the nastin would get rid of the nerves shouting in his mind too. He struggled out of bed and went to his wardrobe, wincing as Hadden rang the bell for his valet. The man entered upright and efficient as always, and hustled past Darrien to pull out the green suit. Behind him came servants carrying a metal tub and several buckets of water. How long had they been waiting out there?

"Do I have time for a bath?" Darrien asked.

"You need one," Hadden said. "You stink like a tavern."

Darrien sniffed his armpits and caught the stench of underarm odour and ale. He recoiled and with a sigh, he stripped, not caring if the servants or his friend were in the room. He climbed into the cool water and washed himself. With his valet scrubbing his back, and a team of assistants scurrying about, it took little time for Darrien to bathe and dress. Hadden hurried him out the door.

"Captain Pelham will be waiting."

Let him wait. The officious man had never approved of Darrien, had worked him twice as hard as anyone else when Darrien had done his twelve months of mandatory military service. Nothing Darrien did would change Pelham's opinion, plus it gave Darrien immense pleasure to annoy the man.

He was halfway to the Great Hall when his stomach rumbled. He tried to detour towards the dining room, but Hadden stopped him. "I'll have food brought to you."

Darrien scowled. "Who put you in charge?"

"You." Hadden grinned. "Last night. You said I had to get you to the courthouse on time, or you'd smear me in fish guts and dump me in the ocean for the grolin."

Darrien frowned. He didn't remember saying that, but he couldn't remember much of last night. They'd been to a tavern in town, had a few drinks, and he remembered something about a drinking game. "How many people do I have to judge?"

"Thirty."

Thirty names. There had to be a way to get out of it, but his mind wasn't cooperating this morning. Why was it that he could come up with a dozen tactics to avoid the enemy when taking part in the re-enactment of the final battle, but couldn't think of a single excuse to avoid presiding over the trials of a few commoners? He hunched his shoulders. "Tell me there are at least some pretty women to look at."

"A whole list of them," Hadden assured him.

That was something. Was it wrong to hope for

attractive criminals?

"You're late!"

Darrien groaned at Kerwin's voice. His brother stood in a nearby doorway, his golden suit an assault on Darrien's hungover eyes. Darrien squinted to block the brightness. "What are you wearing?"

Kerwin straightened the bottom of his jacket, affronted. "It's the latest fashion."

"Then remind me not to be fashionable this year." The suit looked good on his younger brother, fitting him to perfection, and the colour suited his lighter colouring.

Kerwin tilted his nose the way he did when he wasn't amused, and Darrien's mood plummeted further. Kerwin still hadn't forgiven him. "I'm here to remind you to be very careful with Littleton's case. He's got a lot of supporters."

The thought of dealing with Sinclair Littleton was one of the reasons Darrien had gone out drinking. "I remember," he said. "Don't suppose you want to preside in my stead?"

"Father said it had to be you. I'm going to the harbour to ensure everything is ready down there." He walked with Darrien to the Great Hall. "You know what you have to do." With a pat on Darrien's shoulder, Kerwin departed.

Did he really? Kerwin had always loved their classes and had embraced the responsibility of being a royal. Darrien had never seen the point. He'd constantly been reminded he was learning this in case something happened to one of his older brothers, but since Tartalan had no enemies, little disease, and had been at peace for five hundred years, the chance of him becoming king was extremely low.

Outside the Great Hall, several guards and the herald waited. The guards pushed open the great launda wood doors, and the herald announced, "His Royal Highness,

Prince Darrien of Tartalan, Presiding Magistrate."

The swirl in Darrien's belly intensified. He cursed his father and Kerwin. He wasn't born for this. He was the third son of the king, and the Crown Prince had a baby on the way. No one expected anything from him, and he'd done a good job making sure it stayed that way. All that responsibility, the effect he could have on a person's life by a mere word, was too much power. He could easily get it wrong. And yet, for some reason his father insisted he take responsibility. Foolish. Darrien had always been the one to make mistakes.

Darrien swallowed as the hall full of his subjects waited and watched. Far too many onlookers. Were they all here to see him fail? The playboy prince who could never do anything right. Perhaps they were tired of the re-enactments and wanted a better show.

He could do that. He'd been putting on a show his entire life. He squared his shoulders and strode into the hall.

***

The dank walls of Brigette Silksmith's cell were covered in a green mould that had initially discouraged her from leaning against them. However, over the weeks she'd been in there, her resolve faded, as had the hope her brother would rescue her. The wall became a support to hold her up when she was weak from hunger or despair, and the green mould had become part of her dress, almost like war paint, or more accurately like the mark which identified her as a criminal.

No one cared about her innocence.

At least they had segregated the genders. She shivered. The stench of stale urine floated down the corridor from the men's cells. Here, the bucket was emptied every couple of days, and the women used it rather than urinating on the floor like she'd seen a man do when she'd been marched down the corridor and into her cell.

Bree tugged on her long, brown plait. Each morning she defied her situation by combing out her hair with her fingers and braiding it again, using a little of her drinking water to wash her face and hands, but the longer she was here, the harder it was to motivate herself.

She'd done nothing wrong. Her attacker should be rotting in here.

"You're thinking again, Bree," Solain said.

Bree glanced over at the spice fae, whose hair was as red as the bellar spice in the region she came from. The guards were supposed to refresh her bucket of spice, and ensure she had bellar bread to eat each day, but they hadn't, and Solain had faded, her skin growing pale, and her hair lank and dirty. Fae needed to be connected to their region, or they died.

"There's not a lot else to do."

"What are you going to do when you're freed?" Solain asked.

It was a game Bree didn't like to play. She'd been assumed guilty even though her clothes were torn, and she'd been half-hysterical. What chance did she have when the judge saw her in the grey prison dress? She huddled her knees up to her chest and rubbed her arms. "Do you really think that's going to happen?"

"You did nothing wrong," the fae said. "Me, on the other hand…"

Solain had punched the overseer of the bellar spice fields when he'd taken more than his quota of spice. Unfortunately, he'd fallen and broken his arm, and since the incident hadn't occurred on fae land, she'd been arrested. She was looking forward to voicing her concerns about the growing lack of respect for fae sovereignty at the hearing. She hoped to shame him and the exporter he worked for—if she was strong enough to speak when the hearing arrived. Maybe that was why they kept the spice from her.

"Depends on the judge," another woman said. "I heard rumours Prince Darrien was presiding. He doesn't take anything seriously. He's likely to throw you in gaol for a lark."

"At least he's pretty to look at," Solain said. "Prince Kerwin is a sour, humourless sort."

Bree had never seen either prince. She'd spent most of her life in the launda forest, only moving to the capital city of Farlon six years ago when her father opened a silk shop. She scowled. That move marked the beginning of all her troubles, though she hadn't known it then. She'd enjoyed access to the city library, and her mother continued teaching her although it wasn't usual for girls to be well educated. Bree had just taken her exams to get into university when her mother had betrayed her, running off with another man and deserting them all. "Perhaps the king will be home by then." Bree knew better than to rely on a man to help her. After her mother had left, her father had changed, becoming bitter and controlling, not allowing Bree to leave the house unless escorted by her brother or her father. Her daily excursion had been to clean the shop after hours and return straight home afterwards. Her university dreams were a thing of the past.

Solain laughed. "Queen Matana's birthday celebrations will last weeks."

A guard jangled along the corridor, stopping outside their cell. "Your hearing is scheduled for this morning. You'll each be given a clean dress, but you must wash those you are wearing before you leave." With that proclamation, he unlocked the cell and two boys brought in a tub of water, setting it on the ground. The guard handed a pile of clothing to one of the women. "Sort them out amongst yourself. You have an hour."

Bree's stomach clenched. After so many days of waiting, wondering, and fearing, the hearing was here. The other women gathered to get their fresh clothes, and one simply stripped what she wore and dunked it into the water, sitting on the ground in nothing but her underclothes.

Bree shivered. She didn't want to change, didn't want to be judged, didn't want to hear her sentence. Was there even a chance she would go free when her accuser was the wealthiest and most influential merchant in the city?

One woman washed her dirty dress, but splashed water all over her clean outfit. Bree crawled forward. "Let me," she said. "Hand me your dirty clothes, and I'll clean them before I change."

She scrubbed the dresses, wringing them out and then handing them back to their owners so they could hang them on the line the boys had erected.

"Bree, you need to do your own dress," Solain said. "They'll be back soon."

Bree brushed the loose hairs out of her face. "Only one more to go." She handed the outfit to the waiting woman and then stripped off her own dress. The women formed a circle around her so no guards walking past would see her in her undressed state. "What happened to your back?" Solain asked.

She cringed. She'd forgotten about the scars on her back. Those from her father's belt after her mother had left, as if Bree was to blame for it. Now the simple placement of his hand on his belt was enough to halt any of Bree's dissent. "Nothing."

Keys jangled and steps echoed down the corridor. She scrubbed harder at the stains on the back of her dress. She shouldn't have leaned against the wall so much.

"Quickly," Solain urged.

Bree wrung out the cloth and handed it to Solain to hang. Another woman gave her the last clean dress, which she slipped over her head. It was so wide she could have made two dresses out of it, and it fell to her calves, leaving her ankles bare. Her father would be horrified. Only the fae wore clothing which showed off their legs. All the other women had found a better fit. The guard unlocked the door. Bree exhaled, smoothing down the dress, trying to get a little more length out of it.

"Hands out," the guard ordered. They stood in a line, hands in front, and he clamped chains around their wrists, joining them all together. "This way."

Bree was last in the line as they filed out of the cell and along the corridor. "You can leave them in our cell, guard," one of the male prisoners yelled.

"Yeah, we know how to punish them," another called, grabbing his crotch.

Bree flinched and kept her head down, mentally urging the women in front to walk faster. Men were such base creatures, controlled by their emotions, with lust and anger the strongest. They cleared the cells and walked into a lighter, cleaner room. The walls were still stone, but had nothing growing on them, and uniformed men worked at the desks inside. The watchmen. Bree spotted the man who had arrested her, and anger pierced her so fast it took her breath away. He hadn't asked for her side of the story. It was his fault she was here. Filled with outrage, she stepped towards him, only to be brought up by the pinch of the chains on her wrists. What was she doing? She couldn't confront him here. Not without making things worse.

Stepping back into line, she lowered her gaze and shuffled along until they exited the building. She blinked against the bright sunlight. The courthouse was across the yard, but instead of leading them there, several more men joined the guard, surrounding the prisoners on all sides and marching them out of the gate.

"What's going on?" Solain asked.

"It's Freedom Day," the guard replied. "The prince will hear your cases in the castle's Great Hall."

Freedom Day. A celebration of the end of the war between Tartalan and Molanka five hundred years ago. The irony wasn't lost on Bree. People filled the streets waving the Tartalan flag, a brown launda tree on a green background. Some jeered as they walked by, but most were too busy celebrating to notice. Bree's face heated. What if she saw her neighbours, the Feathwaites? Had they returned from visiting family? Had her father told them what had happened?

Just as she was about to lower her gaze, she spotted a familiar boyish-looking face in the crowd. "Samuel!" Surely her brother would come to her defence, would tell the guards they had arrested the wrong person. Perhaps he'd been arguing for her release since she was imprisoned.

Sorrow filled Samuel's expression. Though she couldn't hear him, she could read his lips. "I'm sorry." He turned away.

Shock froze Bree. He wasn't going to help her? They hadn't been close since her mother had left, but she had cooked and cleaned for him, and they'd spent pleasant evenings together. As long as they never mentioned her mother, and Bree did exactly as she was told, things were peaceful at home.

The chains jerked her forward, and she stumbled, falling hard to one knee on the cobblestones. Pain shot up her leg and brought tears to her eyes as she struggled back to her feet and limped to catch up.

If Samuel wouldn't help her, then her father wouldn't either. The only other family who might speak of her good name were her father's parents, but they lived in the launda forest and might not even know of her predicament. She hadn't seen them since her mother had left.

She was doomed.

Bree stared at the dark cobblestones until they reached the castle. They were led through a side gate where people were setting up market stalls, and paused outside a large wooden door. Her shoes had once been white silk, but they were now the grubby green and brown of the cells. Her father would be upset with her for letting them get so filthy. She grimaced. As if that was her biggest concern. Right now, she'd welcome the strapping if it meant she was free of these chains.

A castle guard came down the line, checking that the chains were secured. His green uniform was impeccable, with the mark of a captain on his shoulder, and his brown eyes showed no sympathy as he rattled the manacles.

Finally, they were permitted entry into the palace. When she'd first come to the city, she'd fantasised about being invited to the castle. It looked so grand and imposing, overlooking the harbour on a raised piece of land. It could be seen from all points in the city, a sentinel standing guard, protecting the people of Tartalan.

Entering the castle in chains hadn't been part of her childish fantasies. The stone corridor was cold, and the chill seeped through her slippers as she hurried along after the other women. The prison guard had picked up his pace, and they were led into a room where the captain waited.

"Sit." He gestured to a long wooden bench along one wall. As they complied, he continued, "You will be unchained one at a time and led into the Great Hall where His Royal Highness, Prince Darrien, will hear your case. If you are found not guilty, you will be taken to another room to retrieve your possessions, and then led from the castle. If you are found guilty, you will be sentenced and immediately returned to the gaol."

Bree clenched her hands together. This was it. She wouldn't even discover how the other women fared until she was back in gaol.

No, there had to be some hope.

The prison guard unlocked the chains of the first woman in the line and the captain led her away. Bree closed her eyes and prayed to the Holy Trinity—the Shelterer, the Nourisher, and the Purifier—to protect her.

It didn't take long for the hard wooden bench to become uncomfortable, but Bree didn't dare fidget or shift in case it made her seem guilty. In all the books she'd read before her mother had left, the culprit always did something to give away their guilt. So she waited, and counted the number of paving stones on the floor. None of the women spoke. When it was Solain's time to go in, Bree smiled and nodded encouragingly. Solain shrugged and walked out, head held high. Someone had given her a bucket of bellar spice, and already her colour looked better.

That's how Bree should be. Confident, with nothing to be ashamed of. But would others see it as proof she was the charlatan Mister Littleton had accused her of being?

The woman next to Bree was unchained, and soon Bree was the only female left in the room. Her wrists chafed from the weight of the chain which now lay along the length of the wall. The prison guard paid her no notice, nor did the two palace guards at the door, but being alone, chained at the mercy of the men, made her stomach swirl. If they wanted what Mister Littleton had wanted, she wouldn't be able to fight them off. She shrank back against the wall, wishing she could turn invisible. Time slowed. Either the woman before her had a lot of accusations to address, or perhaps the prince had decided he needed a break. It had to be close to midday.

Her gaze flittered from the men at the door to the prison guard and back again. None of them appeared interested in her, but then again, Mister Littleton had simply said good evening before he'd attacked. She shuddered.

The door opening made her flinch. The captain walked in, and the prison guard unlocked her chains. "You can return to the gaol," the captain said. To Bree he said, "This way."

She followed him into a wider corridor that turned a few times before arriving at a door.

"Name?" the captain asked.

"Brigette Silksmith."

He raised his eyebrows and looked her up and down. "Right." He pushed open the door and announced, "Miss Brigette Silksmith." He signalled to a chair at the front of the room. "Sit there."

She willed her body to move forward but it resisted every step, her movements slow and jerky, as she made her way towards the lone wooden chair. To distract herself, she scanned the room and immediately wished she hadn't. She was in a grand hall with an arched ceiling stretching high above her. The stone flooring had a design on it, the symbols of the six fae groups in a circle. Behind her lone chair sat hundreds of well-dressed people, as if waiting for a show. She flinched. *She* was the show. They were here to see her sentenced and perhaps pass judgement of their own.

Several of the women glared at her with disdain, so she tore her gaze away. In the other direction was a dais with a throne. Lounging on it as if it was a divan and not the representation of power in the island country was a man no more than four or five years older than Bree. His black hair was styled in a gravity defying coif, which she'd seen many men in their twenties wearing. The cut of his jacket and pants was also of the latest fashion, that which her father was regularly requested to emulate. But it was his direct gaze, the way his brown eyes travelled from her eyes, down her body to her naked ankles and back again, which made her feel as if she wasn't wearing anything at all. He was the same as all men. She crossed her arms over her chest as she reached the chair. Was she supposed to curtsy to the prince?

The prince shifted, sitting a little more upright, and his smile was almost gentle. Bree didn't trust him for a minute, though her body reacted of its own accord, warming to the kindness in his gaze. She stared at the ground.

"Sit down, Miss Silksmith."

She assumed the rich, warm command came from the prince and did as he asked, pulling her dress as far over her knees as it would go.

"The plaintiff, Mister Sinclair Littleton," the captain announced.

Bree flinched, but shifted her gaze to watch as her attacker stood from the crowd and strolled up next to her. Confidence oozed from him, and Bree had the urge to scrub herself clean.

"Mister Littleton, you accuse Miss Silksmith of assault and attempted theft," the prince said. "Please tell me what happened."

Littleton cleared his throat. "It was the night of the storm," he began. "I was hurrying home when I saw a woman over by the copse of trees on the central green. She appeared to be hobbling, and I was concerned for her safety, so I approached to make sure she was all right and had a place to go out of the weather."

Someone in the crowd murmured, "What a kind man."

Bree's eyes widened. That wasn't what happened.

"When I arrived, it was Miss Silksmith. I asked if she needed help, and she said she could help me with something, and then grabbed my crotch."

Bree gaped at him.

Littleton chuckled as if embarrassed. "I thanked her politely and told her I wasn't interested. That's when she attacked me, punching me in the groin and trying to steal my money bag. I didn't want to hurt her and fortunately, the night watchman arrived to help. Mistress Silksmith stopped fighting and started crying, saying I attacked her." He shook his head. "She's such a good actress, she almost convinced me."

The crowd tittered behind him.

Bree's entire body froze, and she rubbed her arms. Why would anyone believe her over him? He was a very influential member of society and her father had longed to receive silks from Mister Littleton who always brought the best stock from the silk valley. Perhaps that was why neither her father nor her brother would support her. Littleton could force her father out of business.

"What happened next?" the prince asked.

"The night watchman arrested her, and I returned home to get out of the storm."

Prince Darrien nodded. "Thank you, Mister Littleton. Miss Silksmith, can you tell us your version of events?"

His gaze was direct, speculative. Did he think she was a thief as well?

Slowly she stood, her heart pounding. "Yes, Your Highness." She curtsied. Every moment of that night was burned into her memory. She inhaled to calm her rapid heartbeat. "I was on the way to my father's silk shop to clean that evening. Normally my brother escorts me, however they received a late shipment of silks, and had to unload it before the storm hit." When she'd received the message from a messenger boy, she'd been elated. A chance to go out on her own, maybe pause for a moment or two in front of a shop front and peruse the wares. "As I crossed the green, Mister Littleton was walking towards me. I greeted him and he hauled me against him, and said he needed a warm body tonight."

She shuddered as his phantom fingers pressed hard against her skin. She'd had bruises for days, but the guards hadn't cared. Swallowing, she then continued. "He picked me up and threw me over his shoulder, carrying me towards the copse. I screamed for help and tried to free myself, but he was too strong, and there was no one around to hear my cries."

"What a vicious liar!" Whoever said it didn't make an effort to keep their voice quiet, and the prince glanced at the crowd.

"Quiet."

Bree clenched her hands to stop the trembling. "He threw me on the ground and unbuttoned his pants. I kicked out and hit him between his legs. The night watchman approached and after hearing Mister Littleton's accusations, he arrested me."

The prince nodded. "Can we hear from the night watchman?"

The man walked out and stood next to Mister Littleton. "Your Highness, I was patrolling my area, helping people prepare for the storm and making sure they got home safely. I saw two figures over by the trees on the green, but it was getting dark and difficult to see. I ran over as Miss Silksmith kicked Mister Littleton."

"How did they both appear?"

"Mister Littleton was in pain and Miss Silksmith was crying. Mister Littleton asked me to arrest her for assault and told me what happened, so I arrested her."

The prince frowned. "Did you not ask for Miss Silksmith's version of events?"

The night watchman shifted. "No, Your Highness. The wind had picked up, and it was raining pretty heavily. We all needed to take shelter, and I knew Mister Littleton was an upstanding citizen. I could call on him for more information in the morning, whereas Miss Silksmith was unknown to me."

"Do you have anything else to add?"

"The next morning, I visited Miss Silksmith's residence and spoke with her father. When he heard what happened, he disowned her, said she deserved what was coming to her."

Bree gasped and fell back onto the chair. After everything she had done for him, this was how he repaid her? A tear slid down her cheek and she didn't bother to brush it away.

"Could you find anyone who would speak to her good name?" Prince Darrien asked.

The man shook his head. "Her immediate neighbours weren't home, and no one else knew her."

"Why is that, Miss Silksmith?" the prince asked.

Her cheeks flamed. "My father prefers I stay at home, Your Highness. Our neighbours, the Feathwaites, are friends, but they were visiting Mister Feathwaites' ill sister. I don't know whether they have returned." And their son, Gideon, worked somewhere with the army. What would he think of her being arrested like this?

Prince Darrien leaned back on the throne and steepled his fingers. Bree lowered her gaze as she awaited his decision.

Suddenly a bell clanged from outside. The crowd murmured, and the prince rose to his feet. A guard burst through the door. "The harbour is under attack!"

Immediately the palace guards formed a perimeter around the prince. The crowd stood, each looking at the other as if waiting for someone to make a decision.

Bree stayed seated. Who would attack the harbour? Tartalan had no enemies. It traded with the mainland countries and had strong ties with Sylta because the king's sister was the queen there. It made no sense. Perhaps it was a Freedom Day re-enactment.

"We must get to the harbour," Darrien called. "Kerwin was down there."

Bree raised her gaze, and the fear on Darrien's face struck terror in her. This was real. Someone was attacking Tartalan.

A tremendous bang rang through the hall and the soldier at the door turned. "They've breached the castle."

Almost as one the crowd surged forward, some heading for the main doors, others to those on the side. Bree stood where she was. Would one of the guards stop her if she fled?

Littleton was gone, lost in the mass of people, and at the throne the prince fought with a man who had been in the crowd. "Hadden, let go of me," the prince yelled. "I'm going to the harbour."

"The king ordered me to protect you," Hadden responded. "We're leaving the city."

"I won't leave my brother or my people."

The door behind them burst open and a dark-haired nobleman charged in. "They're overrunning the city."

"Help me get him out of here," Hadden commanded. "Darrien, we've got to regroup. If Kerwin has been captured, you're in charge."

Darrien's face paled, and then he nodded. "Let's go." They ran out of the door the nobleman had entered, followed by the palace guards.

Bree spun around. No one paid her any attention. She wasn't staying here for enemy soldiers to arrive. She ran to the door the prince had exited and pried it open. Shouts came from down the corridor to her right, so she headed left. This corridor was narrow, possibly a servants' passage, and she jogged along it, not wanting to run headlong into a fight.

The corridor twisted and turned until she had no idea which way she headed, but she reached an open door into an empty kitchen. The fire still burned and the stench of burnt food filled Bree's nose. Without thinking, she seized a heavy cloth from nearby, moving the burning pot from the flames. Someone might be able to salvage it later. She placed it on the stone ground and then opened the door opposite, peering outside. People scurried in both directions, fear or determination on their faces. The fighting hadn't reached this area yet.

Her heart pounded. She would go to the launda forest, warn her grandparents about the attack, and they would know what to do.

The sun was directly overhead, giving her no clue as to the direction she should go, but a breeze brought with it the scent of the ocean. That way would be west. She moved in the other direction, joining the flow of people. So many of them were dressed in their finest clothes and didn't seem to know where to go. They were possibly townsfolk who'd come to the castle for the festivities. Freedom Day was the one day a year when the gates were thrown open and everyone was invited.

A perfect day for attack.

She rounded the side of the building. Market stalls were set up in long rows and bunting hung from posts, but people weren't browsing. Here soldiers in red fought guards in green, and common folk were hiding, or running towards the gate opposite Bree.

Red was the colour of Molanka. Why would their neighbour attack them?

An arrow whistled past her, and she ducked back behind the wall, her pulse racing. She couldn't stay here. Safety lay outside the city in the launda forest. She had to be brave, like the warrior, Caitlyn from the legends of old. Taking a deep breath, she peeked around the wall and mapped her passage to the gate. Now.

She sprinted to a tipped cart, its rich red apples spilling across the ground. She gathered two in each hand and then crossed to a nearby stall, taking cover from its wall. And so she crept closer to the gate, moving from stall to stall, her focus on the gate and escape into the city.

"Argh!"

She flinched and ducked out of the way as a soldier and guard crossed in front of her, swords ringing against each other. The guard in green dropped his sword and the red soldier swung.

Bree threw an apple, hitting the soldier square in the chest. The shock of the impact was enough to make him hesitate, and the guard gripped his weapon and thrust it through the soldier's chest. The man fell to the ground, his dying eyes locking on Bree. She fought the urge to be sick.

Her chest squeezed. The guard grasped her arm, shaking her out of her daze. "Get out of here, girl. Go hide in your home." He shoved her towards the gate, and she ran, darting around the fighting and then she was out of the castle grounds and running down the long road which led into the city.

Smoke rose from the harbour and below, the streets were full of fighting and people fleeing.

The eastern city gates, the most direct route to the launda forest which beckoned in the distance, were closed. The other gates most likely were too. But she couldn't go home and risk her father or Samuel sending her back to gaol. How else could she leave the city?

The launda trees on the green towered far above the houses. Before her mother ran off they used to spend afternoons sitting under a launda tree on the southern side of the city. A tree she used to climb to see over the city walls.

She ran down the road, taking the first street left. Her side ached from the exertion, but she dare not stop. Not with the chorus of screams and wails around her. If she was caught, Mister Littleton would seem like a minor inconvenience.

Bree turned a corner and crashed into a large, hard

person. He grunted and turned, his red uniform screaming danger. Before Bree could move, his hand whipped out and clamped around her wrist. "What have we got here?"

The street was empty.

From behind him another man appeared. "Looks like a lush wench to me. We've cleared this section of the city. I reckon we deserve a reward."

Her breath caught. No. No, she wouldn't let this happen to her again. She struck, thrusting her knee directly into the man's crotch and he bellowed in pain, letting go of her wrist. She ran, her feet slapping against the cobblestone ground, pain ricocheting up her legs as her slippers couldn't protect her from the hard ground.

Footsteps pounded behind her, but she didn't look over her shoulder. If she could get to the tree, she'd be safe.

Something hit her feet, and she stumbled, tumbling onto the hard ground. She shrieked, but before she could get up, she was jerked around and found herself face to face with the pair who had attacked her.

"Help!" she screamed.

The soldier she'd hit laughed. "No one's going to help you. They're all cowering inside, or dead."

His friend was already unbuttoning his pants. "Drag her down that alley just in case someone has delusions of being a hero."

No, Trinity help her. This couldn't be happening to her again.

She fought, but the man was too strong. He captured her arm and dragged her along the cobblestones down a space between two houses.

"Don't get to your feet, wench," the friend said. "You're right where we need you to be."

Bree screamed again.

Chapter 2

Darrien plucked another arrow from his quiver. Only two left and then he'd have to use his sword. He aimed at a Molankan soldier who had his sword raised, about to strike a Tartalan guard and released the arrow. It struck his enemy in the heart, killing him. Darrien blocked the revulsion. He had no time to be soft, had to pretend they were animals he hunted, not humans. They had invaded Tartalan and were killing his people. He reached for another arrow, his horse jostling between Hadden's and one of the palace guards' horses as they fought in the street. They'd been forced away from the harbour by the surge of the invading army. It grated to be heading in the opposite direction from his brother, but there was fighting here, and people he had to protect.

An ear-splitting scream wrenched his attention to an alley nearby. He nudged his horse closer, his bow raised. Inside were two enemy soldiers standing over someone on the ground. The woman screamed again as one soldier unbuttoned his pants.

Fury welled in Darrien, and he released his final two arrows in quick succession. Both men fell forward, one on top of the woman. She struggled, weeping, but was not strong enough to push him off. Darrien dismounted. "Watch my back," he ordered Hadden.

He withdrew his sword in case the soldiers weren't dead, but they didn't move. He hefted the man off the woman, and she scrambled away from him, her drab prison-grey dress capturing his attention. His eyes widened.

"You're having a terrible day, Miss Silksmith." Who would fathom her being attacked again? She probably considered her stunning features, almost fae-like in their delicacy, a curse not a blessing. Not even the ugly, shapeless dress she wore could hide her beauty.

He held out his hand and after a moment of hesitation she grasped it. She weighed next to nothing as he pulled her to her feet.

She snatched her hand back and curtsied. "Thank you, Your Highness. I'm sorry for running from the palace. I didn't know what to do."

He almost laughed. They were under attack and she was worried about going to gaol. "I was going to pardon you anyway," Darrien said.

Her eyes narrowed. "I wasn't guilty."

He liked her spark. He had seen no hint of it during the trial.

"Darrien, we've got to move," Hadden yelled.

He hesitated. He couldn't leave her here. "Have you got somewhere to go?"

She nodded. "I'm going to the launda forest."

"You can't. The gates are closed. No one can leave the city." Which meant hopefully they could keep the enemy inside. If he could get a message to the water fae, they could fetch reinforcements from the other ports around the country. He frowned as a horrific thought occurred to him. The water fae shouldn't have let an enemy ship through the reef. Had they betrayed Tartalan?

"I know a way out of the city." Brigette's words captured his attention.

"Where?"

She pointed south.

"Show me." He grabbed her hand and pulled her to his horse. She struggled, fear in her eyes. He swore and let her go. "I won't hurt you. I need your information. Consider it a royal command. Show me how to get out of the city."

She exhaled. "All right." She let him lift her onto his horse. He mounted behind her, trying to ignore the way her buttocks pressed against his groin. "Take the reins," he ordered.

He kicked his horse into a trot, and Hadden and his guard fell in beside him.

The Molankan hadn't made it further down this street, though Darrien withdrew his sword and held it at the ready. People stood outside their houses, uncertainty on their face. "Men, make your way to the nearest barracks," Hadden called. "Women and children barricade yourselves inside."

What was the point? They were woefully under prepared. Darrien prayed whatever the Molankan soldiers wanted, they wouldn't hurt his people once they had control of the city.

They reached the southern wall. A huge launda tree grew nearby, its branches high above spreading shade over a large area.

"We're here." Brigette swung her leg over the front of the horse and slid down. She hurried to the tree trunk and moved around its base, running a hand over its bark. Darrien frowned. What did she think they were going to do—climb it? The trunk ran straight up past the height of the city walls before it branched out. Ten people could encircle it, arms outstretched, and still their hands wouldn't join. There was nothing to hold on to in order to climb the Shelter-cursed thing.

Brigette disappeared from view and then a moment later she was back, gesturing to them. "They're still here. Quickly. Ask the tree's permission to climb."

Perhaps her time in gaol had muddled her mind.

Hadden dismounted and followed her back around the tree, out of sight.

"I ask this tree's permission to climb and beg its forgiveness if I hurt it." Her voice rang out loud and clear.

Yes, definitely a little cuckoo. Only the fae communicated with trees. He nudged his horse around the side. Brigette was already a person's height off the ground. She glanced at him. "There are notches in the bark."

Darrien gazed up. A long way to fall if they slipped. But the only other choice was fighting the men at the gate.

"Bree? Are you sure it's safe?"

She glanced at the palace guard, her eyes wide. "Gideon, what are you doing here?"

"Protecting the prince."

She smiled. "I used to climb this tree when I was younger. It's quite safe."

Gideon nodded and stepped back.

"I'll go next," Hadden said.

"How do you know Brigette?" he asked Gideon.

"She was my neighbour before I joined the guard."

And Brigette had said her neighbours would speak for her good name. "I need to speak with the water fae. You need to gather up as many men as you can and head out the eastern gate. I'll meet you at the launda forest."

Gideon shook his head. "I'm sworn to protect you."

"And I'm sworn to protect my people. To do that I need as many men as possible. Get them out of the city. The Molankan might not have reached the eastern gate yet."

Gideon hesitated then nodded. "The fighting is getting closer. You should go now."

Brigette was three-quarters of the way up, and Hadden wasn't far behind. Darrien dismounted and unstrapped his saddle bag, slinging it over one shoulder. It was always full of supplies because he liked to sneak out of the city whenever he could and go camping in the forest. "Take our horses."

"Yes, Your Highness."

Brigette was at the first branch now and she'd swung her leg over, so she sat on it as if it were a horse. She shuffled along its length towards the wall. The branch of a launda tree on the other side of the wall almost reached the stone. Was that their way down the other side?

"Good luck," Darrien said. He hoped he wasn't sending Gideon to his death by not taking him along. He strode over to the tree and searched for the first notch. The bark was rough, but flat with no handholds.

Running his hand over the trunk, he searched in vain for any lump which could be the first hold.

"Ask for permission," Brigette called.

Weird. What had she said? "I ask this tree permission to climb and beg its forgiveness if I hurt it." As he said the words, his fingers bumped a notch. Goosebumps prickled his skin. The launda fae didn't discuss their relationship with trees but spoke as if they were sentient beings. Which, if he thought about it, would give him nightmares every time he sat at his wooden writing desk.

He climbed quickly, each new notch appearing as he needed it, without requiring him to stretch for it. He peered down to make sure Gideon had left, and then increased his pace. By the time he reached the first branch, Brigette and Hadden stood on the wall and Brigette was pointing to something. Hadden leapt, landing awkwardly over the opposite branch. He kicked and strained but managed to swing up and sit on the branch.

Darrien reached the wall and climbed down next to Brigette. There were no walkways along the walls, no need to defend from outside forces, because there were only a few places on the island people could land. The harbour of Farlon was the only one on this side, and the other ports had a similar defence. The walls were meant to keep people in, as per the treaty with the fae, not out. Not far away the ocean glistened in the midday sun, but there was a headland between this beach and the Farlon port. He wouldn't have to worry about Molankan soldiers on this side.

"Are you going to jump?" Darrien asked.

Brigette hugged herself. "It's a lot further than I remember."

And she wore a dress which would hinder her movement. "You can do it." If she fell, she would be seriously injured. "Do you need to ask it for permission?"

She nodded and with a shaky voice, she repeated the request. A breeze fluttered the dress. What she needed was a belt. He unbuckled his and handed it to her. "Tie this around your waist and use it to pull your dress higher."

Her cheeks reddened, but she took the belt. There was no way she was guilty of Littleton's accusations. As she adjusted the fabric so it folded over the belt, Hadden called, "Darrien, you go next. Show her how to do it." He had already shifted down the branch, so he was almost at the trunk.

Darrien wouldn't leave her behind, not when she'd helped them escape. "Follow right behind me, all right?" He waited until she agreed and then Darrien asked the tree for permission and leapt, hitting the branch mid chest. He clung on and swung his leg over. He reached his hand out to Brigette. "Now you."

She jumped, but she didn't have the power behind her leap. She wouldn't make it. He lunged for her hand, brushed her palm and grasped hold. He slid sideways as her weight pulled him down. They would both fall.

Suddenly her weight lessened, and he hauled her towards him. She clutched the branch and dragged herself on to it, hugging it with her arms and legs. She panted, eyes wide and fearful.

Tarta, that was close. His heart raced. "Come on, Miss Silksmith. Keep moving, we don't want the enemy to spot us." The shouts of fighting were getting closer. He shuffled back towards the trunk to give her more room. "Brigette, follow me."

"Bree," she said. "My name is Bree." She straightened, determination in her gaze, and she shuffled towards him.

"That's it. Keep going." Her speed forced him to move faster. Hadden was already on his way to the ground. Darrien headed down the trunk, Bree right behind him. His breath huffed from him as his feet touched the ground.

"There's no one around," Hadden reported. "It's mostly coastal scrub we have to cut through."

"We need to get to the ocean. I want to know why the water fae let an enemy into the harbour."

Bree reached the ground and hugged the tree. "Thank you."

Definitely a little strange.

"Which way?" Hadden asked.

"The ocean," Darrien said. Bree shifted away, looking east towards the launda forest. "Bree, are there any trails near here?"

She flinched as if caught and cleared her throat. "There used to be a path down to the beach." She pointed. "And there's one which meets the eastern road out of Farlon and goes to the launda forest."

"Show me the path to the ocean."

Her steady gaze held a hint of defiance and she glanced back towards the forest.

Now wasn't the time for her to assert herself. "Why do you want to go to the launda forest?"

"My grandparents live there."

She would be safe there. "All right. Show me to the beach, and then I'll see you're taken to your grandparents."

"Thank you." She moved past him and explored the area until she said, "Here it is."

The trail was overgrown, but there was a gap. Hadden took the lead, pushing through the branches, and Bree followed him with Darrien bringing up the rear.

They pushed through the dense undergrowth. Now and then he caught glimpses of what appeared to be small houses, but when he blinked they disappeared. Maybe he was losing it. It reminded him of the tales his mother used to tell him of the Tarta, the little people for whom the island was named. Legends said they had convinced the fae to help Captain Farlon, who'd discovered the island.

The scrub fell away, and the soil became sandy. Darrien strode out onto the soft white beach and straight down to the water, not caring if his boots got wet. "I demand to speak with High Elder Lachlan." He spoke aloud and also pushed his thoughts out as his father had taught him. Next to him, Bree had taken off her shoes and was knee deep in the water, washing her arms and her face. She probably hadn't bathed in weeks.

He shook his head and focused on the water. "High Elder Lachlan, show yourself."

The water rippled, and a fae breached the surface, his long hair like green and black weed and his skin with a silver shimmer to it. "Who are you to order the king's presence?"

"I am Prince Darrien. I demand to know why he let an enemy through the reef to attack Farlon."

The fae frowned. "We let your father's ship through the reef."

Darrien's mouth dropped open. "My father?" That couldn't be right. "He's in Sylta for my aunt's birthday." Dread filled him. Had his family been captured by Molanka?

Concern crossed the fae's face. "Wait here." He dove back into the water with a splash of his tail and disappeared.

It had been a fortnight since his parents and older brothers had left for Sylta. If Molanka had killed them, it would make him king.

He swore, and for the first time, genuine fear crept in.

The fae returned, water running down his bare chest. "It was your father's ship, but no one has seen him or the rest of your family. The guards assumed he was returning from Sylta and didn't stop to question it."

The relief soothed the fear. Maybe they were still alive. There was time for the ship to have arrived in Sylta and returned. It could have been stolen from the harbour.

The water rippled again, and another fae appeared, this time wearing a crown of coral. As he stood, his body morphed from scales to skin, his tail becoming legs with only his private area still covered in scales. Darrien inclined his head. "High Elder Lachlan."

"Prince Darrien. My apologies for breaching our agreement. I will speak with those responsible."

"How many ships are there?"

"Five. I estimate three thousand sailors."

The garrison in Farlon couldn't hold that many at bay.

"I've sent scouts to check the surrounding seas and I've sent messengers to the other ports to warn them," Lachlan continued. He glanced behind Darrien and his eyes widened. "Brigette."

She gasped and curtsied. "High Elder."

"How do you know her?" Darrien asked.

The king was silent a moment and then answered, "Her mother introduced her to me when she was a baby."

Strange. The water fae normally kept to themselves. Who was Bree's mother?

"What will you do about the invaders?" Lachlan asked.

Darrien had no idea. "What will you do?" he countered.

"While they are on land, we can do little. My people can't spend too much time away from the water or they weaken. I will double the guard to make sure no more ships get through."

It was too late now. He closed his eyes and tried to bring the lessons of Captain Pelham to mind. Communication was key to any successful battle. "How will you get word to me if more ships are coming?"

"Brigette can tell you." Lachlan took her hand and pressed his thumb into her palm. She flinched, and when he withdrew his hand, she had two dark, wavy lines, almost like a birthmark on her skin.

"What did you do?" Darrien demanded. "She's not staying with us."

"She must. It's the only way I can relay messages." To her he said, "Press this mark and think of me. I will hear your thoughts. When I need to speak with you, this mark will tingle and you will hear me."

No, Darrien wasn't putting her in danger. He thrust out his hand. "Give the mark to me. We're taking her to her grandparents."

Lachlan shook his head. "It can only be Brigette. I must go. My people need me." In a splash, he was gone.

Darrien waded over to Bree and grabbed her hand, pressing the mark. "Come back. We're not finished."

Bree winced and yanked her hand back, her eyes wide. "He said it's not a toy to be played with."

"I didn't hear anything."

She placed a hand to her head. "He spoke in here."

He hadn't paid enough attention in class when he'd learnt about the fae. He hadn't known such magic existed.

"Darrien, we might get a good look at the harbour from up there." Hadden pointed to the headland above them.

Bree waded out of the water. "There's a lookout," she said. "It must have been an old defence post, because there are catapults up there." She glanced at Darrien. "Mother used to take us there for picnics. You can see all the way to the launda forest from there."

"Where is your mother now?"

She shrugged, her face red. "I haven't seen her since she ran off with another man two years ago."

That wasn't the behaviour of a fae, so maybe Bree wasn't fae. They were fiercely loyal to any they loved. He remembered that from his lessons because he'd vowed never to seduce a fae. He didn't need the grief.

"Let's go," Hadden said. "We should be able to see what's happening in the city and then we can make plans."

Darrien gestured for Bree to lead the way. She scooped up her dirty slippers and strode along the sand towards the headland. They would have to find her more clothes and some decent shoes, since he would have to keep her with him.

The guilt was sharp. Already he'd stuffed up. He should have taken her straight to her grandparents. How was he meant to make important decisions?

The path up to the headland was a little wider than the trail they'd followed to the ocean. Perhaps it was used regularly. He was panting by the time they reached the flat ground at the top. He walked slowly around the area about two hundred paces wide, partially to control his breathing, but also to examine the magnificent view.

The ocean stretched out in front of him in one direction, and the dark green of the launda forest in the opposite. Below, he had a perfect view of the harbour.

It was eerily quiet. Five large ships docked alongside smaller fishing vessels and merchant vessels. The jetties were empty save a couple of bodies lying on them, probably dead. A few bodies floated in the water and as he watched a fin appeared and circled one. Then a water fae appeared, taking hold of the body and dragging it away. The grolin circled the next body, dressed in red, and then dragged it under with a snap of its jaws.

Darrien shivered.

"Lachlan says his people will collect the Tartalan bodies for burial," Bree said. "He's giving the Molankan bodies to the grolins as a reward for not eating our people."

His skin prickled. He couldn't live next to such vicious creatures.

Closer to the gates into the city there were further signs of fighting, more bodies lying on the ground, and red uniformed men patrolling the area. The harbour had been taken. Behind the wall he could see fewer battles, as if his people had given up.

Where was Kerwin? He'd been down at the harbour today, making sure all the preparations were in place for the afternoon's re-enactment ceremony.

The pavilion lay broken at the end of the longest jetty, some of its structure tilting towards the water. Underneath it lay a body dressed in gold.

Darrien froze. No, it couldn't be. Kerwin said it was the latest fashion, so it would be someone emulating his brother. "Hadden." He pointed.

Hadden always carried a telescope on him. Swore by it.

The click of the device sent a chill through Darrien, and he held his breath.

"It's Kerwin."

Darrien spun to Bree. "Contact Lachlan. Get one of his people to help him." He refused to consider his brother was dead. Kerwin would have been in Sylta with the rest of his family, if his father had trusted Darrien to rule on his own.

"He's going personally," Bree reported.

Darrien's gaze didn't waver from his brother's body, searching for some minute movement which would prove he was still alive. Lachlan launched out of the water and hauled himself onto the jetty, his skin glistening in the sun as it changed. He was followed by two more fae who helped him shove the structure away from the body. Lachlan squatted and turned Kerwin over. The dark stain on his chest was clear even from here. Darrien stumbled back, not needing to hear Bree confirm what he knew.

Kerwin was dead.

His youngest brother, the one he'd teased regularly, but loved for his gentle and structured ways, was gone.

And it was his fault. If he'd proven he could be responsible, Kerwin would be safe in another country. This was more evidence he couldn't be trusted with responsibility.

The grief threatened to overwhelm him, but a movement on the docks, a soldier in red, captured his attention. It didn't matter if he wasn't ready. He was all Tartalan had.

Darrien had to take charge. He swallowed hard,

bracing his shoulders.

The Molankan would pay.

Chapter 3

The sun glistening off the water in the harbour seemed like a harsh mockery of the death lying on the docks and in the water below. Bree's heart ached as Lachlan's words echoed in her head. She swallowed hard, wrapping her arms around herself, before repeating them for Darrien. "I'm sorry, Your Highness, Prince Kerwin is dead."

He said nothing, standing there, staring down at the harbour.

She glanced at Hadden, who also waited for a reaction.

Nothing.

Goosebumps leapt to her skin. This silent, still prince reminded her of her father the day her mother had left. She had scars from the explosion that followed. She backed away. She wouldn't ever let a man beat her again.

Bree, what's going on?

She flinched at Lachlan's voice in her head. How was she supposed to get used to it? *Darrien hasn't said anything.*

He'll be in shock. I heard some of the Molankan guards mention more ships are coming. I've sent fae to confirm.

She dare not disturb Darrien with the news yet, not with him coming to terms with his brother's death.

Hadden lifted his telescope and scanned the city. "Darrien, there are soldiers outside the eastern gates."

Darrien whirled. "Ours?"

"Yes, they're wearing green uniforms. Heading for the forest."

"Gideon must have got them out. We need to meet up with them," Darrien said. "These invaders need to pay."

His tone gave Bree chills. The faster she got away from him, the safer she'd be. "Ah, Your Highness."

His glare turned on her.

She took a couple of steps away from him. "Lachlan believes more ships are coming. He's sending scouts."

"Tell him to stop them entering the harbour this time."

She relayed the message and got the mental equivalent of a grunt back. Tarta! Being forced to communicate between two royals felt far more dangerous than sitting in a dark, dank cell.

"Darrien these catapults could be of use," Hadden said, stripping a creeper off one of them.

"They've got to be centuries old."

"Yeah, but they're covered in launda resin," Hadden said.

The resin increased the longevity of the wood so fewer trees had to be cut down. It was part of the agreement with the launda fae.

Darrien joined him and together they uncovered the catapult. They inspected the gears and the arm still swung back. "All we need is ammunition."

"Like boulders?" Bree asked, pointing to a mound covered in more creeper.

Hadden grinned. "Yep."

"Let's sink some ships," Darrien said.

Hadden shook his head. "We want them to leave," he pointed out. "No ships, no way to leave."

"So we kill them all."

She jolted. Three thousand men. Men who were acting under their king's command. Practically innocent—except for the two who had attacked her. She would not be party to such slaughter. The prince could find someone else to be his messenger. Bree moved away from him, her gaze drawn to the way back to the beach. Maybe she could slip away without anyone noticing. They were still focused on the catapult and the harbour.

"Darrien, you need a plan," Hadden said. "Perhaps we can negotiate."

"They killed Kerwin." His voice shook with pain.

Bree stopped at the edge of the lookout. He was grieving, and he had saved her from the soldiers back in the city. Until they received word from the other ports, Darrien was on his own. How could she justify deserting him? Tartalan was her home too, and the invaders wouldn't stop at Farlon.

"We need to find some horses, and more arrows," Hadden said. "Then we can meet up with the force in the launda forest, and by then Lachlan should have news from Otolon and Nellon. We can arrange a consolidated attack on the city and win it back."

When Darrien said nothing, Hadden waited patiently. Bree moved to the other catapult and began coaxing the creeper from it, uncurling its hold on the wood, but trying not to hurt it.

"We need to get word to my parents," Darrien said. "Bree, ask Lachlan if he can send a message."

She pressed her hand and repeated the request.

I will need to form a circle with my family, and my sons are on their way to the other ports. A ship may be faster.

"We don't have any ships available," Darrien pointed out.

"There'll be one at another port," Hadden said.

Bree calculated the day. "There might be a ship at the

Silk Valley basket," she said. "It anchors offshore until the ocean is calm and then collects the silk."

"How do you know?" Darrien asked.

"Father is a silksmith. He always complains when the silk is late because of rough weather and it's almost every week." The quickest way to transfer silk from the valley to Farlon was by sea, but steep cliffs surrounded the area. A large basket had been erected over the cliff for the silk to be lowered to a jetty at the base, but boats could only get close enough when the weather was calm, otherwise they'd be crushed against the rocks. Even with the weather potentially delaying it, it was faster than transporting it overland.

"Tell Lachlan."

She repeated the message, and he promised to check.

"How can we write a message?" Hadden asked. "We've no paper, and no royal seal, so your parents can verify it's from you."

"Mother always said my terrible handwriting was instantly recognisable," Darrien said. "We just need paper." He dumped his saddle bag on the ground and searched through it but came up empty handed.

Someone cleared their throat behind them and both Darrien and Hadden whirled around, hands on their swords. Bree turned more slowly, fear tightening her skin, picturing a Molankan army at her back.

Instead, her gaze was drawn down to a one-foot-tall person with green hair and overalls made from launda leaves. The person inclined his head at Darrien. "Prince Darrien, I am High Elder Meldrick of the Tarta, here to offer my people's assistance against the Molankan invaders."

Bree blinked. She'd thought the Tarta were a myth, or had died out long ago. She knew of no one who had actually seen them. Quickly she curtsied to the small elder.

Darrien stared at the man until Hadden elbowed him. With a frown, Darrien acknowledged the Tarta. "My Brother, I'm afraid you've caught me off guard. I didn't realise your people still existed."

Meldrick nodded. "This was our agreement with King Farlon and his ancestors after him. Only the king knows so he can keep our towns protected and secret, however we connect with each of his heirs when they are born so we can come to their aid if needed." Meldrick glanced towards the harbour. "You may need our aid now."

"What can you do against armed soldiers?"

Meldrick puffed his chest. "We may be small, but we are many. During the last war we helped King Farlon gather information on the enemy."

Darrien appeared dubious and Hadden bemused. Of course they would dismiss the Tarta because he was different from them. Bree had years of being dismissed because she was female, and trying to please her father had got her arrested and abandoned. She wouldn't let these people feel the same hopelessness. Bree curtsied again. "My Brother Meldrick, if I may speak?"

Meldrick nodded. "Of course, Brigette."

How did he know her name? "We need to send a message to King Jerek who is in Sylta. Could you get us parchment and ink?"

He smiled. "I'll send my people now." He twisted, murmured something as if there was someone behind him. Perhaps there was. If the Tarta moved unseen, there could be countless numbers of them on the lookout now. Bree crossed her arms and moved a little closer to Darrien.

A moment later two Tarta appeared, both wearing armour made from launda bark. One carried a piece of parchment almost the same height as him, and the other carried an ink pot and quill. They bowed to Meldrick.

"Here you are," Meldrick said, gesturing to his men.

Amazing. Bree crouched and took the items. "Thank you." She handed them to Darrien. "Your Highness."

His mouth gaped, and he shut it with a snap. "Thank you." He looked down at the harbour and then back at High Elder Meldrick. "Can you find out what's happening in the city? I want to know who is commanding the attack."

"It's King Tremont of Molanka," Meldrick answered. "He's taken up residence in the castle."

That was quick. It couldn't be more than a couple of hours since they landed.

"I'll write a message for you to take to him." Darrien strode over to the low wall to write his notes.

Meldrick's eyebrows raised.

"Please," Bree added for Darrien. "I'm sure his Highness is thankful for your help. He just discovered his brother, Prince Kerwin has died."

The Tarta's expression morphed into one of sadness. "My condolences. May I ask if there is anything else I can do for you?"

"Can you find us horses?" Hadden asked.

"Yes. I'll send my people to fetch some." He gestured to one of his soldiers and the Tarta disappeared.

It was incredible. How did they vanish and travel so quickly? Bree itched to ask, but she didn't want to offend them.

"Which water fae are you connected to?" Meldrick gestured to her hand.

She rubbed her thumb over the mark. "High Elder Lachlan."

"Will you tell him I'm preparing my people?"

If the fae knew about the Tarta—why didn't humans? She sent the message to Lachlan.

Tell Meldrick I'll visit him by evening. We've found the silk merchant ship. Does the prince have a message to send?

Yes. He's writing it now. I'll bring it down when he's done. My people will be waiting.

"High Elder Lachlan says he'll visit you this evening," she told Meldrick.

"Good." He glanced at Darrien who was still writing. "I must prepare my people. They are frightened. We'll move inland towards the mountains or the launda forest."

"Where do you live now?" Hadden asked.

"We have a town in what you see as scrub below." Meldrick pointed. "As well as other villages in areas where humans don't wander. King Jerek has a map of them in his study." He pressed the remaining Tarta soldier forward. His yellow hair was the colour of spring blossoms and seemed almost as wispy. "This is Joden. I've assigned him to stay with the prince. He can communicate between us and will answer any questions the prince has about our people. He can also take the message to Tremont." Meldrick inclined his head. "A pleasure meeting you, Brigette." He disappeared.

"That will take some getting used to," Hadden said.

Bree agreed. What did it mean for her privacy? No, thinking about it would only upset her. She smiled at Joden. "I'm Bree, and this is Hadden. Nice to meet you."

Joden saluted. "Likewise, though these aren't the best circumstances." He glanced over at Darrien. "We've found horses, but it's best they don't climb up here. They may be spotted."

"Darrien, we should go," Hadden called.

Darrien blew on the parchment in front of him. "I'm done." He stood. "Where's Meldrick?"

"He had to go and help his people," Hadden said. "Joden is his ambassador."

Darrien rolled up both messages and handed one to Joden. "Take this to Tremont immediately. Wait for his response."

Joden scowled and raised his eyebrows at Bree. "Yes, Your Highness." He disappeared.

The prince strode to the path. "We need to get this message to the water fae."

Bree hurried after him. "Lachlan found a ship which can take it," she told him.

"Good."

He and Hadden moved faster than Bree, and she fell behind, her slippers useless on the rocky path. She slipped and winced as sharp points dug into the soles of her feet. The silence was broken by rustling in the bushes. Her heart leapt, and she lengthened her stride, not wanting too much distance between her and the men who had swords and could protect her. The thick brush was on both sides of the path, so it would be difficult for the enemy to pass through, but something was in there. Was it the Tarta preparing to flee?

The pain in her feet was nothing compared to the fear of being captured again. She broke into a jog to catch up with the others.

By the time she reached the shore, Darrien was handing a water fae the note he'd written, and Hadden waited on the beach next to three horses.

"Can you keep this dry?" Darrien asked the fae.

She nodded. "It will get to the ship dry and in one piece."

Darrien waded back. "We're going to the launda forest. We'll meet Gideon's team there." He scanned the area. "Where's Joden?"

"He's not back yet, Darrien," Hadden said.

"How do I call him?" He glanced at Bree as if she knew the answer.

"He never said," she told him. "But I imagine he'll return after he's completed his task. King Tremont might not react well to him suddenly appearing." She hoped he wasn't in any danger. Despite his size, he should be able to vanish—shouldn't he?

"She has a point," Hadden said. "I almost had a conniption when they showed up."

"Let's hope he's not long." Darrien mounted, and his friend followed suit. Bree hesitated. She'd never ridden a horse by herself before.

"Hurry up, Bree," Darrien said.

"I don't know how to ride."

Hadden dismounted. "Your horse should follow the others," he said. "I'll ride behind you in case there are any issues." He helped her into the saddle.

"Thank you." She had no desire to be left alone so close to Farlon. The quicker she got to her grandparents' the better.

They took a path which avoided the city and led around the scrub. The bushes continued to rustle, though there was little wind. It must be the Tarta.

The sun warmed her back as she followed Darrien towards the launda forest towering in the distance, a vast swathe of tall trees which spread halfway across the island. As they got closer, the urge to kick her horse faster was strong. The forest was safety.

Joden appeared on the horse's neck in front of her. "Mind if I ride with you?" His smile was cheeky. "You're far prettier and nicer than the others."

She jolted and then let out a breath. "You're welcome to," she said, "but don't you have to report to the prince?"

"I'd rather wait until we get into the forest. He won't like what Tremont said."

"He didn't try to capture you, did he?"

"Nah, it's not easy to do. This is our land, and it protects us. He did demand Meldrick swear allegiance to him as the rightful king of Tartalan, though. Meldrick wasn't impressed." He twisted to check where they were. "Where are you headed?"

"We saw some of the palace guard come this way, so Darrien's hoping he can find them and plan a counterattack."

"Right. I'll find out where they are." He disappeared.

Bree smiled. She should ask him if there was a way to warn them before he appeared, so he didn't frighten everyone.

They moved out of the coastal scrub and crossed the field which lay between it and the forest. Bree looked back towards the city. The gates were closed, and no one waited outside. Had word spread to the nearby villages and towns? She hoped so.

The launda trees soared above her as she rode under their canopy, and a blanket of calm settled over her shoulders. Home. The last couple of years living in the city had been the most horrible of her life, but here, in the forest, were her happiest memories. They'd lived close to her grandparents, and her family had been happy and whole. She'd spent many a morning with her mother, gardening and learning about the plants in the forest. Birds used to join them if they dug in the soil and turned up worms and insects for the birds to eat.

There was always something baking and the scent of bellar spice bread or berry cakes brought her back to this time and place. If only they'd never left.

Joden appeared again. "Can you take me to speak with his Highness?"

She placed a hand to her racing heart. "Why don't you appear before him?"

He laughed. "Bit scared I'll surprise him too much and he'll swat me like a fly."

Fair point. "Is there a way you can announce your arrival?"

"I guess, but where's the fun in that?"

She chuckled and nudged her horse faster, but it ignored her. "Your Highness!" she called.

He twisted around and she pointed to Joden. "Joden's back."

"Thanks." Joden disappeared, only to reappear on Darrien's horse. Darrien had reined in so she was able to catch up and hear what Joden had to report.

"Captain Pelham has set up camp half a league into the forest," Joden said. "I'll take you to him."

"What did Tremont say?"

Joden winced. "He's reclaiming Tartalan for Molanka and correcting the betrayal of Captain Farlon five hundred years ago. He expects your surrender by morning and for King Meldrick to swear his fealty too."

Darrien swore. "What is wrong with the man? We've always been allies."

"If I may continue, Your Highness?" Joden asked.

"Go ahead."

"I spent some time in Tremont's office listening before I made myself known. It seems his wife is ill, and he was told he would find the solution here in Tartalan. He's ordered his men to go through the library searching for a cure."

"He could have asked for help."

"From what I gathered from the conversation, he did ask for help, and also asked for additional resources, but your father refused. Tremont has ordered the food in the city to be loaded onto a boat to be sent back to Molanka. His people are starving."

Darrien frowned. "It makes no sense. My father wouldn't refuse him help if he asked for it."

"I am merely reporting on the conversations I heard," Joden said. "I'll direct you to Captain Pelham now."

He returned to Bree's horse and whispered something in its ear. It moved deeper into the forest, following a barely there trail through the undergrowth. Bree tugged on the reins to stop it, but it didn't work.

"They can follow us," Joden said. "Don't worry."

She would worry. She was going deeper into the forest towards an entire group of soldiers, and she was the only female. Her prison dress showed an unseemly amount of leg, and she had no other clothes to change into.

She inhaled deeply, the rich, sharp tang of the launda leaves filling her senses and helping to calm her. Maybe she could slip away when they arrived at camp and go to her grandparents' house. They lived further north, but she never got lost in the forest. She'd warn them about the invasion and get something else to wear.

Murmured voices came from the forest in front of her and she rode into a clearing filled with about twenty men. The one calling orders was the captain of the palace guard who had kept an eye on all the prisoners, but Gideon stood next to him. Someone shouted a warning, and they all turned to stare at her. She hunched down and Darrien rode forward. "Captain Pelham."

The man scowled and nodded a greeting.

Hadden dismounted, so Bree quickly followed, not wanting to draw any more attention. As she led her horse over to where the rest of the horses were picketed, she overheard two soldiers speaking.

"The Playboy Prince isn't taking this seriously if he stopped to bring a whore with him."

Shock filled her, and she walked faster, pressing closer to her horse.

"Maybe he'll share."

Her throat closed over. No. She wasn't being attacked again. She wasn't letting these men threaten her or control her life any longer. Bree handed her horse to Hadden and then slipped around the edges of the camp. Most men were sharpening swords or preparing dinner, but the ones who'd made the obnoxious comments watched her. Her skin crawled. She couldn't stay here. It wasn't safe. She didn't care if she was the prince's only connection to the water fae.

She was tired of being at the mercy of men.

She slipped behind one of the launda trees and ran.

Chapter 4

The launda forest was quiet, waiting, watching. Darrien always imagined it held its breath whenever humans entered. Perhaps it was a foolish fantasy, or he'd paid too much attention to the stories his older brothers used to tell him about what mysteries the fae hid in the forest. Which he'd then used to try and scare Kerwin.

Grief threatened to drown him, and Darrien fought to concentrate on Captain Pelham's words. The man's tone had always made Darrien zone out, and sorrow continued buzzing in his head, making him want to rant. He closed his eyes and shoved the grief aside. More would die if he didn't pay attention. This was all on him.

"Wodlon and Sallon garrisons will come to our aid," Pelham said.

But would it be fast enough? "You've sent word?" Darrien asked.

"Of course, Your Highness," Pelham sounded offended. "I sent men immediately, though it will be at least a week to hear back from them, and even longer for them to get here. We must prepare to besiege the city."

Pelham was wrong. It wouldn't take that long. "Joden." He looked around to find the small Tarta soldier sitting on his horse.

"Yes, Your Highness?"

"Can you send a message to all the garrisons? Tell them Farlon has been attacked and we need them to prepare for battle." He ran through possible scenarios. If they got ships from Otolon and Nellon, they'd need the garrisons outside the city to stop the Molankan from fleeing further into Tartalan.

"They should march to Farlon immediately," Pelham ordered.

Joden glanced at Darrien and he nodded, pushing down his urge to disagree with Pelham just for the sake of it.

"Of course." Joden saluted and vanished.

Surely Lachlan had received word from the other ports by now. Darrien glanced around the clearing. "Hadden, where's Bree?"

"Your Highness, now is not the time to be cavorting with women," Captain Pelham said.

Darrien bristled and bit back his flippant answer. His reputation was his own fault.

"I'm not sure, Your Highness," Hadden responded.

"Find her. I need news from High Elder Lachlan." He turned back to Pelham. "That woman is our link to the water fae. Without her, we can't communicate with High Elder Lachlan."

"That woman is a criminal," Pelham responded.

"*Was*," Darrien corrected him. "Now she's an ally and a valuable resource." He was tired of Pelham talking at him. "Tremont is claiming Tartalan as a Molankan state, and searching for a cure for his wife's illness. Maybe if we can help him find a cure, he'll leave." Wishful thinking perhaps, but he would try peaceful means to resolve this if he could. "I need a list of the best healers in the country." Which might be hard to put together. But the fae had healers, and perhaps the Tarta would too. He scanned the clearing again, spotting Hadden speaking with the soldiers, but no Bree. Had she run away?

Damn it. Joden was gone, and he hadn't asked how to contact him. A mistake. Not his first and certainly not his last.

"Tremont won't leave if we find a cure. He wants our resources," Pelham argued. "We must be ready to fight."

"We will be, but we have little information." His father always said knowledge was key. "I need to contact the launda fae." Now he definitely wished he had paid more attention in class. He walked over to the nearest launda tree and placed a hand on its rough bark. "I request an audience with High Elder Astraea." He sent out the thought as well.

Nearby soldiers snickered. "The prince has smoked too many mushrooms."

Inwardly he cringed. How in the Trinity's name was he supposed to lead these men if they had no respect for him? Perhaps he should leave Pelham in charge.

Hadden returned. "Bree's not in the camp," he reported. "One man saw her leave, but thought she was going to relieve herself."

"How long ago?"

"Just after we arrived."

Would it be quicker to send someone after her or wait for Joden to return?

"Your Highness, she might have gone to her grandparents' house," Gideon said, walking over. "They live not far away. I can check if you'd like."

Darrien nodded. "If she's there, bring her back."

"Yes, Your Highness." Gideon went in the direction Hadden had pointed.

"Have you finished talking with trees?" Pelham asked.

Darrien flinched at his snide tone and whirled to him,

lowering his voice. "You will not disrespect me in front of my men."

Pelham scowled and saluted. "Yes, Your Highness."

Damn it, everything was going poorly. This was no mock war. It was real.

"You called for me, Prince Darrien?" The quiet but authoritative voice came from behind him.

A willowy woman stood there, her long brown hair topped with a crown made from entwined twigs and leaves. He bowed in her ethereal presence. "High Elder Astraea, thank you for answering my call."

"We have invaders on our soil," she said. "What do you plan to do about it?"

It all came down to him, what he would do. He wasn't ready for this. He straightened, meeting her gaze directly, faking his confidence. "I plan to remove them," he said. "I am preparing my people now, but I need to know what help the fae can offer me."

"We are little use outside the forest," she said. "But should they make it this far, we will not let them enter."

"Do you have any healers who can heal Tremont's wife?"

"What is wrong with her?"

Darrien shrugged. "I don't know." He'd send Joden with another message and ask him.

"My healers can offer suggestions if you can get us details."

Good. "Can my people use the forest as a refuge?"

"How many?"

"All who need it."

She shook her head. "The forest cannot cope with too many people, but I shall speak with the other fae on the island, and we will find places of refuge for them all, should they need it."

It was a start. Now he needed to figure out what in Tarta's name to do next.

***

Bree ran until her side ached and her breath came in gasps, and then she slowed, taking her bearings and moving north to where her grandparents lived. She wouldn't feel guilty about running away. The prince had promised to take her to her grandparents' house if she showed him the way to the ocean. She hadn't asked to be marked by the water fae. She wasn't anyone important. She simply wanted to find somewhere safe, something she hadn't felt in a very long time. The trees were her sentinels, and she used to pretend they guarded her while she explored the forest near her house.

Finally she came across a small stream which fed into the major river running through the launda forest. She followed its banks until she smelled wood smoke in the air and then spotted the hedge which surrounded her grandparents' garden. Relief flooded her, and she broke into a run, pushing through the gate and into the yard. "Nanna! Granddad!"

As she reached the back door, it swung open and her grandmother stood there, her hair a little greyer than Bree remembered, and wearing a half apron, her hands covered in flour. "Bree! It's so wonderful to see you. What are you doing here?"

Bree flung her arms around her grandmother as tears flowed down her cheeks.

"There, there. Come inside and tell me what happened. What are you wearing?" She raised her voice. "Bert! Come quickly. Bree's home."

Home. The word made her chest constrict and the tears flow faster.

Bree let herself be led into the kitchen and accepted the cloth her grandmother handed her to dry her eyes. Her grandfather strode in, wiry as always, his blue eyes changing from pleasure to concern when he saw the state of her. "What's going on?"

Bree shook, the emotion of the day overtaking her, and she struggled to breathe. Nanna pressed a cup into her hand. "Drink this."

It took a couple of attempts to bring the cup to her mouth, then she sipped the sweet herbal mixture. The shakes slowly subsided. Her grandparents sat either side of her at the kitchen table. Where should she start?

"Tartalan has been invaded," she said. "The king of Molanka has broken the peace treaty and claimed the island for his own. He's already taken Farlon. I almost didn't escape."

Nanna gasped. "Your father and Samuel?"

Bree shook her head. "I don't know. I wasn't with them when it happened."

"Why are you wearing prison grey?" Granddad asked.

Shame filled her. She should have realised he would recognise it. "A few weeks ago, I was attacked on the green. I fought back and the watchman who witnessed it arrested me because my attacker was an influential merchant. I've been in prison since then, but today was my court case at the castle."

"Why didn't your father send word?" her grandmother asked.

"The watch said he disowned me."

"My son wouldn't! He was proud of you. Every time he wrote, he told us how well you were doing at university and how you were too busy for visits."

Bree blinked. So that was the lie he told. "I don't go to university." It explained why her grandparents had never invited her to stay. "I do nothing but clean and cook for him and Samuel."

"Child, you're distressed, but you shouldn't lie," her grandmother said.

Fury welled in her. To be called a liar on top of

everything else was too much. She shoved back her chair, struggling to undo the belt at her waist in her rage. "I'm not! Since Mother ran off with another man, he's kept me a prisoner in our house." She pulled up her dress to reveal the scars on her back. "He beat me when she left, and any time I disagreed with him."

Her grandmother gasped and traced the scars with her fingers.

"He was upset about your mother leaving, but we never suspected he would do this," Granddad said. "Samuel never said a word when he visited."

"It makes no sense," Nanna said. "He knew one day your mother would have to go."

Bree frowned at her. "What?"

Joden appeared on the table. "There you are. The prince is upset with you."

Nanna shrieked and Granddad jerked back. Joden nodded to them. "Greta and Bert, you are well known to the Tarta. I am Joden." He bowed. "We thank you for the gifts you leave."

A memory surfaced of helping her grandparents leave gifts of clothes and food for the Tarta. She'd always thought it was a game they played with her.

Bert recovered from the shock first. "Welcome to our home, Joden. Which prince do you speak of?"

"Prince Darrien, third son of King Jerek of Tartalan. Bree has been travelling with him."

Her grandfather glanced at her, eyes wide, but someone knocked on the back door. "I'll be right back."

A few moments later, he returned with Gideon. "Gideon says you're helping the prince."

She should have realised Gideon would know where she went. She stepped back, her heart racing. "I'm not going back. It's not safe. The soldiers think I'm a whore."

Gideon's expression softened. "Darrien will tell the men your importance. Their words were a reflection of their opinion of the prince, not of you."

"Why should she go back?" Bert asked. "She'll be safer with us."

"High Elder Lachlan of the water fae marked her," Joden explained. "She's the prince's fastest way to communicate with him."

Curse Lachlan. "Can't I stay here and you can pass the messages to the prince?" Eventually one of the men would try something. It was in their nature. She rubbed her arms as chills ran down them.

"I can't," Joden said. "Darrien has me running messages all over the place. I might not be available, and the information might be urgent."

"Then can't King Meldrick send another Tarta to stay with me?"

"Every available soldier is helping our people move inland. Their presence keeps our people calm."

Bree couldn't argue with that.

Brigette, I've received information from the ports. Wodlon and Nellon have both been attacked. Those cities have fallen.

"No," Bree gasped.

"What is it?" Gideon asked.

"Wodlon and Nellon have been attacked and overrun."

"I'll tell Darrien." Joden disappeared.

"How many ships do they have? What is the enemy doing?" Gideon demanded.

Bree repeated the questions to Lachlan.

The Molankan are consolidating in the city. They don't appear to be killing any of the civilians, but they are gathering supplies. But there's more. My scouts report another twenty ships are heading for Tartalan.

Nausea swelled in Bree's stomach. "Twenty more ships are on their way."

Gideon swore. "We have to get you back to Darrien. We can't let those ships land." He grabbed her hand, pulling her towards the door.

"Wait a minute!" Bert said. "I'm not letting my granddaughter go off to war. You tell High Elder Lachlan to find another person to mark."

"He said it could only be me," Bree said. "I don't know why. Maybe because Mother introduced me to him as a baby."

Her grandparents exchanged glances.

"Why would she?" Bree asked.

"We don't have time for explanations now," Gideon said. "How far out are the ships?"

Lachlan, when will the ships arrive?

By morning.

They had very little time. She told Gideon.

"Joden!" he shouted. The Tarta didn't appear. He turned to Bree. "There's no time for Lachlan to mark someone else. If those ships arrive, we'll be overrun. You need to be by Darrien's side to relay messages. I will keep you safe."

Every ounce of her being longed to stay here in the cottage of her childhood, but he was right. She couldn't let Tartalan be overrun. Then nowhere would be safe. "Nanna, can I borrow some clothes?"

Greta looked at Bert, who nodded. "Come with me. Bert, fetch us a bucket of water so she can wash."

Bree followed her grandmother into their small bedroom.

"I don't like any of this," Greta said.

Neither did Bree. "You and Granddad will have to leave," she said. "If the Molankan are after resources, they'll come to the launda forest."

"The fae won't let them take it."

"Then there will be fighting. I want you to be safe."

"I'll speak with Bert." She handed Bree a top and skirt. "These should fit you."

Bert carried in the water. "No, give her a pair of my

pants," he said. "A skirt will only hinder her."

It wasn't seemly for a woman to wear pants, but perhaps it would make her less desirable to the soldiers. She reached for the pants he handed her. "Thank you."

They left her to wash and change, and when she returned to the kitchen, Greta handed her a bag. "Food and a few treatments for you." She hugged Bree, clinging a moment longer than usual. Bree stepped back, blinking away the tears, and hugged her granddad.

Bert gave her a knife. "For protection. Keep it in your boot." He showed her how to store it in the boots he'd given her.

"Thank you." Its solid form against her ankle gave her courage.

Gideon nodded at her grandparents and led her out of the house. When they were clear of the yard, he said, "You should have told me you were scared."

She glanced at him and stifled the laugh of disbelief. "I haven't seen you in years. This morning I was a prisoner wrongfully accused. How am I supposed to know who to trust?"

He sighed. "You'll learn quickly, but you can come to me if you need help."

Gideon set a fast pace through the forest, and Bree didn't have the spare breath to talk as she hurried to keep up with him. Her new boots cushioned her feet, and the pants wrapped around her legs were like an armour against the world. Joden reappeared to say Darrien had ordered her back to camp, and she told him about the extra ships due to arrive in the morning.

By the time they reached the camp, it had been dismantled and men were waiting for their next command. Bree couldn't see Darrien anywhere. "Where's the prince?"

"Over there." Joden appeared and pointed. "He's talking to the High Elder of the Launda Fae."

Gideon weaved through the soldiers and Bree followed, keeping her head down, not wanting to see the looks of speculation on the soldiers' faces. "Your Highness, we're back." Gideon stopped and Bree almost crashed into him.

She stepped to the side and spotted the woman Darrien spoke to. She wore a crown of twigs and leaves, but it wasn't that which made Bree's mouth drop open as she met the woman's gaze.

It couldn't be. It made no sense.

She stepped forward, arm outstretched. "Mother?"

Chapter 5

Bree blinked, trying to make sense of what she was seeing. Why was her mother in the forest wearing a crown, talking to the prince? She was sure her eyes were playing tricks on her, but still her mother stood before her, her long brown hair falling to her waist and her brown eyes wide with surprise.

"Bree. What are you doing here?"

That was her question.

"Bree is our contact with High Elder Lachlan," Darrien said. "She didn't mention she was your daughter, my Sister." He raised his eyebrows at Bree.

My Sister? How? "The man you ran off with was the High Elder of the fae?" She'd never thought her mother would be so shallow as to want a title. They had been so close, and Bree had been so certain of her love. Having her mother by her side had made living in the city bearable.

"What?" her mother asked. "I didn't run off with a man."

Lies. Bree was too tired and too confused to challenge her. This woman had abandoned Bree, and didn't deserve her time. She turned to Darrien. "Are we going back to the ocean, Your Highness? Lachlan wants to know what help you'll provide."

"Tell him we'll man the catapults at the entrance of the harbour. We don't have access to more boats." He turned to Joden. "Can you check whether there are catapults near the other ports? If we attack them in Farlon, they might detour to one of the other cities."

"Be right back." Joden vanished.

"Let's move out," Darrien called. "Bree, I want you to stay near me."

She nodded as she relayed the plan to Lachlan, conscious of her mother so close by. She'd prayed for this for years, and now it was too much.

"I need to speak with my daughter," Astraea said. "She will catch up with you." She lay a hand on Bree's arm.

Bree jerked her arm away at her mother's soft touch. She wanted to burst into tears and throw herself into her mother's arms, but her mother had betrayed her. Had left her behind, had enabled her father to keep her prisoner.

Darrien shook his head. "You're welcome to travel with us, my Sister, but I need Bree nearby in case the situation changes."

"As you wish. We will walk beside you."

Bree shook her head, anger working its way through her shock. "I'm not interested in anything you have to say," she hissed, her cheeks flushed. What would the prince think?

Her mother jerked back.

"Bree, talk to your mother," Darrien said. "That's an order. I can't afford to have you distracted."

She stared at him. It wasn't right for him to order her to do such a thing.

She caught Gideon's gaze, and he nodded. This wasn't just about her anymore. She had a responsibility to her country. Clenching her teeth, she followed her mother to the edge of the group of soldiers, so at least no one would overhear their conversation.

"I am so pleased to see you, Bree," Astraea said. "I was disappointed when you didn't visit."

Bree snorted. "It's hard to visit someone when you don't know where they've gone. You abandoned us."

Astraea's hand went to her throat. "I did not! I had to leave to do my duty. Your grandfather was ill, and I had to nurse him through his final days."

"Granddad is fine. I just saw him."

"Not your father's father. Mine."

Huh? Bree hadn't known her mother's parents were still alive. "Father said you'd run off with another man, that you didn't want us anymore."

Astraea's eyes widened. "That's not true. He knew why I left. Why would he lie?"

Her confusion tempered some of Bree's anger. Maybe there was more to the story. "He was furious and bitter." Hope and fear clashed in her, and her next words were tentative. "Why did you leave?"

"My father was ill and as his only heir, I took over ruling the forest."

Ruling the forest. She shook her head. "How are you fae? Why didn't you ever say anything?"

"Your father didn't want me to. He wanted you to live a normal life until you were old enough to decide whether you wanted to follow your fae kin or your human kin."

The realisation stole Bree's breath. "I'm part fae?"

Astraea nodded. "Only a member of royal fae blood can receive the mark Lachlan gave you." She frowned. "I will have words to him about involving you in this."

So that's how Lachlan and Meldrick had known who she was. "But why didn't you take us with you? Why didn't you at least say goodbye?"

"When I got the message Father was ill, it was urgent.

There was no time to say goodbye, and I trusted your father to tell you the truth."

"It's been years! Couldn't you have visited at least once?"

"No. After I became high elder, it was impossible for me to leave the launda forest. I sent your father messages asking him to bring you to the forest, but they went unanswered."

"Why can't you leave?"

"I'm tied to this place." She gestured to the surrounding trees. "They need a high elder to help them thrive and leaving even for a day is harmful." She sighed. "Now you are grown and have returned, you might find leaving difficult as well."

No. "I have to go. The prince needs me." But that wasn't the point. "You could have asked Nanna and Granddad to send for me," she pointed out. "Father forbade me to leave the house without him or Samuel. I was a prisoner in my home, forced to cook and clean for them. The one time I went out alone, he beat me so badly I couldn't sit for days."

Her mother gasped.

"So, you can make your excuses, but I've seen how powerful the fae are. Lachlan's voice is in my head." She tapped on her forehead. "You could have left me with something, anything." Anger swelled in her. "Do you know why I'm with the prince?" She didn't give her mother a chance to answer. "Because when the Molankan army attacked, I was in the palace on trial. A man attacked me in the streets, and he was so influential, no one believed my story. Neither Father nor Samuel came to my aid."

"I had no idea."

"Because you never cared enough to find out," Bree countered. "It was luck I remembered the tree we escaped from." Her breath left her. "That's why we used to spend so much time under the launda tree."

Her mother nodded. "I needed a connection to the trees." She was silent a moment. "Only one who is attune with her fae blood could have got the tree to reveal its secrets."

"I can't be attuned to something I don't know I have." They were nearing the edge of the forest and a heaviness lowered over Bree, making her steps slow. She didn't want to go on, the desire to stay in the forest pulled at her. "What's happening?"

"You can feel it?" her mother asked.

"Yes."

"It's the trees, not wanting you to leave. They need the fae in the forest to thrive."

"Tell them to stop it." It felt like she was walking through honey.

"I can't. It's the way it is for fae."

Bree's skin prickled and anxiety caused her breath to quicken. She had to go with Darrien, but the thought of leaving made her want to run in the opposite direction.

"Hadden, bring Bree her horse," Astraea called.

She bent over, panting. No, she couldn't.

"What's wrong with her?" Hadden asked.

"She's connected with her fae heritage," Astraea explained. "It makes leaving the forest uncomfortable. Every nerve wants her to stay here."

"She has to come with us."

Astraea nodded. "Help her onto the horse. It will be easier if you can lead her out."

Bree barely registered Hadden dismounting and walking over to her. He cupped his hands, and she placed her foot in them, allowing him to boost her onto the horse's back. She stroked the horse's neck, trying to calm herself.

"Give me your hand." Astraea didn't wait for Bree to respond, simply took it and pressed her thumb into the palm. Bree felt a sharp burn as she had with Lachlan and the mark that appeared was a triangle with a stem, almost like a simplified tree. "Now you can contact me when you need me."

Bree hadn't consented to be the messenger girl for the fae, even if part of her celebrated being reconnected with her mother. "You can't help from here."

"You'd be surprised by what I can do," her mother said. "I am sorry for what has happened, Bree. I hope when the war is over, we can talk." She pressed a launda nut into Bree's hand. "Keep this with you at all times. It will help."

Bree rubbed her thumb over its segmented surface. She clung to the saddle, focusing on the horse's mane as her body wanted to slide sideways and off the animal.

"Lead her out," Astraea commanded. "Slowly so she doesn't hurt herself."

Bree didn't look up to see Hadden's reaction. Right now she didn't care what anyone thought. She prayed to make it out of the forest in one piece. It was no wonder the fae never left their areas if this was what it felt like.

Her horse moved forward, and she closed her eyes, focusing on her breathing. The forest's pull dragged her upright as if she was stuck like glue. She panted, gripping hard to the saddle, and the launda seed centred her. She wasn't leaving the forest, she was taking a part with her. There was a pop, as if the glue had let go and the pressure on Bree released. She slumped forward.

"Bree, are you all right?" Hadden asked.

She nodded. "The pull is gone."

"I've seen nothing like it," someone close by said.

"The fae are strange creatures," another man agreed.

How many of them had been watching her struggle? Bree took a few deep breaths and opened her eyes. When they adjusted to the dark, she made out the silhouettes of the men surrounding her. In the distance, a few lights glowed in the city. She frowned. It was brighter than she expected it to be. The streets she travelled to get to her father's shop were always dimly lit.

Hadden dropped back to ride next to her. "Better?"

"Yes, thank you for your help."

"My pleasure." He lowered his voice. "Gideon told the prince why you left. Darrien asked me to tell you that we'll protect you. He'll ensure everyone knows how important you are."

Bree jolted. Important? She'd never felt important before.

"We'll be heading into the coastal bush soon and Joden's not back yet," Hadden continued. "Can you communicate with the trees and sense if anyone is out there?"

Bree frowned. "I don't know." Though she didn't want to contact her mother so soon, being ambushed would be worse. She pressed the new mark on her skin. *Mother, can I talk to trees now?*

It is a skill which takes some time to master.

Curses. *Is there a way I can tell whether there's an ambush ahead of us?*

We are most connected with the launda tree, though I did feel some connection with the coastal plants. When you enter the bush, brush your hands along the leaves, feel its essence. It will give you a sense if people are nearby, but be aware, the Tarta live there too, so it might not be the enemy.

Thank you.

"I might be able to," she responded to Hadden. "But it will take practice to be accurate."

"It's better than nothing."

She almost laughed. This day had been crazier than an adventure in any book she'd read. She wanted to curl up and sleep and forget everything for a brief while.

They finished crossing the land between the forest and the bush. Bree reached out to brush the prickly leaves and closed her eyes. A vibration ran over her hand as if she was touching a drum which had just been beaten. She sensed bits of activity all around, low to the ground.

"Anything?" Hadden asked.

"I think the Tarta are still packing and leaving," she said.

"We have some people who are reluctant to leave." The female voice came from the top of Bree's saddle and she flinched, gazing down. The small figure standing on her horse's neck said, "I'm High Elder Yasmin." As if drawn to her, a dozen fireflies swarmed around, illuminating the Tarta. Just under a foot tall, with long hair the colour of autumn leaves and wearing a dress fashioned from leaves of the launda tree and shoes made from its nuts, she was the height of fashion.

Bree bowed her head awkwardly. "My Sister, I'm honoured to meet you."

Yasmin waved. "Call me Yasmin. I can't be bothered with all that royal nonsense you humans and fae require. Besides, you're a fae elder."

She hadn't considered that. "Where are you going?"

"North to the mountains."

"Joden can travel wherever he wants in an instant," Bree said. "Can't your people simply move there?"

"To an extent," Yasmin replied. "Joden is a soldier, so he's trained to move fast. Most people only travel short distances to visit family and friends. Plus, we can only carry a few things at a time. Many of my people are struggling to decide what to bring with them. They've lived here for over five hundred years, which is plenty of time to accumulate a lot of memories."

"Five hundred years?"

She nodded. "We live a long time. It was my husband, Meldrick, who negotiated with Captain Farlon when he first arrived."

It was beyond comprehension, but Bree was learning quickly not to discount anything as possible.

"Can we do anything to help with the evacuation?" The question came from Bree's left, and Darrien's voice startled her.

"Actually yes," Yasmin said. "If we can borrow one of your carts and a horse, my people can carry a lot more and they may be quicker to leave. There's a cart at a farm not far to the north."

"It's yours," Darrien said. "Tell the farmer I'll ensure he's compensated and come to me if you have any troubles."

"Thank you, Your Highness." Yasmin bowed and vanished.

Bree smiled. She liked the Tarta High Elder.

They reached the shore and Pelham sent some men to the lookout to scout without even discussing it with the prince. Who was in charge here—Pelham or Darrien? Darrien dismounted and strode down to the water's edge. Bree touched her palm. *We have arrived.*

I will be there soon.

"Come on," Hadden invited as he followed Darrien. Gideon and Pelham joined them, and Bree didn't want to be left alone with the other men, so she hurried over.

"Lachlan's on his way," she told Darrien.

A few minutes later, the water rippled and the water fae high elder appeared, morphing from scales to skin as he stood. "Half of the ships have sailed further north," he reported without preamble. "I suspect they plan to hit the ports of Nellon and Otolon."

"Then you'd better stop them," Pelham ordered.

Darrien glared at him, but addressed Lachlan. "I'm waiting to hear from Joden whether we have similar defences at the other ports."

"I'm back," Joden called next to Bree, making her jump. "There are catapults around the harbour, and some along the coast where there's a channel between the reef. The bad news is, I can't find any soldiers to man them. All the outposts are empty. It seems everyone went into the city for the Freedom Day celebrations."

"Then we'll have to find civilians," Darrien said.

"They won't know how to use the catapults," Captain Pelham said.

"They should have had their training," Darrien countered.

"Could one of us go?" Gideon asked.

"You'd never get there in time," the captain argued.

Lachlan cleared his throat. "I can help you get there, but it won't be a pleasant trip."

"What does it entail?" Darrien asked.

"My people can drag you through the water," he said. "You should make it before any ship arrives. If one goes to Otolon, he can go up the river. Joden, can you arrange a horse to be waiting for him?"

Joden nodded.

"The other person will need to go around the island, with the dolphins."

"How will they breathe?" Hadden asked.

"We'll ensure they have air pockets."

Bree watched Darrien, waiting for him to make a decision.

"Which of your men would you recommend?" the prince said to Pelham.

"You can't be serious. They'll drown."

"I assure you they won't." Lachlan's tone was cool.

"I'll go," Gideon said. "Can another Tarta soldier meet me in Nellon? It would make it easier to send messages if you don't have to do all the jumping around."

"I'll talk to Meldrick," Joden said.

Gideon strode into the water. "What do I need to do?"

Lachlan nodded his approval. "Wait there."

Pelham stiffened and strode over to where the other soldiers waited. "I need a volunteer to lead the defence of Otolon," he said. "You will be transported up the river by water fae."

One man raised his hand. "I'll go."

Pelham nodded as if satisfied. "Come with me." He led the soldier over to Gideon. "You are to head the defences of Otolon and Nellon. I'll send garrisons to you, but you'll need to recruit civilians. Your aim is to stop ships from landing and prevent the soldiers from leaving the cities."

Darrien stepped aside and let Pelham take over. The captain was asking a lot of both men. Surely the enemy in the city would attack the men manning the catapults the moment they started firing on the ships.

"My people are ready, Your Highness," Lachlan called.

Two dolphins were harnessed similar to harnessing a horse. Bree stared at the animals. She hadn't realised they were so big. Gideon stepped forward.

"One of my people will accompany you," Lachlan said. "You'll need to change dolphins about halfway."

Joden appeared next to Bree. "Tarta soldiers will meet you both when you arrive. They'll transport messages to the prince."

Lachlan gave the soldier going to Otolon instructions, and Gideon walked over to Bree. "Will you be all right here with these men?" he murmured.

She tensed. "The prince and Hadden have promised me protection."

"Can the prince be trusted?"

Could any man? Darrien had pronounced her important. She would be safe at least until he no longer had need of her. "I believe so."

"Gideon," the prince called.

"Take care." Gideon returned to the prince and

Lachlan, who explained how he was travelling. The other soldier had already gone, only the barest of ripples showing where he was underwater. Bree rubbed her arms. It wouldn't be a comfortable ride.

After Gideon left, Darrien, Lachlan and Pelham talked tactics. Bree wandered further down the beach. The bushes rustled behind her and occasionally she heard voices. She imagined the Tarta packing up their houses and moving inland. She hoped they wouldn't lose their homes, but the country was at war. They'd lost the first battle, and the next one would be significant. If they couldn't stop the ships arriving, it wouldn't take long before the island was overrun.

She sat on the sand using a log as a back rest and watched the waves flow in and out. With the reef surrounding the island, the waves were not large and their shush against the shore was soothing. Her eyes grew heavy. It would be nice to rest. Could she risk closing her eyes?

The drag of sleep pulled her under.

Chapter 6

Darrien's head thumped in a dull ache as he struggled to concentrate. They'd been discussing strategies for over an hour and getting nowhere. It was difficult to plan when you had so few resources against twenty ships and a city overrun by the enemy. He sighed. Both Pelham and Lachlan had far more experience than he did, but he would have to make the decision. The thought had him eyeing the coastal scrub for an escape route. Would anyone notice?

The scouts Pelham had sent to the lookout returned and saluted Pelham, ignoring Darrien.

"It's a good, defensible spot, Captain," the first man said. "Plenty of ammunition for the catapults, and underneath the plants there are waist-high stone walls the whole way around. We can hold the position."

"There's only one path up," the second soldier continued. "And the bush is far too thick for the invaders to cut through it. Should they send men to stop us, we can pick them off one by one."

Like collecting fish from a rock pool. Good.

Pelham nodded. "Take the men now, clear the area. Then get some rest before the morning."

Both men saluted and left.

Would they have been so cavalier if Kerwin or one of his other brothers had been here? They hadn't even acknowledged him. And Pelham hadn't asked for his input or agreement. "We should set traps on the path up," Darrien said.

"They'll just become obstacles for us to avoid on the way down," Pelham countered.

"Or they'll slow the soldiers and mean there are fewer for us to fight." They were twenty men against thousands.

"It's unnecessary," Pelham said.

Darrien didn't have the energy to argue. What did he know? This man had taught him military tactics. "When will the ships arrive?"

"Early morning," Lachlan said. "I don't think they'll try to navigate the reefs in the dark, but they might."

So they needed to be ready. "Let's go," he said. "You can keep us updated through Bree." He squinted in the darkness but didn't see her amidst the men preparing to leave. "Where is she?"

"I hope you haven't let her escape again," Pelham said. "She's vital to this campaign."

Darrien ignored him. Hypocrite. Gideon had explained why she'd left, and Darrien understood. He should have been the one to make sure she was comfortable, but his initial rage at Kerwin's death had left him numb, and then terrified of the task before him.

"I can't contact her," Lachlan said. "She must be asleep."

That could be a problem. He scanned the beach. In the dark, it was difficult to make out more than shapes. He spotted Hadden and gestured him over. "Have you seen Bree?"

"She was sitting by the log." He pointed.

Probably more exhausted than he was. He wandered

over to where a dark shape was curled up. "Bree, wake up."

No response.

He crouched and touched her arm. "Bree."

She shrieked and jerked away from him.

"It's Darrien," he blurted. "You're on the beach, safe."

She placed a hand over her heart. "Sorry. I must have fallen asleep."

"We're moving to the lookout now."

She stood. "Of course." She brushed down her clothes. "What are we doing with the horses?"

A good question, and one he hadn't considered. She was better at this than he was. The horses would give away their position and get in the way if they took them to the lookout. "Joden."

"Yes, Your Highness?"

"Can your people take our horses somewhere safe?" he asked. "Not too far away should we need them, but so the enemy can't capture them if they come this way."

"We can take them to the farmhouse where Yasmin got the cart," he said.

"Thank you."

The soldiers had already dismounted, and had taken their gear from their bags. Pelham was leading them up the slope.

Darrien sighed as he and Bree joined Hadden and Lachlan. "We should arrange a regular contact time," he said to Lachlan. "You and Bree will both need to sleep and if you can't wake each other through your mental connection, it might be a problem."

Lachlan nodded. "I will rest now. When the ships are a mile out, wake Bree." He paused. "Then if we're both awake at dawn, dusk, midday and midnight we can ensure communication is open."

He glanced at Bree. "Is that all right with you?"

"Yes."

"Then it shall be," Lachlan said. "If I may have a word with you in private, Your Highness."

Darrien followed the water fae away from Hadden and Bree.

"With your father away, I feel it is my duty to say you must have more faith in yourself," Lachlan said.

Darrien blinked and ran a hand through his hair. "What?"

"Your father and I spoke regularly, and he expressed concern about you before leaving—not in your ability, for he was confident you could do the job, but in your tendency to let others take charge. Pelham might be captain of the city, but your instincts are strong. My people will set traps for the ships to hinder them from entering the harbour, and you should set traps as you suggested."

Darrien had no words. The idea his father had spoken to Lachlan about him made him feel… uncomfortable. He hadn't realised his father had noticed his actions. He'd thought he'd hidden it well.

"I hope I haven't overstepped, Your Highness."

Darrien shook his head. "No, thank you, my Brother. I appreciate your advice." Now was the absolute wrong time to trust his instincts. The consequences of getting it wrong would destroy his entire country. He fought the urge to be sick.

"I will go now. Good luck." Lachlan waded back into the water and dived under the surface.

Darrien wished he could swim away. With a sigh, he joined the others.

"What did he want?" Hadden asked.

"He was giving me advice." Hadden was the only other to give him advice. Ahead, the soldiers had left the beach, and the horses were being led away. Was Lachlan right and he should insist on traps? They'd always helped during his mock battles—but this was real. Could he really draw comparisons?

"Let's go."

It took a couple of hours to prepare the defences of the lookout. Darrien found one soldier who would obey him, and had sent him to set traps down the path, then he found Bree a place out of the way to sleep. The coming battle would be terrifying and exhausting, but he would do what he could to make it easier on her. Now he did a final lap around the area. Most soldiers slept, or pretended to, while a couple stood guard. Defences were tight. It would be near impossible for anyone to sneak up on them without warning. He gazed down at Farlon, seeking out the place Kerwin had died. His lungs squeezed so tightly it was impossible to breathe. Darrien sucked in air and moved his gaze on. The docks were lit with coal lamps, but aside from a couple of soldiers standing guard, it was quiet. The rest of the city slept, and smoke from the lamps hung in the air. Tremont must have brought them with him. He'd heard Molanka had embraced coal-powered energy, but when the technology had been brought to Tartalan, his father had rejected it. The smoke had polluted the air, and sailors reported dense smoke clouds hung over Bermont these days. It would go against the treaty they had with the fae and the Tarta about keeping a balance in nature and resources.

His father had been right. The Molankan had only been here a day, and already the air smelled off.

"You should get some rest," Hadden said, coming up to him.

Impossible. Too much was at stake. Could he stop the ships? How many of his men would die? His mind raced through the scenarios repeatedly. "I can't."

Hadden patted him on the back. "Try. You'll be

leading these men, and that requires a clear, rested mind."

Around them the soldiers had made makeshift beds around the walls of the headland. Pelham was already snoring. "All right. You should too."

"I'm going to bunk near Bree," Hadden said.

A good idea. He hoped now the soldiers had seen Bree with both Astraea and Lachlan, they would realise she was here for a reason, and treat her with respect.

She was a fae princess. Though he'd wondered about her heritage, he couldn't quite comprehend it. He had heard little of the conversation she'd had with her mother, but he hoped it meant after the war, she would have somewhere safe to live.

He went across to one guard. "Wake me when you sight the ships."

"Yes, Your Highness."

He joined Hadden, and Bree didn't stir as they lay on the ground beside her.

Despite his belief he wouldn't sleep, he was dragged under almost immediately.

***

When Darrien woke, it was to the dusky light of dawn. He blinked and rolled over, spotting Pelham facing the ocean with a telescope to his eye, the night guard with him. Had the ships arrived? He stood and jolted at the ten ships anchored outside the reef. Anger filled him and he strode over. "Why didn't you wake me?"

The guard stammered, "The captain said to let you sleep."

Pelham didn't even glance at him. "They haven't made any movement into the harbour yet."

"That's not the point. Bree needs to be awake for Lachlan to communicate with her, and I promised him I would wake her when the ships were spotted." Nerves and anger clashed. This was it. The battle would begin soon.

"I didn't know."

He glared at the guard. "I expect my orders to be followed. I outrank the captain." Disgusted, Darrien hurried back to Bree. Gently, he touched her shoulder. "Bree, you need to wake."

Her eyes flickered and then opened. They widened as she recognised him, and she sat. "Is it time?"

"The ships have arrived. Please ask if Lachlan needs anything."

She pressed her palm. Next to her, Hadden stirred.

"He's not happy," she reported. "He's been trying to get in touch with me for over an hour."

Darrien helped her to her feet. "Send my apologies." He led her to where Pelham stood.

"The sailors on board have been talking," she continued. "They will make their run through the harbour as soon as the sun is above the horizon. They want to have good visibility before attempting it."

The calm, glassy ocean should have been an advantage, but smoke belched from the ships, so they didn't need wind in order to attempt the passage.

Darrien's skin prickled as his brain kicked into gear, assessing the situation. "It will take a couple of shots to determine the catapults' range," he said. "Warn Lachlan. His people need to be clear of the area when we fire." The last thing he needed was to kill his allies. To Hadden he said, "Wake the soldiers. I want them alert and ready."

The sun appeared on the horizon above the launda forest in the distance. They would have the advantage. The ships would sail into the sun, making it difficult for them to see. He'd take every advantage he could get. He exhaled as the realisation hit him. He'd given orders without waiting for Pelham's approval. Perhaps the trick was simply being too angry to care.

When Hadden returned, he handed Darrien a bellar spice roll. Astraea had provisioned them with enough food for a few days, but the idea of eating turned his stomach. His people weren't warriors, despite the mandatory year of military service they were all required to undertake. It had been a rite of passage forever, and though it was gruelling, it had also been a lot of fun. It had cemented his friendship with Hadden.

He stared down at the ocean. Perhaps that was the key. He'd had no trouble ordering people around when it wasn't a real conflict. Could he pretend the same now? He clenched his teeth. People would die today. It wasn't at all the same.

He studied the ships' route. The gap between the reef was wide enough for two ships, though only one ever attempted it at a time. "Bree, ask Lachlan how deep the passage is."

"Fifteen metres."

His mind ticked through the options. "If we can sink three in the passage, they should block it, and prevent any other ships from entering."

"They can still row in," Pelham pointed out.

"Yes, but it will be slower and more difficult for them," Darrien said. And they could pick them off with arrows. Thankfully, the Tarta had supplied them with more arrows overnight. "Bree, can Lachlan's people stop the ships from moving?"

She was quiet for a moment. "Not easily. The steam power makes it more difficult. The best they can do is slow them or position them in line with the catapults."

That would work.

"Not much of an ally, are they?" Pelham said.

What was his problem with the fae? "They're better than none," Darrien told him. He remembered Lachlan's words. He needed to get the captain on side. If they were both issuing orders when the battle came, it would be a disaster. But either he had to let Pelham take charge, or he had to be brave enough to insist on leadership. His gut swirled as he pulled the man aside. "Pelham, we need to work together. When the ships enter the harbour, do you agree we need to block the passage?"

"Yes."

"Good." He swallowed hard. "I'll need your advice, but I'll issue orders."

"You want to be the hero?" The disdain was clear on the older man's face.

If only he knew how little Darrien wanted to be here, but his answering smile was automatic, a habit long ingrained. "Of course."

"My men don't respect you," Pelham spat, disgusted.

Neither did Pelham, but it was Darrien's own fault for encouraging the lies and rumours. "They don't have to respect me," Darrien said. "They just have to obey me."

Pelham hesitated, a deep frown on his face. "You'll issue my orders?"

"As I see fit." He shouldn't be goading the man, but it was second nature. "I always win the mock battle each Freedom Day."

"This isn't a game."

"No, it's not, but I will win." He poured all his arrogance into the words. "My father will hear about your role."

Pelham studied him for a long moment, his unhappiness clear. "All right. You give the orders."

"Thank you." Unease and uncertainty piled on top of the nerves instead of the relief he'd hoped for. His orders would save or kill his men.

He turned back to the ships and waited for them to make the first move.

*****

The waiting was interminable. Bree didn't want the fighting to begin, but until it started, it also couldn't end. She sat with her back resting against the stone wall, and took the launda seed from her pocket, rubbing her thumb over its segments. The motion soothed her. Darrien discussed tactics nearby with Pelham and Hadden, while the other soldiers ate breakfast. In the light of day, she realised how young they all were. At least half had to be only eighteen and on their mandatory year of service. They didn't speak as they ate, but the signs of nerves were there. One tore his roll into tiny pieces before chewing each bite as if it was the last thing he would ever eat. Another kept pulling on his bow string to make sure it was taught. Several patted their leg or shuffled their feet, unable to stay still.

Three older men, perhaps in their thirties, were sharpening their swords and the scrape of metal against stone set Bree's teeth on edge.

"Why are you sharpening your sword?" one young soldier asked. "We'll shoot them with the catapults."

The man closest to him looked up. "Do you think Tremont's going to let us sink his ships without a fight?" He gestured to the city. "There are thousands of Molankan soldiers down there ready to protect their gains."

The boy paled.

"We've got arrows," another said.

"They won't last long," the man said. "I'd suggest you all sharpen your swords."

High-pitched scraping soon filled the air. His words made Bree withdraw the knife from her boot and check its blade. She hissed as it bit into her skin, and she sucked the blood from her finger.

"What have you got there?"

She flinched at Darrien's voice. "Granddad gave me a dagger for protection."

He crouched next to her. "I should have considered that. Do you know how to use it?"

Was there a trick? "Don't I just stab someone with the pointy end?"

He chuckled. "Yeah, but if you can, go for the most vulnerable spots; neck, eyes, belly, groin." He indicated each area.

She remembered the men who had attacked her and wished she'd had the dagger then. "All right. Thank you."

Darrien hesitated. "I'm sorry you're here," he said. "I wish I could have left you safe with your grandparents."

His kindness made her pause. "Tartalan is my country too," she said. "I will not hide away while others try to take it."

"You are braver than me," he murmured.

Before she could ask what he meant, her palm tingled and she pressed the mark. *Bree, the ships are moving.*

She gasped. "They're moving." She didn't need to tell Darrien what she meant as they both stood to look over the ocean. Sure enough, two of the boats made their way into the passage.

"Man the catapults," Darrien called. He pointed to one of the young soldiers nearby. "I want you to monitor the city and the path up. Tell me the minute you see evidence they are organising a counterattack."

"Yes, Your Highness." The boy saluted and moved away from the catapults to a spot which overlooked the city.

"Tell Lachlan to get his people out of there," Darrien ordered Bree.

Bree passed on the message.

They're out.

The men loaded the two catapults.

The early morning sun had a touch of warmth and Bree closed her eyes, tilting her face towards it, and breathed deeply. It would be a beautiful day with not a single cloud in the sky, and yet here they were about to attack boatloads of people.

In the harbour, two ships sailed forward, one behind the other, keeping a reasonable distance apart.

"Wait until they're both in range," Darrien said. "We don't want one to turn around."

Pelham nodded.

The ships sailed closer to the docks.

Pelham gave the signal.

"Not yet!" Darrien called.

Too late. Two boulders hurtled through the air with a loud twang, one curving towards each ship. The first sailed over the target and landed in the water with a splash. The second hit the ship dead on, and the crack of splintering wood was like a whip. Sailors yelled as water rushed on to the deck.

Watch my reef!

Bree winced. "Watch the reef, Darrien."

He didn't look at her, his eyes narrowed on the scene in the harbour. "We're adjusting the range now. Get back to your spot, Bree."

Her gaze fixed on the sailors jumping overboard to swim to shore. Fins broke the surface and circled the swimmers. Grolin. Screams filled the air, and the water turned red. Her stomach roiled and Bree stumbled away. Putting a hand to her belly, she hurried back to her spot. She'd known the day wouldn't end without death, but the reality was horrifying.

She retched over the wall. Behind her, they released another boulder, and the crack and cheers which followed told her they'd hit the ship. So many would die.

Eight ships left. They stayed where they were as the sun rose in the sky. They would have to try again at some stage or go home. Bree hoped it would be the latter.

Pelham spoke to Darrien. "They'll be preparing an attack on the lookout," he said. "We have to get those ships sunk before they do." He gestured Bree over. "Ask Lachlan if he can move the ships towards us."

It will wear out my people, but we can.

"Tell him to do it," Pelham ordered.

Bree glanced at Darrien, who nodded, and then repeated the request. One ship broke away from the group, and moved towards the harbour, very little smoke coming from its chimney. It was eerie. The sailors ran back and forth, throwing an anchor over, but it made no difference.

"Fire!" Pelham ordered.

Darrien flinched and scowled at the captain, but said nothing. Shouldn't he be in charge?

The boulder hit the ship, and water rushed on board. Then the next ship moved forward. They were helpless. The sailors couldn't jump into the water, not without being attacked by the grolin. It didn't seem fair.

"We should give them the opportunity to surrender," Darrien told Pelham.

Pelham barely glanced at the prince. "They never gave us such courtesy."

"Joden!" Darrien called. The Tarta popped up next to him. "Tell Tremont if his ships retreat, we'll help his sailors."

The Tarta disappeared.

"Movement on the docks," Hadden called.

Bree walked over, needing to see for herself. Molankan soldiers were pointing to what was happening in the harbour. One soldier ran towards the castle while sailors shot arrows into the water, aiming for grolin and fae alike.

Behind her, the catapult fired, and another ship sank. The screams of the sailors in the water turned her stomach. She wanted to block her ears and close her eyes.

My people are exhausted, Lachlan said. *The ships we have sunk are blocking the harbour's entrance, but we can't do any more until we rest.*

The ships were enormous. No wonder it was exhausting. Bree relayed the message.

Pelham scowled. "Not much help, are they?"

Darrien turned to Bree. "Thank Lachlan for his help and tell him to let his people rest. We appreciate all their efforts."

Hadden spoke. "It won't be long before we have to fight them here."

Joden reappeared. "Hadden is right. Tremont won't surrender. He's arranging his men as we speak."

Bree's skin prickled as a cold sweat washed over her. The soldiers bragging about the defensiveness of the lookout seemed to be just words now.

Watching the sailors die from a distance was bad enough. How would she handle the bloodshed when it was up close?

She didn't want to be here, but there was no escape. She peered over the lookout. The sheer cliffs fell all the way to the ocean below. Would a person survive such a jump? On this side, they'd hit the reef. Bree strode over to the other side, which faced the beach where they'd met Lachlan. The water was as distant but a clear light blue which meant there was no reef below. Still, she didn't like her chances.

"Stop pacing," Hadden said. "You're making the soldiers nervous."

Bree glanced around. No soldier was still. Some counted the arrows in their quiver, others tapped the hilt of their sword or plucked the string of their bow. She sat, willing herself to be calm.

Darrien and Hadden discussed in low voices how many soldiers Tremont would send against them. He would have to keep some behind to keep control of Farlon.

"He'd be foolish to send more than five hundred,"

Hadden said.

Five hundred. Close to twenty-five men for every one they had here.

Bree checked the lookout path. It was narrow, but would it be enough to keep them away? Her skin grew clammy. What was she doing here?

"Movement at the gates!" the soldier monitoring the city cried.

She joined Darrien as the red-clothed soldiers marched out of the city. They kept coming and coming, and she lost count. Definitely over five hundred soldiers. They had no chance against so many, would all be slaughtered.

Next to her, Darrien swore. "It's at least a thousand."

"The ships are moving," a soldier called.

"You ten, man the path," Pelham ordered. "The rest of you, arm the catapults."

Darrien growled and said under his breath, "Damn that man."

Why wasn't he asserting his authority? He was prince, he was in charge of the whole island. If Bree had that kind of power, she wouldn't let it go.

She returned to her spot, brought her knees to her chin and closed her eyes. She would risk the jump before she'd let Molankan soldiers capture her again.

Bree, what does the prince want us to do?

At the sound of Lachlan's voice, she opened her eyes. Darrien and Pelham were arguing about something. She moved over to them. "Lachlan wants to know what to do."

"Keep the ships within the catapult range and we'll do the rest," Pelham said.

He couldn't. He'd said his people were exhausted. When Darrien scowled, but said nothing, Bree didn't relay the order.

From down below came a scream, a noise full of pain

before it was cut off. Wide-eyed, she scanned the lookout, but no one had attacked.

"Traps?" Hadden asked.

Darrien nodded.

"I told you we didn't need traps," Pelham said.

Darrien shrugged. "It will slow them down, and it's at least one less person to fight."

Bree traced the Molankans' progress up the path by the screams. It seemed as if Darrien had organised a lot of traps.

"They're here!" a soldier called.

Darrien gave the order. "Fire!"

A whooshing noise filled the air as arrows were released, and the answering grunts as they hit their targets. Bree tried to block out the noise. Her heart beat faster and tears pricked her eyes. This was a reality she'd not contemplated. Each scream stabbed her heart.

"They'll have to clear the path of bodies soon," Hadden commented.

Bree closed her eyes against the image that provoked and then quickly reopened them. She cursed her active imagination.

"Incoming!" a soldier manning the catapults yelled.

Bree glanced towards him. Her eyes widened, and she pressed herself back against the stone wall, a sharp edge digging into her spine.

A ball of flames flew straight towards her.

The ships weren't as defenceless as she'd thought. There was nowhere to run.

Chapter 7

King Tremont of Molanka stood at the window overlooking the harbour as the battle unfolded. His hands clenched at his sides and rage bubbled inside him. The Tartalan were supposed to be defenceless, and with only the playboy prince in charge, they should have surrendered without a fight. His contact had been mistaken, again. Tremont would have to deal with him later. Luckily, his ships also had their defences.

The anger simmered into satisfaction as the fireball hit the headland. Though he couldn't hear anything, he could imagine the screams. They deserved it for daring to defy him.

He was doing them a favour, reuniting their lands under one ruler. Ensuring resources were shared equally. Tartalan wouldn't have been discovered had it not been for his ancestors.

"Excuse me, Your Majesty."

He jolted and found the tiny man standing on his desk again. That the Tarta were real had come as a shock, and he still wasn't sure what to make of them. "You have news for me, Joden?"

"Prince Darrien says he will stop attacking the ships

if you order them to leave."

Tremont laughed. "He's in no position to make demands." Already his men were gathering at the southern gate to launch an attack on the lookout.

Joden frowned. "But surely you don't want your men to die."

He grimaced. "There is only one person's fate I care about." Emeline. He had to find a cure. He eyed the Tarta. "What healing magic do your people possess?"

"Magic? None, Your Majesty."

"Nonsense." He strode closer, and the Tarta moved to the opposite side of the desk. "You appear out of air. That is magic."

"No. It's our connection with the land. We've always done this. It is not magic."

"To me it is. My wife is ill, and I need a cure. Find one and I will leave this land." He would take the cure to his wife personally, but he'd leave his men behind to consolidate his control.

Joden inclined his head. "What are your wife's symptoms?"

"She is weak, lethargic. Has no energy to eat or stand. She loses weight and fades away each day."

"She isn't being poisoned, is she?"

As if anyone would dare! "Her food is tasted, and my daughter doesn't leave her side. It is not poison."

"I will speak with my king." He vanished.

Tremont waved his hand over the desk where the Tarta had stood to ensure he was gone and then called to his guard who waited outside the room. "I want an update from the men in the library, and bring Littleton to me."

The guard saluted and closed the door.

Tremont settled in his chair. This was Jerek's study. A portrait of the royal family hung on one wall, and there were several reports on the desk. They spoke of successful harvests, plentiful food and resources. Somehow Jerek had figured out how to rule the fae, and get exactly what he needed.

At the knock, he called, "Enter."

Sinclair Littleton strode in and bowed. "How may I be of service, your Majesty?"

"You didn't tell me about the catapults on the headland," Tremont said.

Littleton frowned. "Catapults?"

Tremont gestured to the window. "Look for yourself."

The man's sharp gasp was satisfying, as was the concern on his face. "I had no idea, Your Majesty. I doubt anyone has been up to the headland in decades."

"You didn't know about the Tarta either," he said. "Perhaps you don't know your country as well as you said you did. Don't make me regret working with you."

"You won't." The scowl smoothed into a smile. "Everyone I've spoken to believed the Tarta were a myth."

Tremont ignored his excuse. "What progress have you made with the healers in town?"

Littleton handed him a list. "These are their suggestions."

Tremont scanned it and dropped it on the table, disappointment filling him. "Useless," he said. "We've tried them all."

"I'll keep asking."

"Do that. I want you to reassure the citizens they are safe to go about their business as long as they don't attack my men. I also want another ship of supplies ready to leave as soon as we've dealt with the men on the headland."

Littleton bowed. "Yes, Your Majesty."

Tremont watched him leave. He would have to monitor the man. He had far too many ideas, and would likely lead an uprising the moment Tremont returned to Molanka. As it was, he'd betrayed his own king. Ambition would lead to his downfall.

The scholar Tremont had brought with him appeared in the doorway. He bowed lower than Littleton had. "You wanted to see me, Your Majesty?"

"Have you found anything?"

"There is a lot of information, Your Majesty. The doctor is reading every book I can find on healing. It will take us weeks to go through."

"I'll send you more men."

"Thank you, Your Majesty."

Tremont waved a hand, dismissing him. The cure was vital. When they'd exhausted the information in the palace library, they would expand through the city and then the country. The city had enough resources to help Molanka in the meantime. And his wife's health was paramount.

***

Time slowed as the flaming ball flew inextricably towards the lookout. Men pushed and shoved each other, trying to get out of the way. There was nowhere to hide now the lookout had been cleared of debris to make fighting easier.

Bree was hypnotised as the ball got larger and larger before crashing to the ground in a wave of flames spreading from its centre. She ducked her head to protect her eyes. Stray sparks burnt through her trousers, and she patted them out.

Screams filled the air. Two men were aflame. One dropped to the ground and rolled while the other leapt over the wall and off the lookout towards the ocean below.

No! Bree raced over in time to see the splash made by the man hitting the water. She pressed her palm.

Lachlan, someone just jumped. Can you check if he's all right?

"Bree, get Lachlan to turn the damned ship around!" Darrien yelled.

Bree jumped at the command and relayed the order.

My people are still recovering from moving the ships. I don't know if they have enough energy to help.

Bree told Darrien, and he glanced at Pelham. "Sink that ship," he commanded the men manning the catapults.

"They're attacking up the path!" a soldier yelled.

The men reacted quickly. Avoiding the flames, which weren't spreading on the sandy ground, they rushed back to their positions to take on the fresh attack. One catapult launched a counterattack, but only grazed its target.

The one who jumped is badly burned. One of my people will take him to safety. Lachlan's voice filled Bree's head.

The man who had been rolling on the ground stopped in front of her, the flames out, his face screwed up in agony. Black clothing hung on him, and his blistered skin showed through the holes. He groaned.

He needed treatment fast, but there wasn't enough water on the lookout to help. *Lachlan, I'm sending someone else down.*

She helped the injured man to his feet. "You need to jump off the cliff. The fae will pick you up and help."

The man nodded. Bree helped him over the wall on the cove side, careful not to touch his blisters. Down below, she could make out the shape of a fae. It was a long way down. Her head spun, and she swayed a little.

The soldier stared at her in disbelief.

"The other man survived," she said.

He closed his eyes, muttered something under his breath and jumped.

"Bree, get back in here!" Darrien yelled.

She turned and spotted another missile arching

through the air. "Look out!" She ducked behind the wall as the flame ball hit the lookout, and there was a resounding crack.

She waited for a moment to allow the shrapnel to land, and then peered over the wall.

One catapult was split in two, its arm lying broken to the side. In front of her a man clutched at the wooden stake embedded in his thigh while another lay on his back, eyes open, a stake in his chest. Dead.

Bree stared, unable to look away as her body went limp. She clutched the wall, her hands shaking. She didn't want to cross the protective barrier.

"Miss, can you help me pull this out?" It was the soldier with the stake in his leg.

No. She wanted to follow the burnt man over the edge into the relative safety of the water where she would be free of danger.

"Please, Miss," the man beseeched her.

Bree pushed away the selfish thoughts. He needed her help. She climbed over the wall and knelt by him. The wound wasn't too deep, but the wooden stake had to come out. "We need something to bandage it with."

She had no idea what was in the packs, and everyone was busy either fighting the men attacking from the land, or preparing the remaining catapult for attack. "Joden!"

The Tarta appeared before her, his face pale. "Yes, Bree?"

"I need bandages." She scanned the lookout. Other men were bleeding. "As many as you can bring."

"Of course." He disappeared.

The remaining catapult fired, and she heard the responding crash of it hitting its target. Relief filled her. She pressed her hand against the man's wound. "We'll wait until Joden returns."

"I've got to get back there. They need my help."

He was right. They were rapidly running out of

arrows. Soon they'd have to fight hand-to-hand. Joden reappeared and dropped a stack of bandages on the ground. "Here."

"Thank you. We'll need more arrows if you can find them."

Joden nodded.

Bree wadded up a bandage. "On the count of three," the man said.

Bree pulled at the stake when he reached three. The man bellowed in pain and then gritted his teeth as she firmly wrapped the bandage around the wound.

"Help me up." The man raised his hand, and she pulled him to his feet.

He tested his weight on the leg and grabbed his bow and arrow. "Thanks. Why don't you help the others?" He limped towards the lookout entrance to risk his life again.

Bree couldn't watch him go. Was this what she had to do? Heal them enough so they could get killed the next time they were attacked? She dug her nails into her palms. This was war. She had to help.

A few men around her were bleeding, but their wounds were superficial. Across the other side of the lookout a man sat, his back against the wall, slumped over his stomach. Checking to make sure she wasn't in firing range, Bree ran to him and squatted down. She put a hand on his shoulder when he didn't look up. "Can I help you?"

The man slowly lifted his head. His hands were covered in blood as he pressed the wound in his chest. Next to him was a bloodied sliver of wood. He grimaced at her. "I don't think you can help, lass." He coughed and blood sprayed over her.

She flinched, wiping her face. He was dying.

No, she wouldn't let him. She grabbed a bandage. "We just need to stop the bleeding," she told him. "If you shuffle from the wall, I can wrap this around you."

"Tell my wife, I love her," he said as he did as she asked.

"You can tell her yourself when this is over," Bree said, keeping her voice light.

Quickly she wrapped the bandages around his torso as tightly as she dared. He was silent throughout.

"There, you can sit back now."

The man didn't stir.

Her heart leapt to her throat as she gently pushed him back.

His eyes were open, staring at nothing.

Tears ran down her face, blurring her vision. She shook him. "Wake up!"

No response.

"I said, wake up!"

"He's dead, Bree."

Darrien touched her shoulder. She could barely make him out through the tears. She shook her head. "No."

"Yes, you need to leave him here. There are others who need your help." He pointed.

One soldier had an arrow sticking out of his shoulder while another was bleeding from his head.

"But he gave me a message for his wife. I don't even know his name."

"I'll find out for you," Darrien promised.

"Darrien, we need your help," Hadden called.

Darrien pulled Bree to her feet. "Go, your bandages are needed." He turned, notching an arrow to his bow as he did so, and moved into the fray, his movements confident as he released arrow after arrow.

Taking a shaky breath, she wiped her bloodied hands on her pants. She would save as many men as she could.

"They're retreating!" someone called.

The sun was two hand spans above the launda forest, and the fighting had been relentless, but they had kept the army at bay. The path up had become a funnel full of dead bodies which had to be dragged out of the way before the soldiers could advance. And many tasked with the removal joined the dead bodies. Now the Molankan moved back down the slope of the lookout to gather at its base. The men were exhausted, and Bree sank to the ground to rest her legs. Their numbers were dwindling. Five men had died, and several were injured. Plus, their arrow supply was almost non-existent. Joden had some Tarta ferrying new arrows to them, but they couldn't carry many at once, so it was a stop-gap measure more than a solution.

What would happen now? They couldn't stay up here indefinitely.

Darrien ordered a couple of men to stand watch as the rest grabbed food and rested. The bodies of the dead men were moved close to the shattered catapult where they had a semblance of protection.

How would they get the bodies back to their loved ones?

Darrien had discovered the name of the soldier who had died, and she would find his wife when this was over, tell her he loved her. She hated the thought the men who'd fought so bravely would rot up here. Perhaps the Tarta could help. "Can you protect the dead men?" At Joden's confused expression, she added, "Can you transport them to a safe place to await burial?"

Darrien walked over to hear the answer.

Joden shook his head. "We can't move anything larger than us." He paused. "What I can do is hide them from the enemy and protect them from the elements. The Molankan will see nothing on the ground. Then we can return for them when we can."

"Please do," Darrien said. "I don't know how long we're going to be up here."

There was no escape, they were under siege. How

long could thirteen men hold off the army? "Smoke!" a guard called.

Bree moved with Darrien and Pelham to the top of the path. At the bottom of the lookout, smoke rose above the thick bush.

Darrien swore. "They're setting the bush alight." He looked at Pelham. "We've got to get out of here."

Pelham scowled. "Where are we supposed to go? They're guarding the only path down."

He was right. It would take too long to cut an escape route through the thick bush and with it soon aflame, far too dangerous.

But what good would burning the bush do? The flames wouldn't spread to the lookout because there was nothing to burn in the clearing.

Bree gasped as the realisation struck. When the surrounding bush was burnt, it would be easy for the Molankan to push through the burnt flora, and they would have access to the whole lookout. They wouldn't be filtered down the one path. As soon as the fire burned down, they were all as good as dead.

"We have to jump," Darrien said as he turned to Bree. "The burnt men survived, didn't they?"

Bree pressed her finger to her palm. *How are the men who jumped?*

The first man died from his burns. The second is injured, but recovering.

We need to get off the lookout. Can your people take us to safety if we jump?

There was silence for a moment. *It's dangerous. You need to make sure you hit the water with your feet, otherwise you may break bones.*

Bree told Darrien.

"So we get off the lookout and none of our men are in any state to fight?" Pelham asked.

"At least they'll be alive." Darrien coughed as the

smoke drifted over the lookout. The fire was halfway up the hill and moving fast. He called the men together and explained the situation. "We can take a chance and jump, or wait and fight the Molankan. I say we jump."

"I say we stay. A good soldier never abandons his post," Pelham said.

Why was Darrien even giving them a choice? He was in charge and it was obvious they had a better chance of survival jumping.

Hadden spoke. "I'd prefer to live and fight another day. I'll jump."

"I'll be no use in a fight," an injured soldier said. "I'll jump."

One by one, the soldiers agreed to jump until Pelham was left with two others.

"Pelham, three people can't defend the lookout. It's suicide."

Pelham said nothing.

"Bree, ask Lachlan when they'll be ready for us," Darrien ordered. "We need to move fast before the fire reaches us."

We're ready.

"I'll go first." Hadden moved to the edge of the cliff.

Bree clenched her hands together.

Without a backwards glance, Hadden jumped. The next soldier took his place and peered down. "He's safe."

Her breath whooshed out as the following five men jumped in quick succession. The smoke stung her eyes and made it harder to see.

"The enemy is charging the hill," a guard yelled.

Seven left.

"Faster," Darrien ordered, and the men jumped, barely waiting for the ones before to clear before leaping.

An arrow whizzed past the men, missing them. Three men to go.

Darrien raised his bow and arrow and fired off arrow

after arrow in quick succession as more men jumped. There were yells as the arrows hit their marks. Bree had never seen anyone fire so fast.

"Pelham get moving," Darrien ordered.

Pelham was at the path, braced for a fight. The fire crept its way along the shorter grass on the outside the wall. The yells of the Molankan army were getting closer.

The soldiers who had agreed to stay looked at each other.

"Jump," Darrien ordered.

They followed the others off the cliff.

Bree glanced over to where they had left the bodies. There was nothing. Only Darrien and Pelham were left on the lookout.

"Pelham, I order you to jump."

No response.

"Curse it, man, that's an order."

Pelham was an idiot, but they needed every man, and it didn't look like Darrien would leave without him. Bree ran to Pelham, anger coursing through her. She yanked on his arm, getting his attention. "Your prince gave you an order and you defy him? What would the king say if he found out?" The smoke haze blocked the view of the path. At any second, she expected the Molankan to burst through it.

"What in the Shelterer's name are you still doing here?" Darrien demanded. "I thought you'd gone." The anger in his voice made her stride back towards the wall.

"You should be," she retorted. "We need someone alive to take charge."

Their eyes met and she saw his realisation that she spoke the truth.

Pelham shook himself as if coming to his senses and charged over. "Over you go." He lifted her over the wall and followed. "Come on, Darrien."

"I'll be right behind." He fired more arrows.

Her heart leapt to her throat as she stared down, down to the ocean below. It was easy to talk about jumping, far more difficult to take the leap. The fire crept towards her. Dark shapes moved through the water, and she hoped they were fae and not grolin. A whoosh brushed her face, and she ducked. They were shooting at her! Her head spun.

Darrien stood on the wall now, firing as quickly as he could. "What are you waiting for?" he yelled.

"Now!" Pelham yelled.

She inhaled and braced herself before she jumped. Something smashed into her side, and pain stole the air from her lungs. Her hand collided with the arrow as she fell, her other hand flailing, the water rushing up to meet her. She hit the ocean hard.

Everything went black.

Chapter 8

Darrien watched helplessly as the arrow slammed into Bree's side, and she screamed in agony. Holy Trinity. Was she dead? Another arrow rushed past him, bringing his attention back to the battle. "Go, Pelham." If he had obeyed Darrien's orders, Bree would be fine. If Darrien had been able to leave a man behind, she would not have been shot. He fired his last two arrows at the invading army, and pushed Captain Pelham off the cliff. As soon as he was clear, Darrien jumped.

His stomach flipped as the ocean rushed to greet him and he hit it hard, feet first, his bow almost ripped from his hand. The impact stole his breath and the cold water dragged him down. He struggled to the surface as arms grabbed him and kept him under.

"Breathe." The voice sounded next to his ear.

Impossible. He was still underwater. His lungs hurt as arms encircled his chest and pulled him through the water.

"Breathe."

Trust. It could only be a water fae. He inhaled, expecting a mouthful of water, and instead received a breath of air. Darrien opened his eyes. The water glistened above him, but didn't touch him, as if a bubble of air surrounded his face. The sensation was uncomfortable, as was the speed he was pulled through the water, but at least for the moment he was safe. Through the transparent liquid he spotted the nearby reef. Hopefully, the grolin who had feasted on the enemy were satiated.

The fae slowed and dragged Darrien through a narrow gap in the reef before surfacing, pulling Darrien with him. Darrien stood, wiping his eyes. "Thank you." They were in a large limestone cave and the rest of his men were on the white sandy shore, seeing to each other's injuries. Several water fae helped.

Where was Bree?

He found her on the shore, surrounded by several soldiers and Lachlan. He waded out of the water. "How is she?"

"The arrow's penetrated deeply," Lachlan said. "I don't want to pull it out. It will cause too much damage."

"You can't leave it in there." The cloth pressed around the wound was already red with blood.

Lachlan nodded. "But her mother will heal it better than I can. They have the kinship bond which we do not."

Bree's eyelids fluttered, and then her eyes opened. She groaned and her hand went to the arrow. Lachlan stopped her from pulling it out. "Leave it. We need to get help."

"Do we have time?" Darrien demanded.

Lachlan glanced at the wound and then at Darrien. "I don't know."

Pelham was a medic. He was talking to some men. "Pelham! Over here."

The captain strode over. "How is she?"

"Bleeding," Darrien said. "What can you do?"

"Best I can do is stitch her."

"Will it help?" he asked Lachlan.

Lachlan opened his eyes. "It will have to. Astraea can't leave the forest."

Darrien held Bree's hand. "This is going to hurt."

Her wide green eyes contrasted against her pale skin.

"Relax if you can, Bree." Lachlan pulled out the arrow.

Bree's scream was cut off as her eyes rolled back into her head and she fell unconscious. Pelham worked quickly with the thread while Lachlan placed his hands on Bree's stomach, his eyes closed, lips moving without a sound.

Darrien hesitated, his thumb rubbing the back of her cold hand. She'd been through so much already, had come back to him though she wanted to stay safe at her grandparents' place. She was braver than him, getting through to Pelham when he could not. He owed it to her to stay by her side, he wanted to stay here. But she'd been right. Someone needed to lead his men.

No, *he* needed to lead his men.

His gaze shifted to scan the cave. His soldiers were wet and exhausted, many staring with the blank gaze of horror from their first battle.

Bree twitched and he squeezed her hand. Pelham worked fast, and was almost finished. Darrien exhaled. He had other soldiers to see to. He left Bree, and moved to the back of the cave where one of the water fae helped a soldier with a cut on his arm. "Is it bad?"

The soldier looked up and shook his head. "Just a scratch. A bit of shrapnel hit me when the catapult broke. I didn't feel it until I hit the water."

Too focused on the fight. "You fought well." He turned to the water fae, and rubbed his arms against the cold. "Where are we?"

"About half a league from Farlon. There's no easy access to the cave from the shore."

So, they'd have to go back into the water in order to leave. The Molankan had seen which way they'd gone. Some would be scouring the shore for them. They couldn't stay here waiting for the enemy to find them. They needed their horses. "Joden," he called.

The Tarta appeared before him. "Yes, Your Highness."

"Can you arrange for our horses to be brought to the shore?"

"Of course."

Before he disappeared, Darrien asked, "How are your people? Has Meldrick seen them to safety?"

Joden was sober. "Yes. They are out of immediate harm and will continue to travel north to the mountains. The cart you loaned us has been vital. Without it, many of my people would have died in the fire the Molankan lit."

Darrien jolted. Their whole village may have been destroyed. He had to remember he was fighting not just for his people, but for all the peoples of his land. The heaviness of the responsibility almost overwhelmed him.

He closed his eyes. Focus. One step at a time.

His short-term goal had to be getting his men to real safety—the launda forest was their best option. They could recover from their injuries and then deal with the thousands of Molankan invading. Darrien scanned the men for Hadden, and found him sitting with a soldier who had burns down one side. "How bad are the injuries?"

"The fae say the salt water will be good for the burns, Your Highness," the soldier said, cradling his arm with his opposite hand.

He wouldn't be able to fight again. Perhaps Astraea could shelter him until he was healed. "Good. Hadden, can I have a word?"

Hadden got to his feet, and they walked to the front

of the cave, the waves lapping at their feet. Thirteen soldiers were all he had. "Where do we go from here?" Hadden asked the question Darrien was thinking.

"We're no match for the force in Farlon, and it will be a quarter moon for the soldiers from Wodlon garrison to arrive."

"At least we've stopped most of the ships," Hadden pointed out. "Maybe Lachlan can tell us how the other ports fared."

Lachlan was still, bent over Bree, his hands over her wound. Pelham spoke with other soldiers, making the rounds to check how they all were.

"We're outnumbered and the Molankan can spread from the cities before we can put any defences in place."

"Then let's worry about what we can control," Hadden suggested. "We can get these men out of here, regroup with the Wodlon garrison, and any men Gideon and the Otolon soldier recruit."

"They'll need those men for their battles at the other ports." He needed information. Joden appeared before him. "The horses are on their way."

"What's the status at the other ports?"

"The ships haven't arrived yet." He was silent a moment, his head tilted as if listening, and then said, "Gideon has reached Nellon, and is gathering farmers to man the catapults, but the soldier is still on his way to Otolon."

Perhaps Gideon would sink the ships before they reached either port.

Pelham walked over. "I've stitched Bree, but Lachlan says her injury is deeper and still bleeding. He suggests we move to the launda forest where her mother can heal her." Lachlan spoke with one of his fae, who replaced him by Bree's side.

"My people will continue to fight the sailors on the remaining boats," Lachlan said. "But there is little we can do to help you with those already on land."

Darrien nodded. "We will regroup. Do you have a connection with Astraea?"

"Yes. I'll send updates through her until Bree is healed." He glanced at Bree, his face full of concern. "She needs her own kind, quickly."

Darrien jolted. They needed to move fast. "Thank you for your help." Darrien inclined his head.

"This is our home too." Lachlan called to his fae and then said, "Follow the gap around these rocks to get to shore. It's not too deep."

"Joden, where are the Molankan?"

"They've taken over the lookout, and are searching the shoreline. If you go now, you should get away without them catching you."

"Where are the horses?"

"They'll be here soon. We're taking them a different route, so the Molankan soldiers don't spot them."

His nerves trembled. If he got the timing wrong, his men could be slaughtered. But it was time he took control. Pelham's decisions weren't always the right ones. He braced himself and called the men together. "You fought well today." Not a single man was without a bandage or wound on his body. "There will be more battles to come, but we will regroup in the launda forest. Follow Pelham out of the cave where our horses are waiting."

A couple of soldiers nodded as if they approved of the orders, and all got to their feet at his order without looking at Pelham. Darrien pressed his lips together as a surge of confidence swept through him. Perhaps he'd proven himself.

Bree still lay on the ground, unconscious. Carefully he picked her up, and was last to leave the cave, Hadden by his side. They waded around the rocks to the shore and relief filled him to see his men had already claimed their horses and were mounted.

"I'll take her on my horse," Hadden said, mounting.

Darrien hesitated, wanting to keep Bree with him where he could monitor her. No, his friend was right. Better he be unencumbered so he could lead his men. As it was, there were far too many horses without riders.

His stomach clenched as he passed Bree to Hadden. He wouldn't think about the dead yet. At some stage, he would send people to collect those who lay on top of the lookout, but he suspected Tremont would leave a force up there to stop them from retaking the strategic position.

He sighed. They had done what they needed to do—many Molankan sailors were dead. There were fewer who could harm his people.

He mounted, and Joden stood on his horse's neck before him. "The attack in the north has begun," he reported. "The water fae have forced the ships into a channel within reach of the catapults, and many have been sunk already. If they can block the channel, the remaining ships may not have room to turn around. It will delay them."

Relief filled Darrien. Perfect. "Good. Keep me updated, please."

"Of course. There are other Tarta monitoring the Molankan movements. We'll warn you if you come close to them."

"Thank you."

The scrub surrounded them, and it would a quarter league or more before they reached the open farmland between the ocean and the forest. They'd be easily spotted, but the Molankan hadn't brought any horses out of the city. At least they'd be able to outrun them.

But for how long?

Chapter 9

Bree struggled through the haze in her mind, trying to break free of the fatigue which kept her under. Pain pierced the fog, sharp and insistent, and she opened her eyes with a groan. She swayed and arms around her tightened.

"Bree, you're safe. Don't move."

She twisted, gasping at the pain.

"It's Hadden."

The tension in her muscles released, and she took stock of the situation. She was on a horse, and green countryside stretched before her with the launda forest beckoning. The last thing she remembered was being on the shore. "What happened?" Pain thumped a beat in her side.

"We're going to regroup in the launda forest," he said. "Lachlan says your injury needs to be seen by your mother, and we hope the launda fae will shelter our injured men."

That's right. They had shot her as she jumped off the lookout. Her head spun and she swayed as she brushed her wound. Her eyes closed of their own accord. It took too much effort to keep them open. She leaned into

Hadden.

"Don't fall asleep, Bree. We're nearly there."

She was just so tired.

"Bree, talk to me," Darrien ordered from her right.

She forced her eyes open. He rode next to her, no longer the pristine prince he'd been in the castle. His dishevelled hair and crinkled clothes would send his servants into a panic, but the biggest change was the weariness and authority in his gaze. "Any news from the north?"

"The battle has begun near Nellon, and we have people manning the catapults to attack the ships."

Just like they had. "Are they in danger?"

"The enemy in Nellon can't see the coast where the catapults are," Joden said. "They don't know their ships are being attacked."

Good.

"They've sunk half a dozen," Darrien continued.

More dead. They might be the enemy, but she would not celebrate their deaths.

Her palm tingled, and she rubbed it.

Bree, how far away are you?

She jolted at her mother's voice in her head. She'd forgotten about the connection. *We'll be entering the forest soon.* Too soon for her to figure out how to deal with her mother.

I'm waiting. Your pain radiates through our bond.

Was healing something else she could do as part fae? There was so much to learn, and she'd had no time to come to terms with it. She yawned, and the weight of fatigue dragged her under.

Tell whoever is with you to move faster, her mother ordered.

It was an effort to speak. "Mother says, move faster," she murmured.

"Go," Darrien ordered, and suddenly the horse

broke into a trot, and it jerked her about, the pain making her groan. The horse accelerated into a gallop. Bree had no strength to hang on, but Hadden had one arm tight around her.

She moaned.

"We're almost there, Bree. Your mother should be able to take the pain away."

It was impossible to speak through the agony in her side. The forest loomed before her, and when they rode under its boughs, Hadden slowed his horse to a walk. "Where do we go from here, Bree?"

She had no idea, but a soft breeze brushed her skin, and some of her pain receded.

"Bree?" Hadden shook her and the pain returned.

"I don't know."

"Lift her from the horse, Hadden."

They both flinched at the voice coming from the shadows, and Astraea came into the clearing. Hadden lifted Bree down, laying her on the ground. "What do you need me to do?"

Astraea smiled. "Go with Danja. She will show you where your men can rest."

Behind her mother was another launda fae, tall and willowy with black hair, who gestured to Hadden.

Hadden hesitated.

"I will bring Bree back to you when she is healed."

Bree wanted to reassure him she would find them, but her mother placed her hands over Bree's wound and the agony was the last thing she knew.

It was dark when she awoke, but fireflies hovered around her mother, who stood nearby. "How are you?"

Bree placed a hand on the wound, but there was no pain. She prodded, expecting tenderness, and it felt like any other part of her body. "It doesn't hurt."

"I've healed the injury. I will have words to the prince

about putting you in such a dangerous position." The anger in her voice was clear.

Bree sat up. "It was necessary. We blocked the harbour."

"You could have died."

Annoyance filled Bree. "Many more would have if I hadn't been there to communicate between Darrien and Lachlan." Her mother was a fine one to talk. She'd left Bree with an abusive father.

Her mother scowled as she handed Bree food. "Eat. You need to get your strength back."

She bit into the cake-like morsel, and a tart flavour exploded on her tongue. After swallowing, she said, "This is delicious."

"Rogueberry cake," her mother said. "It was your grandfather's favourite."

Bree sat. "Why didn't we ever meet him?"

"You should have. He died unexpectedly. Simply faded away before we discovered what was wrong with him. It was as if the forest had died around him, leaving him powerless, but the launda trees are strong and healthy."

A sense of loss filled Bree for what she hadn't known. She had a million questions, but they would have to wait until later. "Where are Darrien and Hadden?"

"With the rest of their men. I will take you to them in the morning. There is still much we need to discuss."

Bree shook her head. "Now is not the time, Mother. We are at war, and I need to be with the prince in case Lachlan needs to speak with him."

"Lachlan tells me all is quiet," her mother said. "And I can have you to the prince in a matter of minutes. This is something I need to teach you—how to move at speed through the forest."

Interest tickled Bree's skin. Moving fast had definite advantages. "What do you mean?"

"You are connected to the trees and they to you. You can use their energy to propel yourself across the ground." Her mother vanished and then spoke from behind Bree. "Like this."

Bree spun around. "How?"

"Will you allow me the night to teach you powers, which may be of use to you in this fight?"

Interest and excitement shimmered through her veins. She wanted to protect herself and be of more use to Darrien. But a part of her fought against learning about her fae heritage. Being kept from her mother had caused much of Bree's anguish. She sighed. Now wasn't the time to let her emotions rule. "All right."

Her mother returned to her side. "Close your eyes, feel the tree's essence brushing against your skin."

Bree did as she was asked, and a gentle breeze swept past her skin. No, not a breeze, as no leaves rustled.

"Open your mind, listen to them."

She frowned. How did one open their mind? Maybe like she did when she spoke to Lachlan. She tried it and heard faint murmurs.

Hello, Brigette. The voice was aged, full of wisdom.

She jolted and opened her eyes.

Her mother smiled at her. "You heard her?"

"Yes."

Astraea brushed her hand over one of the tree trunks. "This is who is speaking to you."

"What's her name?"

"Trees don't have the concept of names. They are individuals and yet they are one."

"Then how do they know if you're speaking to them?"

"You speak to their essence. Each has a slightly different feel. Reach out again."

Bree reached out with her mind. *Hello?*

We are pleased you have returned to the forest. A different voice this time, just as aged, but a little more playful.

Thank you. A thought occurred to her. "Mother, if the trees are sentient, does it mean we're murdering them if we chop them down?"

"In a way. They can pass their essence into a seed and be reborn, but they lose some of their knowledge and there is a risk the seed won't germinate."

Horror filled Bree. "But we light wood fires every day for cooking."

Her mother laughed. "People gather firewood from the wood the trees discard. They regenerate and leave their old wood behind. It's why we have an agreement with the royal family that only certain trees may be felled. They are trees who choose to be reborn, ones which have grown so old they want to start again."

"That's a relief." She fingered the launda seed her mother had given her before she'd left the forest. "What about this seed? Is it waiting to be reborn?"

"No, it is one of the many potential children the trees scatter on the forest ground. Here in the middle of the forest they have little opportunity to grow, so when a tree is ready to be reborn, we take their seed, nurture it, and plant it on the edges of the forest, or in a clearing where it has a chance to grow."

"Is that why fae exist? To ensure the trees don't die?"

"The relationship is so old, no one really knows. As long as there have been launda trees, there have been launda fae."

"What about the other trees?"

"They are like babies compared to the launda," her mother said.

"Do the fae not nurture them too?"

"We don't leave our forest. Few have thought to venture further and attempt a relationship with them."

Strange. Or maybe not. The uncomfortable dragging sensation when she'd left the forest had been hideous.

"You must learn to use the trees' essence to move faster and hide yourself. That will be the most useful to you in your travels with the prince."

"But there are only two launda forests in Tartalan."

"You may be able to use the techniques with other trees. It is something you will need to experiment with."

Intrigued, Bree asked, "What do I do?"

"First, speak with the tree nearest to you. You want to connect with its essence and ask it to cover you." Astraea placed a hand on the tree trunk and disappeared.

Bree glanced around, squinting in the dark.

"I'm still here." The voice came from the same location, and as Bree watched, her mother reappeared. "You try."

Bree placed her hand on the rough bark and said, *Are you there?*

Of course we are. The tree sounded amused.

Could you please hide me?

A tingly sensation brushed her head and then swept down her body as if she was being covered with a piece of silk.

"Good," her mother said.

Bree looked at her hands. "I can still see myself."

"Yes, you are inside the bubble."

"Then how will I be sure it has worked?" She'd get into all sorts of trouble if she thought she was invisible and stayed still instead of running.

"Ask the tree."

Oh. Her cheeks heated. *Am I covered?*

Yes.

Can you cover someone who is not fae?

Yes, as long as a fae is with them. We helped the prince and his friend escape because you were there.

Bree gasped. "So that's how it happened."

"How what happened?" her mother asked.

Bree asked the tree to stop covering her, and

explained about escaping the city.

"Then you know it already," Astraea said. "I'm pleased you remembered it."

"So am I."

"Let's continue. It is getting late, and you will need to rest before morning. We'll return to your camp, but first I want you to tell me where it is."

"How?"

"Ask the trees. Be specific about who you are looking for, picture them in your mind."

Darrien's face appeared before her, and she sent his image to the tree. *Where is he?*

She sensed the message go out, almost as if the trees whispered to each other, passing the question out, and then a message returned, and she felt pulled in one direction. She pointed. "They're that way."

Astraea beamed. "Correct. Now the last thing to learn is how to move fast. You can connect with the trees' essence, and they will pull or push you in the direction you want to go."

Bree frowned. "I don't understand."

"Walk with me." Her mother held out her hand and after a moment's hesitation, Bree took it. "Open your mind and ask the trees to help you move."

Will you help me move faster?

She wasn't ready for the sudden push and pull, and she stumbled, her hand wrenched from her mother's. She was over ten metres away, despite not having taken a single step.

Her mother chuckled. "It takes a bit of getting used to. The trees in front of you pull and then as you go past, they push until the next tree connects to you."

Bree panted, her head spinning, and placed a hand on her stomach. "It's disorientating."

"At first," her mother agreed. "Try again."

Bree exhaled and prepared herself. She stepped

forward, this time ready for the extra propulsion, and kept walking as the trees helped her. After taking five steps, she stopped and turned. In the distance, the fireflies glowed around her mother. Incredible.

No one would catch her now. She wouldn't have to fear being attacked or captured as long as she was in the forest. Elation filled her, as did a newfound confidence. She strode back to her mother. "Can others travel with me like that, if I hold their hand?"

"Only if the trees agree to it," her mother said. "It takes a lot of effort for them, so only use it when necessary."

Thank you, Bree said to the trees.

"Practise when you can," her mother suggested. "It should become second nature to you, but for now, I should get you back to the camp so you can sleep." She smiled. "You can lead us back to them."

A test. She could do this. Bree took her mother's hand and opened to the trees, finding the camp site. Then she asked for speed and walked towards the men. It took only a minute to arrive, but this time she had some concept of how far she'd travelled.

Her mother squeezed her hand. "Stop here. If you appear in the middle of camp, you'll startle them and they're on edge as it is."

Good idea. Bree coughed and approached the campsite. A fire burned in the centre and the trees leaned away from the heat, unease in their essence. "They don't like the fire."

"No. Fire is one thing which can kill them."

"Should I ask Darrien to extinguish it?"

"Tell him our fears, but it is unnecessary to put it out. The men need the comfort and warmth it brings. As long as they only gather wood from the ground, it is fine."

A guard called, "Who goes there?"

"It's Bree and High Elder Astraea," Bree answered,

moving closer.

The guard bowed. "I'm glad you are well, my Sister."

It took a second for Bree to realise he was talking to her. "I'm not royalty."

"Actually, you are, Bree," her mother said. "Elder Brigette of the launda fae."

That was far too weird to deal with. Yesterday she was in prison. "Call me Bree," she said to the guard.

Most of the men were asleep, but Darrien was speaking with Pelham and Hadden. Suddenly she remembered how she'd yelled at Pelham before leaving the lookout. Would she be punished?

Darrien glanced over as she entered the camp and studied her for a moment before smiling and striding over. "You're well?"

His smile lessened her worry. "I am. Mother healed me."

"Thank you, my Sister." Darrien bowed.

"No need to thank me, Your Highness. She is my daughter." Astraea continued towards the other men. "Tell me what is happening beyond the forest."

"We have men from surrounding villages coming here," Darrien said. "Can your people direct them to us?"

Astraea nodded. "How many ships landed?"

"Three made it to Nellon, and another three were spotted further out to sea, on their way to Otolon." He glanced at Bree. "Can you ask Lachlan if they've found any more?"

She pressed her mark but received no response. "What time is it?"

"About an hour before midnight," Hadden said.

"He might be asleep. I'll try again at midnight."

Darrien nodded. "Five ships remained at Farlon, and Lachlan was going to do what he could to ensure those sailors didn't make it to the shore."

"How many on each ship?" Astraea asked.

"We estimate six hundred," Pelham said.

"How will you stop the Molankan from leaving the cities?" she asked.

"My soldier will gather troops as he goes to Otolon," Darrien said. "I instructed the Sallon garrison to head there, and the Wodlon garrison will come to our aid."

"And in Nellon?"

Darrien said. "We're gathering everyone we can, but the north isn't well populated."

"At least the enemy has nowhere to go," Pelham said. "The mountains are almost impenetrable."

Astraea frowned. "They can pollute the river, and they can mine the mountains. It could do significant damage to the fae who live there."

Darrien held up a hand. "We're not leaving anyone to fend for themselves, but we must prioritise. Tremont wants resources, food foremost. He'll be after the bellar spice farms and the crops. I imagine he'll head south from Farlon first, since most of his men are here. The ships will take another couple of days to arrive in Otolon."

Bree bit her lip. "He doesn't need wood, does he?"

"Why would he?" Astraea demanded.

"If he needs resources, launda wood is highly sought after."

"He has his own forests in Molanka," the high elder said.

Hadden cleared his throat. "Maybe not. I heard a rumour a few months ago when I was drinking in the tavern. A merchant sailor spoke of how much of the launda forests had been chopped down. He was in awe of our forest, which you can see as you sail in."

Astraea paled. "That's not possible. The launda fae would die if he chopped down the forest."

"Can you contact fae on the mainland, Mother?"

Bree asked.

She shook her head. "Only by letter. We can't journey to each other in order to give them the mark they need to communicate, and the distances are too great to travel without much preparation."

Darrien spoke. "Then we may need soldiers in the forest. Your Majesty, are your people trained to fight?"

"No. There's been no need."

"The fae don't do one year of military service like humans?" Bree asked.

"The agreement was humans would protect us if the need arose."

"If Hadden and Bree are right about the lack of resources, then your people might need to fight," Darrien said. "Pelham, can you train them?"

"Yes, Your Highness."

His immediate and respectful reply made Bree blink. Perhaps her accusation had got through to him. "Mother, Pelham should understand what we can do, so he can include it in his plans."

Darrien glanced at her. "What?"

"It is fae knowledge only," Astraea said.

Bree frowned. "We're at war. If fae skills can stop people being killed, then we must use them."

"We're a peaceful people."

"And war has come for us." Without waiting for an answer, Bree requested the tree's help, and brought its essence over her. The men gaping at her proved she was covered. She released the essence.

"That could be very useful," Hadden said.

Astraea sighed. "We can also use the trees to locate people, and to move quickly," she said. "For instance, I know farmers are camped at the edge of the forest about a league from here."

Darrien nodded. "Thank you. Pelham, go with the high elder and work on tactics which will protect the forest."

Bree's palm tingled, and she pressed the mark.

The Molankan are attempting to sneak ashore using the cover of darkness, Lachlan said.

Can you stop them? Bree asked before she passed the news to Darrien.

"Can Lachlan stop them?"

Lachlan answered, *My people are weary, and the grolin have had their fill.*

She shuddered as she told Darrien.

"Ask him to do what he can. We're in no position to stop them. We'll have to face them when they exit the city."

Bree told Lachlan and then asked, *Have you discovered any more ships?*

No, but I have scouts patrolling the ocean.

"Lachlan is patrolling the waters in case more ships come."

"Tell him we may need his people in the rivers going forward, but thank him for his help."

We are at his service, Lachlan replied.

While Darrien and Astraea discussed tactics, Bree wandered over to the base of a launda tree and sat. She recognised its essence as it brushed against her, and she drew comfort from it. She wasn't tired, and needed to be awake so Lachlan could report back on their attempts to stop the sailors reaching land. Hadden joined her.

"You did well today," he said as he sat next to her. "Not many women would have kept such a level head."

There had been little option. "Do you know many women?"

He chuckled. "I simply wanted to ask how you're coping. We've faced a lot in the past couple of days, and Darrien asked me to take care of you."

It was sweet Darrien cared. "It's been a lot," she admitted. "But Tartalan is my home. I don't want it destroyed.”

The tree's essence expanded, brushing Hadden's ear as if examining who he was. Hadden waved his hand. “Damned insects.”

Bree laughed. “It wasn't an insect. It was the tree.”

His eyes widened, and he turned to look at the tree. She opened her mind.

He has the mark of my child, the tree said.

Where is your child?

In the city near the walls.

Bree smiled. *Your child helped us escape.* It might have stopped her falling when she'd leapt from the wall.

Pride burst from the tree and Bree's skin tingled. Hadden rubbed his arms. “What's going on?”

“This tree recognised her child on you. It must have left a residue or a scent or something, I don't know. Her child is the one we climbed to escape the city.”

“Then thank her for us.”

“I have.”

Her mark tingled. *All but one boat reached the shore,* Lachlan reported. *I'm sorry. My people are spent, and many have died.*

Thank you, my Brother. Rest now. Bree stood and went to give Darrien the news.

It was up to them to fight again.

***

Tremont listened to his general report on the attack on the headland. One thing resonated in his head. They'd got away. Jumped from the cliffs into the ocean far below.

A reluctant respect wormed its way through Tremont's annoyance. They had been defeated, and yet they still fought. The playboy prince, as Littleton had called him, showed far more spirit than Tremont had expected.

"We've destroyed the remaining catapult," said the general. "The headland will no longer be a threat. Prince Darrien's men number less than a dozen. I've men scouting the shore for them."

"They have the water fae on their side," Tremont said. "They'll be long gone."

He hadn't expected the fae to take part in the fighting. The fae in his harbour rarely had anything to do with humans. Their complaints consisted of concerns about the water clarity, and he'd told them there was plenty of ocean for them to live in.

The general straightened. "What now, Your Majesty?"

"Bring me every healer in the city and find out whether we can get any ships out of the harbour. I want more food sent to Molanka."

The general hesitated. "Your Majesty, shouldn't we move to attack the garrisons to the south?"

Tremont shook his head. "Let them come to us," he said. "We have a quarter moon at the least before they will arrive. That gives us time to consolidate our control of the city and get the information we need. Take a few men and scout outside the city. I want to know how you would attack Farlon. We can then set up defences."

The general nodded. "Yes, Your Majesty."

After he left, a Tarta appeared on the desk before Tremont. Meldrick inclined his head. "I have spoken to my healers, Your Majesty."

Tremont shifted, giving the little creature his full attention. "What have you discovered?"

"The High Elder of the launda forest had similar symptoms two years ago," Meldrick said.

"How was he cured?"

The sorrow on Meldrick's face held an answer Tremont didn't want to hear. "He wasn't, your Majesty."

Tremont gritted his teeth. "Well, my wife isn't fae.

Did they discover what was wrong with him?"

"No."

Anger blazed and the king dashed the papers off his desk. Meldrick disappeared, reappearing on top of the chair across from him.

"I want answers," Tremont yelled. "I was told Tartalan would provide me with them."

"I'm sorry, Your Majesty. Perhaps if we could see the queen, we could help."

"I'll arrange for you to leave on a ship immediately, if the cursed water fae will let us through."

Meldrick shook his head. "No. We cannot leave Tartalan. We are tied to it. We will die if we leave."

These magical creatures were liars, all of them. The fae in Molanka had sworn to be tied to the land, and yet most of them had now left. All he had to do was figure out how to catch a Tarta. Maybe there was something in the library which spoke of such things.

"So be it," Tremont said. "You may go."

The Tarta High Elder scowled and disappeared.

Restless now, Tremont strode to the library. He burst into the room and the scholar in charge hurriedly stood and bowed. "Your Majesty."

"What news have you?"

The scholar's eyes shone with excitement. "Their library is extensive, Your Majesty. There is much to learn."

"You're here to find a cure for the queen, not satisfy your curiosity," he growled.

The scholar nodded. "Yes, Your Majesty. It seems the fae can heal to varying levels," he said. "The closer the blood relation, the more they can heal."

"Can they heal humans?" The launda fae in Molanka had sworn they had tried to heal his father's injury, but he didn't believe them.

"There are some accounts of this occurring."

"And what of the Tarta?"

"The information on them is more obscure." The scholar reached for a book on the table.

"Can they be captured and taken from Tartalan?"

The scholar frowned, flipping through the pages. "I have found no reference to that."

"Well, look for it." Time was running out, he knew it. Emeline was growing progressively worse, not better, and he would get no news of her until he returned to Molanka.

"Yes, Your Majesty."

Tremont strode from the room and up to the tower to look over the city. All was quiet now the harbour battle was over. Broken planks floated in the water and the remains of many of his ships blocked the only passage through the reef.

They would have to clear it in order to get his ship of supplies through. Perhaps Littleton could negotiate with the water fae.

He'd had very little trouble from the populace after the initial invasion. Most were happy to be left in peace to go about their normal lives. He would show them he was a benevolent king.

They would be pleased to be part of Molanka once more.

Part 2
Sylta

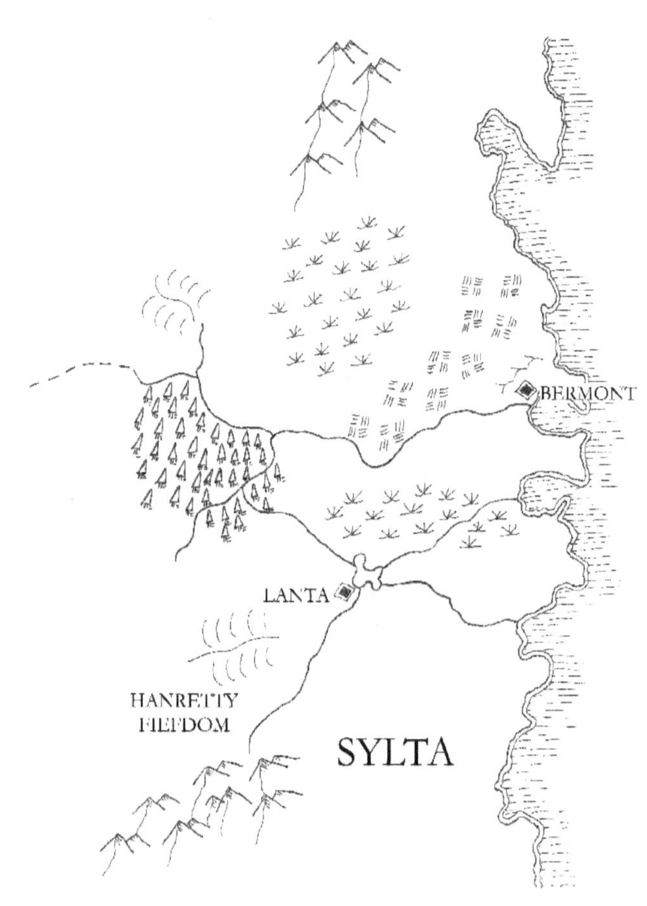

BERMONT
LANTA
HANRETTY
FIEFDOM
SYLTA

Chapter 10

Madeleine Hanretty absent-mindedly tapped her finger on the desk as she went through the numbers in front of her. The grain harvest would be down this year, but not by too much. She would have to ensure she left her villagers enough for their own use, before she sent the rest to the capital for the king to distribute.

A bird chirped nearby, and she glanced at the window where a willy wagtail sat on the sill, preening in front of its reflection. She wasn't sure whether he thought another bird was inside, or if he realised it was his reflection, but he was often there while she worked in her father's study. She sighed. Perhaps she should call it her study now. Her father had gone to the palace a decade ago and returned only once or twice a year. Being the prince's tutor held a lot of responsibility.

But Prince Godric was older than she was, close to five and twenty, and hardly needed a tutor any longer. An advisor maybe, because the man had had little concept of what life was like outside the palace when she'd first met him.

She smiled at the memory. King Orion had been touring the fiefdoms with his son. She'd been about eleven and returned from visiting her mother's family in the silk valley to find a strange teen sparring in the courtyard with their stable boy, Kiril. Madeleine had grabbed a wooden training sword and run to join in, only for the teen to refuse to spar with her. "Girls don't fight."

Fury had overtaken common sense, and she'd disarmed the boy, and stabbed him in the stomach with her sword before storming off. Only later did she discover she'd injured the crown prince.

Godric had wanted her punished, but somehow her father had managed to convince the king that she hadn't meant any real harm. Then he'd told Madeleine she had to entertain Godric while he and the king discussed business.

At first, Madeleine had thought it a far worse punishment than she deserved. Godric had little idea about country life, or how to treat those who ranked lower than he did. She'd yelled at him more than she'd care to admit now, with all the righteousness of an eleven-year-old, but at some stage they'd reached a truce.

The willy-wagtail chirped and flew away, down towards the river.

That had been the location of their truce. Godric had insisted on going fishing, and since she was his companion, she'd had to go with him. She thought it would be tremendously boring, but he'd taught her the peace that could be found listening to the river and being quiet in her thoughts. It was then she'd caught a glimpse of the lonely youth he was, and from that moment on, she was determined to befriend him.

She'd taught him about the silk valley fae, taking him to meet the High Elder, who was also her grandmother. Then she'd introduced him to their villagers, and all the staff.

He'd lost some of what she'd called his royal stiffness, and at the end of their stay, had impressed the king with his knowledge of the fiefdom.

To Madeleine's horror, the king was so pleased he'd ordered her father to return to the capital to be Godric's tutor.

Which left Madeleine without a father.

She sighed. She'd insisted on taking her father's place running the estate because it was her fault he was gone. Her mother had agreed she could learn, and the steward had taught Madeleine about taking care of her tenants and running a fiefdom. Parvan had been reluctant to teach a young girl at first, but when both Madeleine's parents insisted, he relented. She was half-fae and fae had less defined gender roles than humans. Now she had his respect, but it had taken years to earn it.

Someone knocked on the study door. She glanced over at the maid who stood in the entrance. "Come in, Casey."

"I have a letter, Madeleine."

"Thank you." Her father's handwriting on the front of the thick envelope made her smile.

"Will Lady Lorelei and Nadia be home for dinner this evening?" the maid asked.

"I believe so," Madeleine said. Her mother and sister were visiting High Elder Lanley of the Silk Valley fae. She ignored the tug of jealousy about Nadia learning more about their fae heritage. She had enough to keep herself busy without adding fae duties to her schedule.

"I'll tell Cook."

Madeleine nodded and reached for the letter opener. Carefully, she slid the blade under the thick paper and withdrew several letters. She put those addressed to her mother and sister aside, and opened the one addressed to her. Another letter fell out and her heart jolted. From Godric. Despite their inauspicious meeting, they'd parted on friendly terms, and being a young, optimistic child, she thought they would be best friends forever, even though he was four years older, and the crown prince. So she'd written to him when she'd written to her father, and he responded. As she'd grown older, she wondered whether her father forced him to write to her, or if he'd made a servant write on his behalf. She imagined he had far too many responsibilities to worry about one girl's feelings.

She hesitated, her hand hovering between the two letters, and then picked up her father's. Not for the first time she wished he was fae, so she could communicate with him through her mind the way she could communicate with her mother.

My dearest daughter,

Preparations for the Queen's fiftieth birthday celebrations are in full swing, and by the time you receive this I will be surrounded by dignitaries and very important people. The King of Tartalan is due to arrive with his family, and that adds to the chaos as servants fret about how exacting he will be in his needs. I do not worry, for he was not demanding the last time he visited his sister.

Thank you for your last report on the estate. I have told the king your concerns about the harvest, and he says to make sure our people are not left without.

She smiled. She hoped he would say that, but it took time for news from the rest of the country to reach her in the south, and she didn't know how other fiefdoms fared.

I have something to raise which you will find distasteful. In your mother's last letter to me, she spoke about finding you a suitable husband.

Madeleine blinked and reread the sentence. A husband. Why would she want to marry a man who would then take control of the estate and tell her what to do? Her father may be progressive, but most men believed a woman's role was to have babies and see to their needs. Both of her parents knew her feelings on the subject.

Your mother hopes she will find someone when she visits her kin in the valley, but has asked that I pave the way for you to visit the capital should she find no one you like.

Her mother had been scheming behind her back. Madeleine knew something was up when she'd left a fortnight ago, but thought she was simply excited about going home. Besides, if she married a Silk Valley fae, she would have to move there, and would no longer be able to run the estate. Most fae, those without royal blood, couldn't go far from the valley without harm.

As half-fae, Madeleine didn't have those issues, though unlike Nadia she hadn't embraced her powers. Madeleine's duty was to the human side of her heritage since she'd left them without their lord.

With a sigh, she continued reading.

I tell you this, so it doesn't come as a surprise when I invite you to Lanta. Since I received your mother's letter, I have been considering young men, but I fear you will find them all a little vain, and they will not know what to do with your independence. There is only one whom you might consider, but I shall tell you about him if you do indeed visit. For now, know your mother and I will never force you to marry anyone who doesn't meet your approval, and we only want the best for you.

Your loving father,

Shelton

Madeleine flipped the letter over, looking for more. Normally her father wrote longer letters telling her about what was happening around Sylta. Perhaps he had no time amongst the birthday celebration preparations. She closed the letter and slid it into the wooden box with the other letters from her father. She'd known this day would come, though foolishly she'd hoped it wouldn't be for another few years. As the eldest child, her duty was to produce an heir, to train him or her to take care of their people so that everyone on the fiefdom was educated, fed and clothed. Some of the workers told her tales of other fiefdoms where the tenants were treated badly, starved and whipped if they didn't produce. She wouldn't allow it to happen on her land.

In the fae world it wasn't uncommon for a woman to have a child without marrying, but if Madeleine did, it would be a horrible scandal. Her child would be a bastard, and her reputation would be ruined.

She carried the prince's letter over to the chair by the window. It was a glorious day outside, blue skies, and as she opened the window, a gentle breeze blew in.

Madeleine smiled. If she had time later, she'd go fishing to let her mind wander. Her fingers brushed the letter. Godric had been right all those years ago. The gurgle of the stream, the hush of the wind through the trees and the birds singing, plus the sweet scent of sugar blossoms was magic.

Madeleine opened his two-page letter and settled into her chair. That was more like it.

Madi,

Your last letter arrived at the perfect moment, for I was in need of a bit of cheer. Both our fathers had just sat me down and told me it was time I took a wife. They suggested Princess Amber of Molanka would be a suitable candidate, as it would bring our two countries closer together. Then Father and Shelton outlined a number of other women, listing their political value and their virtues as if they were horses at auction. I imagined your reaction if you'd heard your father talking as such and pointed it out to him. He asked me not to tell you.

Madeleine grinned. She'd have a word to her father about it in her next letter.

I refuse to marry anyone whom I have not yet met, so they have invited every candidate to Mother's birthday celebration. Only today we discovered Princess Amber would not be in attendance as her mother is ill. I guess it gives me an excuse to prevaricate.

But speaking of Mother's celebration, it is the biggest hullaballoo. I've been fitted for at least a dozen new outfits and have a list as long as my arm of events I must attend. The only bright side is my Tartalan cousins will be coming, and it will be nice to see them.

She was glad. Over the years, she'd noticed he didn't speak of friends and frivolity, only duty, or tales of what his valet or servants did. The only time he'd been involved in shenanigans was when his cousin Darrien had visited. Perhaps his next letter would be full of hijinks.

The rest of the letter reported the latest palace gossip. She was smiling by the time she finished it. Over the years, he'd told her so much about the people in the palace that she felt she knew them. Everyone from the stable boy who was now a man and dating the scullery maid, all the way up to the priests and nobles with whom he interacted on a daily basis.

The teen she'd met so long ago hadn't known the names of many of his retainers when he'd arrived, though she made certain he knew them all by the time he'd left. So perhaps something she taught him had stuck.

She tucked the letter into her belt. It would go into a box in her bed chamber.

Casey returned to the study. "Madeleine, a messenger arrived to say Mistress Blacksmith had a healthy baby girl."

Madeleine grinned, getting to her feet. "Wonderful news! Could you ask Cook to arrange a hamper of bread with a jar of jam, and ask Kiril to saddle my horse?"

"Yes, ma'am."

Madeleine went upstairs to change into riding breeches, and tucked Godric's letter into the little wooden box on her dresser. Then she took her hat and trotted down the stairs. The kitchen was uncomfortably warm with the fires blazing. "Good afternoon, Cook."

"Mistress Madeleine." Cook curtsied. "Hamper's on

the table." After years of trying, Madeleine had finally given up asking Cook to stop curtsying and calling her mistress. Some things she couldn't change.

"Thank you. I'll be gone about an hour." She picked up the hamper, greeting the other workers in the kitchen, and went outside to the stables. Kiril led her black mare out to her.

"All ready for you, Madeleine." He wore a flat cap over his dark hair, though the ends poked out of it.

"Thanks." She dragged his cap from his head and tousled his hair. "About time you got your hair cut, isn't it?"

He shoved her away with a grin. "I'll ask Cook to cut it for me later. Where are you off to?"

His smile lit up his face and her father's words came back to her. Though Kiril was only a couple of years older than her, she'd never seen him as more than a surrogate brother. He'd been her sparring partner when they'd been younger, had laughed at her naming her sword Caitlyn, after a heroine in stories of old. Then he'd refused to fight her any longer after his growth spurt, afraid he would hurt her. More likely he was afraid she'd show him up. Whatever the reason, they were still friends.

"The village. Mistress Blacksmith had her baby." She allowed him to give her a leg up, though she didn't need the help.

He passed the hamper to her. "Give the Blacksmiths my congratulations."

"I will." She kicked her horse into a trot and headed out.

Only yards from the gate, her palm tingled. She halted her horse and touched the spiral mark there. *What's wrong, Mother?*

Her voice sounded in Madeleine's mind. *I need you to come to the silk valley immediately.*

Madeleine glanced at the hamper she held. The valley was in the opposite direction to the village. *Why? Is someone hurt?*

You're needed to form a communication circle.

Strange. She wasn't usually involved in things like that, but the concern in her mother's tone was enough to stop her asking questions. *I'll be there soon.*

She looked around. Kiril was coming out of the stable with another horse. She rode over to him. "Can you take this to the Blacksmiths?" She held out the hamper.

"Of course. What's wrong?"

"Mother needs me in the silk valley."

Kiril took the hamper from her. "Is everything all right?"

"I'm not certain. I should be home by dinner."

She kicked the horse into a canter and rode the two miles to the valley where the silkworms lived side by side with the fae. As she grew closer, the valley pulled at her like a whirlpool dragged water to its centre. She was used to the sensation and welcomed its embrace. The difficulty came when it was time to leave, and the pull became something weighing her down, trying to keep her there. At the top of the valley, Madeleine spotted dozens of silkworms, the size of small dogs, grazing in the grassy meadow below. With them were fae who cared for them.

As she rode down the trail into the valley, she scanned for signs of what had her mother so upset. No trees had been cut down, nothing was blackened, signifying a fire had passed through, and the stream still sparkled in the sunlight as it wove its way along the valley floor. The burrows where the fae lived were dotted along the slopes and people wandered along the paths between them, but no one looked panicked. It was life as normal.

Where are you, Mother?

At the silkworm nursery.

She stiffened. If something was wrong with the

babies, it was serious.

She rounded a bend and took the path which ran along the slope rather than further down. It had been a while since she'd visited the silkworm nursery, but she still remembered the way. She urged her horse faster. The babies were the lifeblood of the valley.

The path opened into a large, grassed meadow surrounded by trees. Her mother stood in the middle speaking with High Elder Lanley and her two brothers, and Nadia spoke with their cousins nearby. Seeing them all together made Madeleine aware how little she resembled her mother's side. They were all smaller than her, with delicate features, long fingers for unravelling silk and larger ears for hearing the babies' cries.

Madeleine dismounted, leaving her horse at the edge of the meadow, and carefully approached, watching where she placed her feet. The grasses were long enough to hide the babies, and baby silkworms were small and soft, not yet having formed the protective shell around their bodies. It was easy to step on one if she wasn't watching where she was going. Around them the babies squeaked, and Nadia picked up one, soothing it against her chest. There were far more babies than normal.

"Grandmother." She bowed her head in respect. "Mother, what's going on?"

"Madeleine, thank you for coming so quickly. We need your help." High Elder Lanley reached out and pulled Madeleine towards her. "We're trying to reach the silk valley fae in Molanka, but no one is responding. Our link has grown weaker over the past year, and I hope with the addition of you, we'll be able to reach them."

All of this rush so she could speak to Madeleine's uncle, who had married a Molankan fae elder? Madeleine frowned. "What's so urgent?"

"The babies aren't growing," her mother said. "Some hatch, but don't get any bigger than the one Nadia is holding, and many more aren't hatching at all."

"Are the fae well?" The silkworms and the valley fae were connected. If one was sick, the other would become sick as well.

"Yes," Lanley answered. "That's why we need to contact our kin in Molanka, to ask if they've experienced anything like this before." The others joined them; her two uncles and five cousins, as well as her mother and Nadia.

It had been a long time since Madeleine had tried to communicate with the fae this way. She closed her eyes and cleared her thoughts. Lanley's voice sounded in her mind.

Nikolas, we seek your help. Can you hear us?

Her voice echoed as if in a deep chasm.

From a distance, Madeleine felt a tug, so faint, as if a fish was nibbling on a bait. She focused on it as she was taught but heard nothing.

Nikolas, we beg an answer.

Another tug. "Did you feel that?" she asked.

"What?" Lanley asked.

"A faint tug." In her mind, she showed them the direction.

Her grandmother called again, sending her plea towards the tug.

Nothing. Eventually the queen let go and sighed. "I don't like this. We've never had trouble connecting before."

They had a full circle of royals. It should have been enough to push the message to the other side of Molanka.

"We'll have to send a letter," her mother said.

"We could also send word to the king," Madeleine said. "The Tartalan royals are visiting for the Queen's birthday. They might agree to take word to the silk valley fae on their island."

"Good idea," her mother said.

"I'll write to them now." High Elder Lanley strode across the meadow and Madeleine's family followed. None of them watched their footing, as they had an innate knowledge of where the silkworms were. Madeleine hunched her shoulders. She'd never managed to master that skill. After her father left for the palace, her duty had been to the manor house, not to her fae side. She'd long ago squashed her desire to learn more.

At the edge of the meadow, Madeleine collected her horse from one of the fae. "Thank you." Her face flushed. The others were already far ahead of her.

She arrived at the High Elder's residence, which was in a place of more prominence so she could be accessible to her people. It was something Madeleine always admired about the fae. There were no people to go through to get to the leaders. Perhaps it was because they were all tied to this place, unable to leave, and that encouraged everyone to get along and problems to be solved quickly without them escalating. Those who disagreed with each other tended to live at opposite ends of the valley.

Inside were several nooks where the silkworms nested, a dozen or so eggs surrounded by the most delicate silk. A couple of adult silkworms came to greet them.

Madeleine crouched to pat them. They had lived with her grandmother for years. They butted her arm, their armour cold against her skin. "Hello, again."

Welcome.

The silkworms had a limited vocabulary, but it was enough.

The queen sat at her desk to write the letters, and Nadia joined Madeleine. "If the babies don't grow, the fae will become weak," she murmured.

Madeleine nodded. She'd made that connection. The

older silkworms would eventually die and without others growing to maturity, no more babies would be born.

"We need to decide who will take the messages," Elder Aralon announced.

"I'll get Kiril to take them," Lorelei said.

Madeleine felt a twinge of jealousy. When she was younger, she had longed to explore the world.

Aralon shook his head. "He is not one of us. He will not understand the severity of the issue."

"There's no one else," her mother said. "We can't go more than a league from the valley without significant preparation, and we don't have that much time."

"Half-fae can travel further," Aralon said. They both looked at Madeleine and Nadia. Nadia stiffened. "I can't," she said. "It grows harder to leave the valley each time I return to the manor house."

Madeleine frowned. Her sister hadn't mentioned it, though she had been spending more and more time in the valley.

"I'm needed to run the fiefdom," Madeleine said, though she longed to say yes.

Lorelei hesitated. "Parvan is capable of managing in your stead."

Madeleine blinked. "You want me to go?" Excitement and nerves fluttered in her stomach.

"No. It will be an arduous journey and the thought of you so far away makes me nauseous," she said. "But your uncle is right. Only a fae can take one of the eggs and show our kin what is wrong."

Madeleine was torn. Would her tenants be all right without her? "The graduation ceremony is next week."

"Your sister or I will go," Lorelei said.

"Harvesting is only a few weeks away." There were celebrations to attend and deities to pray to. All the duties she'd taken over for her father at such a young age.

"I will ensure Parvan manages everything."

The Queen folded the letters and sealed them. "Your mother is right. Your duty to your fae heritage is as important as your duty to your human side. It is time you recognised that."

Madeleine stepped back at her tone. She'd never seen it that way. Her work at the manor house was her penance, and Nadia was their mother's representative with the fae. She glanced at Lorelei, who pursed her lips and then nodded.

Guilt, hope, and duty clashed. She straightened. "When do I leave?"

The queen handed her the letters. "At first light, tomorrow."

Chapter 11

His Royal Highness Crown Prince Godric of Sylta hated formal occasions—the pomp, the ceremony, being the centre of attention. He stood stiffly in his blue suit, the starch in his white shirt collar scratchy enough to cause a constant itch on the back of his neck. Next to him stood his mother, father and two sisters as the Tartalan royal family were formally introduced. The great hall was full of onlookers and invited guests, all at the capital for his mother's fiftieth birthday celebration.

Crown Prince Ethan of Tartalan stood next to King Jerek and Queen Isabelle, alert and resplendent in his green suit. By his side was his pregnant wife and then Prince Rainier, but Princes Darrien and Kerwin weren't there. Had they stayed in Tartalan? Disappointment filled him even as he told himself it was for the best. Darrien had got them all into trouble the last time they were together. Godric had fun until his father's disapproval bore down on him.

Finally, the announcements were over, and the polite greetings began, the small bow, the air kisses, all for show. Everyone would die of shock if he ran over and hugged his uncle like Madeleine had done with her royal fae relatives.

Godric air-kissed his aunt. "You look well, your Majesty."

"And you look far too handsome not to have a wife," she murmured.

He stifled a groan. If she worked with his mother, they'd have him married before the festivities ended.

"I hope you've got a good bottle of whisky," Rainier said under his breath as they bowed to each other.

"I might," Godric replied, glancing at the stern expression on his father's face.

"You both had better behave," Ethan said. "We left Darrien behind for a reason."

Godric bit his tongue to keep his impersonal 'royal' face on as he followed his parents into the private sitting room, out of view of the public. When the door closed behind the two families, both queens sighed and hugged each other with genuine affection. "It's so good to see you," Queen Isabelle said.

Rainier slapped him on the back. "The whisky?"

"Boys, it's far too early," Queen Matana said.

"It's celebratory, Auntie. A toast to your good health."

She shook her head, smiling.

Godric waited until his father nodded his approval, before retrieving the glasses and pouring each man a shot. "Where are Kerwin and Darrien?"

Ethan glanced at his father, who was already talking with King Orion. "Father left Darrien in charge, hoping it would spark some responsibility in him. But then at the last minute, he left Kerwin there to keep him in line."

It had been a few years since he'd last seen his cousins. "What has Darrien done?"

"Nothing but whoring and hunting," Rainier said. He winced. "Sorry, ladies." He ducked his head as Godric's sisters and Ethan's wife moved to talk with the queens.

Godric frowned. He always forgot how much more relaxed his cousins were in private. They could behave however they wanted, but Godric's father always insisted he behave appropriately, because servants gossiped. He tugged at his collar. "I guess being younger has its advantages."

"Yeah. The sooner Ethan's baby is born, the happier I'll be," Rainier said. "So how many royals have been invited to this shindig?"

He winced at the phrase and moved across the room, away from his father. "Molanka sent word they won't be coming as the queen is ill. You won't be able to meet Princess Amber."

Rainier screwed up his nose. "I don't want to. Mother will arrange a marriage."

Godric smiled, glad he wasn't the only one going through the marriage market. "Mother suggested her to me as well. There are a few more ladies in her arsenal, and if we're not careful, they'll have us both married before you leave."

"Hey, you're the one who needs to produce heirs," Rainier said. "I'm covered as long as Ethan's baby is born healthy and well."

"It will be," Ethan said firmly.

His wife looked well, showing only a small baby bump. Godric tossed back his whisky, and it burned all the way to his stomach. He wasn't ready for marriage, and he wouldn't know what to do with a child. He wanted to live, to experience real life rather than the duty that suffocated him in the palace. The only time he'd had a measure of freedom was visiting Madi at Shelton's estate.

Rainier clapped him on the shoulder. "You've gone pale. Don't worry, we're in this together."

He smiled. At least he had someone on his side.

Three days later Godric was revising his optimism. His feet hurt because he was constantly on show, his royal smile was stuck on his face, and he'd barely had time to talk to his cousins after the first evening due to all the balls and dinners he was forced to attend. With a different girl on his arm at each one.

Where had his mother found so many vapid women?

They had no personality of their own and spent half their time curtsying and simpering about doing whatever he wanted to do. They'd faint if he suggested fishing or galloping across the countryside in a race.

His father stormed into the library where Godric hid, looking as if he wanted to murder someone. Shelton, Godric's advisor, was right behind him. Godric jumped to his feet. "What's happened?"

The moment the door closed his father cursed loudly. "Jerek's ship has been stolen."

Godric blinked. He must have misheard. "What?"

"The ship that brought Jerek and his family to Sylta is gone, and my harbour master can't tell me how long it's been missing."

Shelton nodded a greeting at Godric. "So many ships have been in and out of the harbour over the past few days, they only noticed today, and sent an urgent message with the water fae."

Who would steal a royal ship? "What about the sailors on board?" Perhaps they took a sail while the royal family was busy upriver.

"Missing," his father snapped. "This reflects badly on us. We must find it immediately."

Godric straightened. "What can I do to help?"

"Nothing. You should be at the afternoon tea in the water gardens, not hiding in here."

Trust his father to know Godric's precise schedule. Before Godric answered, Orion continued, "Shelton, travel downriver to the harbour and investigate. I want answers."

"Of course." Shelton bowed, though there were no servants around.

Godric hated the formality. Surely in private they could drop their guard.

Orion turned to Godric, irritation on his face. "If you don't choose a wife by the end of the celebrations, I'll choose one for you, no matter what your mother thinks." He walked out.

Godric winced and clenched his hands to stop himself from running his hand through his hair.

"Take heart," Shelton said. "He only wants you to have what he and Matana have."

Annoyance filled him. Shelton was always defending the king. "No. He just wants me to produce an heir."

Shelton shook his head. "He's hard on you, because he doesn't know any other way. He wants you to be happy." He smiled. "Just like I want my daughters to be happy. I'm going to ask your father if Madeleine can come to court after the birthday celebrations."

"Why?" He couldn't picture Madeleine enjoying dressing for every occasion, though it would be nice to see the young girl again.

"Like you, it's time she found a spouse."

Godric did a double-take. "Little Madeleine?"

"She's one and twenty."

No. She couldn't be. In his head he still pictured her as the eleven-year-old girl with pigtails and a determined attitude. "How did that happen?"

Shelton chuckled. "The same way you became five and twenty. You'd better not keep your mother waiting."

Godric nodded and left the library, his thoughts on the red-haired girl who had charmed him as a teen. Her letters always entertained him, and he looked forward to receiving them, but he'd still kept the image in his mind of her as a scrappy, joyful child, with her hair always falling out of its pigtails. What would a grown-up Madeleine be like?

Three hours later, Godric was ready to drown himself in the tea. His mother and aunt had amassed several tables full of ladies and their daughters for him to meet. At least he wasn't alone. Rainier sat at the next table looking white around the eyes.

"Your Highness, did you know the silk we wear comes from worms?" a young blonde woman whose name he couldn't remember asked him.

"Yes, I did."

"Oh." She seemed disappointed, as if it was some amazing titbit of information no one knew. He'd seen the silkworms when he'd visited Shelton's home and first met Madeleine. He'd held one of the squishy babies, terrified he would accidentally squash it, and it had squeaked at him. Shelton entered the garden and caught Godric's eye. He shouldn't be back so soon.

"Excuse me, ladies. I must have a word with my advisor." He stood, waiting impatiently for them all to stand and curtsy, and then strode across to greet Shelton. "Save me."

Shelton didn't smile. "You need to come. I've sent for the king."

Not good news, then. He glanced back and caught his mother's eye, giving her a hand signal that meant something had come up. She inclined her head and then turned back to the table.

As they walked through the garden, he asked, "What is it?"

"In private," Shelton said. They returned to the library and Orion entered the room with King Jerek. "What's this all about?"

Shelton bowed. "I intercepted more news from the coast."

"What?" Orion barked.

"A water fae stopped the boat on my way downriver," he said. "The bodies of King Jerek's crew floated in on the tide this morning."

Jerek's face darkened.

"The fae said their king has people searching the waters for the ship."

"Anything else?" Orion said.

"When I asked him if the fae had noticed anything unusual, he said a lot of Molankan traders were coming to port with empty hulls, wanting to purchase goods to take home." Shelton continued, "Elder Phillipe of the water fae is travelling upriver so we may communicate more quickly with the coast."

Godric frowned. Traders never came empty-handed.

"That's irrelevant," Jerek said. "I want the men who killed my people and stole my ship found."

"It might not be irrelevant," Orion said. "Molanka has been struggling since the plague swept through their country. Perhaps someone was desperate enough to steal the ship hoping to sell it."

"If that was the case, why wouldn't King Tremont ask for help?" Godric asked.

"He's stubborn and won't allow negative opinions about his country," Orion said.

"Why isn't Tremont here?" Jerek asked.

"His wife is ill. Perhaps we can get the fae to search the Molankan harbour for the missing ship." Orion looked at Shelton.

"I'll see to it."

"Get back to your party," Orion ordered Godric.

"Yes, Your Majesty." He bowed and exited the room. It didn't matter who was responsible for the theft of the ship. His father would consider it as a stain on his honour. And Godric would have to be even more perfect to make up for it. He hesitated at the junction. One corridor led to the garden, the other to his bedroom where he could hide. Before he could even contemplate his choice, he heard his father's voice in his head and saw the look of disappointment.

He sighed and continued back to the garden, keeping his chin up the entire way.

Chapter 12

Madeleine set off for the capital city, Lanta, the next day. With her rode the manor house's weapons master, Brogan, Kiril, and three other guards. She carried a letter of authorisation from High Elder Lanley which should allow her passage through to the Molankan silk valley without trouble. Otherwise, women riding without a female escort would be frowned upon and stopped. Tucked into her jacket pocket were two additional letters; one for King Jerek to take to Tartalan, and the other to give to High Elder Cilla of the Molankan silk valley fae.

In a backpack, she also carried one of the silkworm eggs, to show the Molankan fae what was wrong. Nerves jangled inside her. Taking an egg so far from the valley was a risk, but the High Elder had faith Madeleine's faint fae powers would be enough to keep it healthy. She hoped her grandmother was right.

They rode as fast as their horses would allow them, stopping at night at inns on the side of the road. The first day was uneventful as they travelled through her lands, but she had to resist stopping at the villages to check how everyone was. She would have to do that on her return. This mission was far too important. She couldn't miss

King Jerek.

The only excitement came when a group of brigands tried to stop them, but Brogan fired warning arrows as they thundered through, and the men didn't follow.

Almost a week after Madeleine left, she rode through the huge wooden gates of Lanta. The streets were paved with white stone and decorations hung from buildings proclaiming the queen's birthday. Madeleine's eyes widened. So many buildings built on top of each other, and so many people. The mood was jovial, and people danced in the street, calling out greetings as they moved towards the centre of the city.

"It must be the Queen's birthday today," Kiril commented as the third person toasted the queen's good health.

That would make it more difficult to visit her father. He would be busy with duties. She spotted a woman dancing nearby, and waved her closer. "Excuse me, can you direct us to the palace?"

"Straight down this road and left at the end," the woman said. "Are you attending the festivities?" She looked them up and down with suspicion.

"No, just taking a message."

They continued slowly through the streets as people weren't inclined to get out of the way. More than once, a drunken man stumbled in front of her, and she had to rein her horse in sharply. They reached the end of the street and turned left. Madeleine gasped. In front of them lay a huge, glistening lake, and on its shores stood the palace. The white stone stretched several storeys high, with circular towers at the corners, and bright red tiles on the roof.

"Holy Purifier," Kiril breathed.

"It's something all right," Brogan agreed.

Madeleine had never seen any building so large before, but it was the massive lake which caught her attention. Sail boats and fishing vessels criss-crossed its surface, and the opposite bank was a shadow in the distance. It felt magical, and her fae blood was drawn to it.

Startled by the intensity of the feeling, she halted her horse and blinked.

"Something wrong?" Kiril called.

She shook her head. Perhaps she'd take the silkworm egg to its shores in the morning, but right now, the sun sank towards the horizon. She wanted to be inside before dark. "Let's go."

People streamed towards the lake as if something were happening on its shores. Madeleine ignored the urge to follow. The letters from her grandmother were a constant presence against her chest, and she wanted to be rid of them.

The palace gates were open, but a metal portcullis blocked the way and guards stood at the entrance, their blue uniforms clean and pressed. Madeleine dismounted, handing her reins to Kiril, and approached on foot.

"Name?" the younger guard barked.

"Madeleine Hanretty," she replied.

He checked a book in front of him. "You're not on the list."

She smiled. "No, I wouldn't be. I'm not here for the queen's celebrations. I'm here on behalf of High Elder Lanley of the Silk Valley fae."

"We've already received the high elder's gift," the older one said, his moustache thick and greying.

"This is on another matter." She passed him the letter of passage.

He read it and handed it back. "Nothing there says you need to come inside."

She read the letter. It only dealt with travel into Molanka. Filthy bog marsh. "Please. I have a letter for King Jerek." She showed it to him.

He took it and screwed up his nose. "I'll ensure he gets it." He went to tuck it into his jacket.

"No!" She snatched it back. "I have to deliver it myself. Please, it will only take a moment. If you call for Shelton Hanretty, he'll vouch for me. He's my father."

The guard studied her. "He'll be with the royal family today."

She gritted her teeth. "I understand, but the matter is urgent." If she could deliver the message today, she could be on her way to Molanka tomorrow. The sooner she found an answer to the problems with the silkworms, the safer her family would be.

A guard ran up to the gate. "They're coming. You need to clear the way."

Both guards jumped to attention, and the moustached one shooed her backwards as the portcullis rose, and a contingent of guards marched through the palace grounds towards them. "Go. The royal family are coming."

Madeleine smiled. She'd get Godric to help her. She returned to her horse, and allowed the guards to push her out of the way.

"You need to dismount," the younger guard called.

She gestured for the others to do so as the palace guards strode out of the palace, lining the street between the palace and the lake. People were pushed back, so the street was cleared.

A few minutes later, trumpets sounded, and more guards preceded a royal carriage. She recognised King Orion sitting next to his wife and across from them sat Prince Godric and his sisters.

Madeleine stared. There were hints of the teenaged boy she'd met—this man had the same black hair, now worn long to his collar as was the latest fashion, and a strong nose she'd teased him about—but the stiffness of his posture and his expressionless face was like a sculpture made from marble. He nodded regularly to the crowd who had flooded out of the nearby buildings to see him.

Madeleine waved, trying to get his attention. "Godric!" Her call was drowned out by cheers. Curse it. She scanned the other carriages, hoping to glimpse her father in the procession which followed. Another carriage full of royals judging from the crowns they wore. They must be from Tartalan. Where was her father?

More carriages flowed out of the palace, but they were enclosed, and she couldn't see who was inside. It took almost half an hour for them to pass, and when they were done, the guards still lined the streets. Probably to keep it clear for their return.

Madeleine sighed. "Let's find somewhere to stay the night." They could return before the procession and try again.

Brogan spoke to a guard who directed him back down a street to an inn.

"It's no wonder they didn't let us in," Brogan said as they unsaddled their horses. "None of us look as fancy as those people."

He was right. Unlike at home, here she was unimportant. If she wanted an audience, she needed to dress the part. Thankfully her mother had insisted she pack a high-quality dress, the type she only wore if neighbouring lords paid her a visit. It had been difficult to fit in the saddle bag, but she'd managed it.

"I'll wash and change. You find dinner and have the evening free."

Brogan and Kiril both shook their heads. "You're not wandering around the city unaccompanied," Brogan said.

Kiril crossed his arms and grunted in agreement.

"Fine. If you're accompanying me, you can bathe too, and put on your best clothes." She swept inside and asked the landlady to bring her some water. "What is the royal family doing at the lake?" she asked.

"The water fae have put together a show for the Queen."

Madeleine glanced at the door. She'd like to see that, but by the time she got the creases out of her dress it would probably be finished. Besides, that wasn't why she was here. At least it should give her enough time to change and be back at the gate before they returned.

Half an hour later, Madeleine was cursing her mother, the dress, and the fact she had no other female accompanying her. She could not get this stupid dress tied correctly.

A knock on the door. "Madeleine, are you almost ready? The procession is returning." Kiril.

She flung open the door and dragged him inside. "Do me up." She spun around and gestured to the ties.

"Madeleine!" He sounded shocked. "I'll get the landlady."

"Please, Kiril. There's no time."

He groaned. "This isn't appropriate." But he tugged on the stays and did as she asked.

"Thank you. Come on." She picked up the bag with the silkworm egg, feeling its essence as she did so, and raced out of the room and down the stairs, gesturing for Brogan who waited at the bottom to follow.

Her heart thumped as they reached the main street, and she took a second to smooth down her yellow dress. The Royal carriage was only metres away and this time Godric was on her side, facing the crowd. She stood on her tiptoes and waved. "Godric!" His eyes passed over her without stopping. "Ric!"

A tiny frown crossed his forehead before he smoothed it out.

Maybe he couldn't hear her over the other calls. There

was one thing which might get his attention. She took a breath and yelled, "Ric, you filthy bog marsh toad, over here!"

Beside her, Kiril laughed. Godric flinched and turned back towards her, scanning the crowd. She waved, but the carriage moved into the palace, and she lost sight of him.

Curse it.

She waited impatiently for the rest of the carriages to pass through the gates, still scanning for her father, but didn't see him. The guards came next, filing back into the courtyard. The rest of the crowd went back to their celebrations, and Madeleine followed the guards, but at the gates she was stopped.

"No, you don't." The moustached man grabbed her arm as she walked by him.

"Please, I need to speak with King Jerek, Prince Godric, or my father, Shelton Hanretty."

He hesitated, and glanced towards the palace.

The courtyard was full of people disembarking their carriages and slowly moving towards the main doors of the palace. Had Godric already gone inside?

No one was familiar, but she kept scanning the crowd, hoping to see her father's red hair, or Godric's blue suit. A commotion broke out amongst the crowd and heads bent as someone walked through them. The guard swore and she took the opportunity to push past him, only to be yanked backwards. She stumbled into Kiril who caught her, stopping her from falling to the ground. She scowled at the guard. "No need to get violent," she snapped.

"Madeleine?" The question came from behind the moustached man.

They both turned, and the guard cursed quietly, bowing low. Godric's eyes were wide, staring at her. She jolted at seeing the dark blue rim around his turquoise eyes. Warmth filled her, and she beamed. "Godric! I wasn't sure if you heard me." She remembered her manners and curtsied.

A tiny twitch of his lips, though his voice was cool. "You're the only person to insult me to my face."

Her cheeks flushed. "It was the only way to get your attention. The guard wouldn't let me in."

"She wasn't on the guest list," the guard said.

His gaze went from her face to her toes and back. "You look… different."

She laughed. "It's been ten years, what did you expect, pigtails and a dirty face?"

"What are you doing here?" Godric asked.

"I have an important message for King Jerek."

His eyebrows raised. "Come with me." He glanced behind her. "Kiril, Brogan. Good to see you. Do you want to get a meal in the kitchen while I take Madeleine inside?"

She was impressed he remembered their names.

Brogan nodded. "Thank you, Your Highness."

"Follow me."

***

Godric's mind raced, and he wanted to stare at the self-assured woman striding next to him. Instead, he kept his shoulders back, posture straight, and expression passive as he made his way through the crowd searching for Shelton.

Little Madi had grown up.

He'd been sure he'd heard someone call 'Ric' on his way back to the palace, and the only person ever to call him that was Madi. When it had been followed by the name calling, he was certain, but he hadn't been able to spot her before they'd arrived inside. He'd excused himself and searched for her, but he never would have recognised her. It wasn't until she'd snapped at the guard that the recognition hit, and memories came tumbling back. She didn't suffer fools.

His family was already on the steps of the palace waiting for him, and though King Orion seemed calm, the way his finger occasionally twitched against his side told Godric he wasn't happy. Hopefully he'd forgive Godric after he'd explained. He cast a quick glance over Madeleine's bright yellow dress. It wasn't the latest fashion, but it was nice enough not to cause too much of a stir.

"This way." At the bottom of the steps, he caught sight of Shelton. Good. Their gaze met and Shelton shifted his eyebrows up and down in a move that meant hurry. "I've brought you a guest," he said as he walked past, and smiled at Madi's shriek of delight behind him. Shelton would take care of her and take her into a room where they could talk.

Godric joined his family and his mother murmured, "Who is that?"

"Shelton's daughter. She needs to speak with King Jerek." Seeing the two hug so affectionately in public made him envious.

"Later," his father muttered, and they swept into the ballroom where dinner would be served.

It took another hour of pomp and ceremony before all the guests had entered and were mingling. Across the room, one of the more insistent mothers was dragging her daughter towards him. Someone touched his elbow. "You should hear why Madeleine is here," Shelton said.

Relief filled Godric. "Shall I get my uncle?"

"Yes. I'll find your father."

A few minutes later, they gathered in his father's study and Shelton made the introductions. Madeleine curtsied low to both kings. "My apologies for interrupting the Queen's birthday," she said. "High Elder Lanley has tasked me with carrying two messages, one of which is for King Jerek. I must continue my journey tomorrow."

Eloquent and confident, her red hair fell down to her waist, and the gown clung modestly to her breasts and hips. The tomboy fighter from his youth was gone.

He didn't mind the replacement at all.

"What message?" King Jerek asked.

Madeleine handed him a sealed envelope and waited until he had read it.

"The situation is bad?" the king asked as he passed it to Orion.

"Yes, Your Majesty. If the silkworm babies don't continue to grow, the fae will become weak and die. And if they die, the silkworms will die as well."

Godric blinked and stopped marvelling over Madi's change of appearance. "The fae are in danger?"

"We hope our kin in Molanka or Tartalan might have a solution," she said. "High Elder Lanley asks King Jerek to contact the Tartalan fae on her behalf, and I am to travel to Molanka to speak with our kin there."

"Alone?" Orion asked.

"No, your Majesty. I have five guards with me for protection."

It wasn't much. Since Jerek's ship had been stolen, more reports had returned about the situation in Molanka being more dangerous than they had suspected.

"I forbid it," Orion said. "Such a journey is not appropriate for a woman. I'll send some of my men with the message."

Her scowl was fleeting and so familiar, Godric swallowed his smile. "With all due respect, Your Majesty, you do not have the authority to stop me. I am under orders of the High Elder of the Silk Valley fae, and as part fae, I must obey."

"You're part human too," the king pointed out.

She nodded. "But your men cannot describe the situation with enough detail, nor can they carry the silkworm egg with them." She gestured to the bag she carried.

Orion turned to Shelton. "Are you going to let your daughter travel like this?"

Shelton smiled. "My daughter is capable. I have no doubt she will take the required precautions to travel safely."

The king's fingers twitched.

Godric studied Madeleine. She would be a target dressed the way she was. Any brigand along the way would view her as a prize. He clenched his hands. "Perhaps we can provide her an escort." Could he convince his father to let him join her? Some weeks in Madeleine's company would be a welcome change from the women he'd been forced to dine with lately.

"It is vital we take care of all fae," King Jerek agreed. "It is part of the Tartalan Treaty."

"Shelton, arrange an escort for your daughter." Orion turned to Madeleine. "You will return here on your way home to advise me of the outcome."

She curtsied. "Of course, Your Majesty. Thank you."

Orion strode to the door. "Come, Godric. You still have a wife to find."

Godric hesitated. He wanted to catch up with Madeleine, ask her more about her mission. His father twitched his fingers.

Duty called. Filled with disappointment, he followed his father out.

***

The next morning, Godric woke early and hurried down to the courtyard. By the time he'd sneaked away last night, Madeleine had already returned to her inn to sleep. Shelton had said she would be back at dawn to fetch the escort from the palace and then continue to Molanka. Godric wanted to see her again before she left.

Shelton was already there with a dozen Syltan soldiers. He smiled. "What are you doing up so early, Your Highness?"

"I'd like to wish Madeleine well on her journey."

"I'm sure she'd appreciate it. She was sorry she didn't have time to speak with you last night."

A group of riders entered the courtyard, and he paid them no mind until they stopped in front of Shelton and one rider slid off. Dressed in rough pants and a tunic, flat cap on, it wasn't until Shelton stepped forward and hugged her, that Godric recognised Madeleine. She'd tucked all her glorious hair under the cap, and the loose tunic hid her shape. A quick glance hadn't identified her as female.

Good. It would be safer for her.

"You take care," Shelton said. "The roads may be more dangerous in Molanka."

"I have my sword and bow," she answered.

"Do you still know how to use it?" Godric asked.

She raised an eyebrow. "Would you like to test me?"

It was difficult to stop the smile on his face. "Perhaps when you return."

"Of course." She hugged him. "It was good to see you, Ric."

He froze, the shock of this public display of affection too great, and before he came to his senses to hug her back, she'd stepped away, her cheeks red. "Sorry, that was inappropriate." She faced her father. "Are these my escorts?"

Godric wanted to tell her he liked it, but she was right. A prince shouldn't act that way in public.

There was a commotion over by the gates and a voice yelled, "I have an urgent message for the king. Can't you see I'm a water fae, man?"

Godric recognised the voice and strode over. "Elder Phillipe?"

"Godric, thank Tarta." The fae bent over, puffing. Godric led him over to the water fountain in the centre of the courtyard, and Phillipe stepped into the water.

"What's wrong?"

"Your father and King Jerek need to hear this."

Shelton ordered a nearby guard to fetch both kings. It took a few minutes for them to arrive and by then, Phillipe had his breath back. He stood and bowed at the kings. "News from Tartalan, Your Majesty."

Jerek stiffened. "What is it?"

"The island has been invaded. Word is Molankan soldiers stormed Farlon on Freedom Day."

Godric's mouth dropped open. They had been at peace for five hundred years. Why would Molanka attack?

"My sons?" Jerek demanded.

The fae took a deep breath. "Prince Darrien escaped, but I'm sorry, Your Majesty, Prince Kerwin was killed in the initial wave. He was at the harbour when they attacked."

Jerek flinched, the only sign he was upset.

Sorrow filled Godric. His cousin had been a good man. Young and enthusiastic, wanting the best for his land and his people.

"Why did the fae let them through the reef?" Jerek's tone was ice cold.

"They were in your ship, Your Majesty. The fae thought you were arriving home early."

So that's why the ship had been stolen.

Jerek addressed Orion. "I call on our alliance for Sylta to come to Tartalan's aid."

Godric froze. He'd thought the worst thing he had to deal with during the birthday celebrations was vapid women. But this would mean going to war.

"There must be some kind of mistake," King Orion said. "Tremont has no reason to go to war with you."

"No mistake, Your Majesty," Phillipe said. "We received word from High Elder Lachlan. He saw it with his own eyes. Molankan soldiers attacked the city. There have been no demands yet."

"Did you have a disagreement with Molanka?" Godric asked his uncle.

Jerek shook his head. "We've been trading as normal. I had a meeting with our main exporter, Mister Littleton, just before I left, and he said business was going well, and our partners were happy. I was looking forward to discussing things with Tremont while we were here."

But they hadn't come. "Do you think the Queen really is sick?" Godric asked.

Orion nodded. "She's been unwell for some months now."

"We've got to get back," Jerek said. "Darrien isn't prepared for holding the country against invasion. We must ready some ships." He turned to leave, and Orion blocked his way.

"We must find out more before we decide," he said. "We need to know how many ships and men Tremont has, where they've landed, whether he still has men in Molanka ready to attack Sylta if we get involved."

Jerek scowled. "Are you saying you won't come to our aid?"

Godric exchanged a glance with Shelton. Sylta wasn't prepared for war either. They had a standing army whose job was to deal with any highway men terrorising the countryside, and any disputes between fiefdoms, but they had little experience.

"I'm saying I need more information. While I gather it, I will send word to the lords to prepare. We need to know the best place to attack—Molankan soil or to sail to Tartalan."

Jerek grunted. "I want to know the minute further news comes," he told Phillipe. "Are you able to contact

High Elder Lachlan from here?"

Phillipe shook his head. "It's too far," he said. "We'd need several royal fae gathered together in order to reach him."

The Tartalan king looked at Orion. "Arrange it, while I tell my family the news." Jerek strode back into the palace.

Orion asked Phillipe, "You can arrange it?"

"It will take time."

"We'll come down to the lake when you're ready." Orion gestured to Shelton and Godric and moved inside.

Godric was worried about Phillipe's pallor. "Do you want me to get you a horse?"

"Yes, please."

Godric ordered one of Madeleine's escorts to take Phillipe to the lake. Where was Madi? He scanned the remaining soldiers and couldn't find Madi or her five guards. "Where did the other group go?" he demanded. Surely she hadn't been so stupid as to leave.

"They left when they heard of the invasion."

He wanted to swear. Rash. That was the Madeleine he remembered. "Find them, and bring them back."

He hurried inside to his father's study, where the king and Shelton were discussing options. "Madeleine's gone."

Shelton whirled around. "What?"

"She's not in the courtyard. I've sent men to find her."

He swore. "She can't go to Molanka now."

"The bigger problem is what we do about the invasion," Orion said.

Godric's heart raced. "We need more information. Why would they invade Tartalan? Has Jerek kept something from us?"

Orion shook his head. "Over the past year there has been quite a lot of movement at the border. People have been leaving Molanka in search of food and traders are arriving with fewer goods."

"Do you think Tremont's been preparing for war for that long?" Godric asked.

"Something is happening in Molanka. I didn't contact him because he's so Shelter-cursed prickly."

"What about our people in Bermont?" Godric asked.

Orion shook his head. "My men died during the plague last year and I haven't sent more."

Which now seemed like a huge mistake.

"I need to write messages to my lords, preparing them," Orion continued. "Shelton, get me some scribes, and send the captain of my guard to me."

"Yes, Your Majesty." He left the room.

"What do you need me to do?" Godric asked.

His father sighed. "We're far enough from the border to be safe for now, but I want you to arrange for your mother and sisters to go to the summer palace in the mountains. Then tell your mother we need to wrap up her birthday celebrations. Whether we have to fight here, or in Tartalan, we're going to war."

Chapter 13

Madeleine's heart raced as she eased away from the palace courtyard fountain. They were talking about war with Molanka. If that happened, it wouldn't be safe to cross the border. She'd never get the answer to what was wrong with the silkworms, and the fae might die. The war might last years. Moving slowly so as not to attract attention, she reached Kiril, who held her horse.

"What happened?" Kiril asked.

"We need to leave," she said.

"Madeleine, what news from Tartalan?" Brogan said.

"I'll tell you on the way," she answered. The kings, her father and Godric were in hushed discussions with the water fae, too busy to pay attention to her. She hoped her father would understand what she had to do. It would take another week to reach the border, and if the king declared war, they'd never get across it.

She gestured to her men.

"Are we not taking the guards?" Brogan asked.

"They'll only slow us down," she responded. It wasn't far to the gate and walking would attract less attention. Her back muscles bunched as she moved as quickly as she dared away from the men who ruled multiple countries. But not the Silk Valley. Her backpack was a comfort, the weight of the silkworm linking her to her fae kin. She could feel it alive inside the egg, but it was almost as if it was in hibernation, waiting for something. A constant reminder of her mission.

They cleared the palace gate, and she mounted and trotted through the streets. They were quieter this morning, and litter sprinkled the path. A couple of people swept outside their shops.

Her ears strained for sounds of pursuit, and she fought the urge to kick her horse faster. It wasn't far now. The gates were just up ahead. She glanced behind. Kiril and Brogan looked worried. Further behind them, turning onto the street, were Syltan soldiers.

"Come on." She nudged her horse into a canter, exiting the city gates and taking the road which led around the lake.

Thundering hooves and a loud cry. "Stop!"

Was there any point trying to outrun them? At least now they couldn't trap her in the city. Madeleine sighed and pulled up, waiting for the captain to reach her.

"Prince Godric orders you to return," the captain said.

Madeleine pulled out the letter from High Elder Lanley. "I have different orders." She handed them over and the captain read them. He hesitated.

"Madeleine, what's going on?" Kiril asked.

She faced her men. "Molanka has invaded Tartalan. The kings were discussing what to do about it."

Brogan scowled. "Sylta has treaties with both countries."

"Exactly. We need to reach the silk valley before they declare war."

"I don't like this, Madeleine," Kiril said. "Perhaps we should return home."

She shook her head. "Not without answers. We can't

let the arguments of kings affect the fae."

"It will be even more dangerous," Brogan said. "I asked around at the inn last night. People say Molanka is dangerous, brigands on every corner robbing you for food."

Would they have to fight every step of the way? She closed her eyes briefly. To think she wanted this kind of adventure as a child. "We must still go. Mother will contact me if the High Elder changes her mind."

The captain was still in her way. "I must take you back."

She took the letter from him and folded it, tucking it into her jacket. "Tell the prince his orders don't outrank the high elder. I will visit him when I return."

She was disappointed she hadn't seen him last night, but he was no longer a youth away from palace responsibilities. At least he'd recognised her.

Madeleine nudged her horse forward, and the captain spluttered, following her. "I have my orders," he said.

"Your original orders were to accompany me to Molanka," she said. "Send one of your men to the prince with my message, and then if he is still displeased, he can send more men."

The captain looked unhappy but ordered two soldiers to return to the palace. "I'm Captain Sanders. It appears as if I'm coming to Molanka with you."

Madeleine breathed a sigh of relief. "Madeleine." She introduced the others and then said, "Your company is welcome." Then she kicked her horse into a canter to put more distance between her party and the city.

By the time they reached the marshland around midday, the riders hadn't returned. Madeleine stopped and pulled out the map. The dense scent of rotting leaves made her turn up her nose and breathe through her mouth. "Are you familiar with this area?" she asked Sanders.

"There's a canal through, but it runs towards the coast, not in the direction you want to go. Otherwise, a path is marked by white poles, but most traders go around because the path is not wide."

"How long will it take?"

"It will add another two days to the journey."

"And if we go through the marsh?"

"A day, but if we enter now, we'll have to travel through the night as there aren't many places to camp."

They couldn't afford the delay. "We'll go in." They had a marsh near the Silk Valley, and she knew what to expect. Plus, there might be marsh fae who could help. "Do fae live here?" she asked him.

"Not that I know of."

She dismounted and handed her reins to one of her men. Carefully she stepped over to the marshy ground. Though the soil looked solid, it could be thick mud which would suck her down. She crouched and placed a hand on the ground, grimacing as it sank into the mud. Sending a thought out, she called to any marsh fae in the area.

No response. Why hadn't she spent more time with her mother's kin?

With a sigh, she used a couple of leaves to remove as much mud as she could from her hand. She would smell for days.

"Any luck?" Kiril called.

"No." She mounted.

Brogan rode his way to the front. "Kiril and I will go first," he said. "You stay back with the men."

"All right." He wasn't pleased they were continuing, so she would let him take charge when she could.

Sanders left two guards at the fork in the road in case the king sent a rider after them.

Madeleine kept a few lengths between herself and Kiril in case they wandered off the path. The first few poles were easy to see, and it wasn't long before they were deep in the marsh.

Several hours later Madeleine was second-guessing her decision. The marker poles were difficult to spot, and her party had been reduced to leading their horses single-file along the path because they'd gone the wrong way too many times. Bitey-flies swarmed around them and her skin itched. The breeze rustled the leaves on the trees to her right and whistled through the reeds of the marsh. Aside from the chirp of insects and the occasional frog croaking, it was silent. Then voices came from the bend in front of them. Brogan raised a hand for them to stop and took his bow from his back, notching an arrow.

It would have to be a dedicated or desperate brigand to choose the marshland as a place to set a trap, but Madeleine waited as he went ahead to scout.

A minute later, Brogan was back with a marsh fae and a couple of men who drove a cart full of long poles. "They're remarking the path," he called, a smile on his face.

Thank the Purifier. She dismounted and greeted the fae. "My name is Madeleine Hanretty, and I'm on a mission from High Elder Lanley." She went to take the letter out of her jacket and realised her hand was still dirty. The fae took her hand and the residual mud dropped away. "Thank you."

His smile vanished as he read the letter. "What is so urgent?"

"Few of our silkworm babies are hatching and those that do are not growing."

He glanced at the two men he had with him and moved away off the path. She followed him. "How long has this been happening?"

"A month, maybe two."

"And your kin are well?"

She nodded.

"I shall tell the Marsh fae High Elder. If he has an answer, you will get it before you leave the marsh." The fae waved his hand and the stench surrounding them disappeared. "The path ahead is well marked and wider. You can travel at speed for the rest of your journey."

Strange. The marsh fae usually didn't encourage travellers. "Thank you."

Brogan chatted to the blond who was with the fae. He had an odd accent, but as Madeleine rarely left her fiefdom, it wasn't one she recognised. "We must continue," Madeleine said.

They both mounted. "May the Trinity be with you," she called to the marsh fae.

He led them around the cart and waved. "May the Shelterer grant you answers."

Beyond the cart, the path was marked by poles on both sides and was wide enough for two carts. They cantered through the marshland, making good time as the sun sank low. At the edge of the marsh, Madeleine halted and scanned the surroundings, to see if a fae waited for her with answers from the high elder. No one.

"Thank you," she called.

They rode for another ten minutes before Brogan called a halt. "We'll set up camp here."

This ground was far preferable to a night in the marsh. She dismounted. "Did the man you spoke with say why they were widening the path?" she asked Brogan.

"The merchants have come to an agreement with the fae," he said. "They'll be able to distribute goods from the river into Sylta more quickly."

"And probably pay a high toll for it," Sanders said.

Madeleine frowned. "The fae have little use for coin, and a canal already runs through the marshland."

"Perhaps they've decided to join the rest of civilisation," one of the guards grumbled.

She had heard some people didn't like the way fae

kept to themselves, but in her fiefdom they were few. The silk valley fae encouraged visitors.

She shook her head. Right now she had more important issues to worry about. She dismounted and helped set up camp. It was then she realised they were two soldiers short. Ten men had come with her, two had stopped at the entrance of the marsh to direct any men coming after them, but only six set up camp.

"You're missing two men," she told the captain.

"I sent them back," he said.

"Why?"

The man hesitated. "Those two with the marsh fae sounded like Molankan. They carried high quality swords."

It made no sense. "Molanka has invaded Tartalan."

Brogan growled. "Wouldn't take much of a force to do that."

Sanders nodded.

But why would there be Molankan men in Sylta? Her mouth dropped open. "You think they might invade Sylta?" It made no sense. They were on good terms.

"Few people go through the marshland," the captain said. "If they could make the marsh fae their ally, they could sneak further into Sylta without anyone being any wiser. I've heard the marsh fae travel widely with their coal in Molanka."

It was troubling. If Molanka was to invade, Brogan would be needed to rally her people and defend the country. She took Brogan aside. "You should return home."

"No. Your mother gave me orders to protect you."

"I have the captain and his men," she said. "If war comes, you'll be needed at home."

"If war comes, you shouldn't be going to Molanka."

"I'll travel quicker and with less notice with fewer people accompanying me."

He scowled. "Sanders might be overreacting."

She studied him. "But you don't think he is."

A moment's hesitation before Brogan said, "No, I don't. It's too much of a coincidence for the marsh fae to be widening the path through their land now, when they've discouraged passage previously."

Her skin prickled. "In the morning, you will return home. Travel around the marshland, in case the men we saw try to stop you. I'll tell Mother to prepare."

"I can't leave you. It's far too dangerous."

"You must organise the defence of our land." Parvan was a good administrator, but he knew nothing of warfare.

Brogan frowned. "Kiril will stay with you."

She'd rather go alone. Less chance of anyone she cared about dying, but the uncompromising expression on his face made her nod. "All right."

That night they set several guards, but no one slept much.

*****

Godric spent the next two days with his father and Shelton, planning the fastest way to get to Tartalan, but he couldn't help worrying about Madeleine. Two of the guards he'd sent to find her had returned to say she refused his order and was heading into Molanka with little protection. Shelton contacted High Elder Lanley using Elder Phillipe, but the High Elder, while worried, had said Madeleine's mission was too important to call her back.

Madeleine was riding towards danger, while the women in his family were journeying to the summer palace, away from potential harm.

Godric bade his mother, aunt and sisters farewell that morning and the palace was far quieter with all the guests dispersing to prepare for war.

Now they gathered in his father's study, a map of Sylta spread across the table. "We leave at dawn tomorrow," King Jerek said.

"We've received no word from Tremont," Orion said.

"And you aren't likely to get one if he's in Tartalan," Jerek pointed out. "I need your help."

"It will take at least another week to receive responses to all our messages. We can't react as fast as you would like us to."

Jerek scowled but didn't comment.

Godric turned as someone knocked on the door. The boy bowed low, and behind him was Brogan, the weapons master who had taught Godric while he'd been visiting Madeleine. "A messenger for the king."

Orion glanced up, but it was Shelton who said, "Where's Madeleine?"

"She continued to Molanka, my lord," Brogan answered.

"Why didn't you go with her?" Godric asked.

"She ordered me to return home. Did the captain's men report what we saw in the marshland?"

The king shook his head. "I haven't heard anything since the men reported Madeleine wasn't returning."

Brogan muttered something under his breath. "Your Majesty, we cut through the marshland after we left here. The captain left two men at the entrance in case you sent more men after Madeleine. Halfway through the marsh we met a fae and two men who were widening the path and marking it clearly."

"But they hate people cutting through," Shelton said.

"The captain thought they sounded like Molankan. He sent two soldiers back here to inform you. Did they arrive?"

King Orion shook his head. "No. They didn't."

That wasn't good.

"Shelton, send scouts to the marshland, and I want

men scouting the border," Orion said.

"Surely Molanka wouldn't start a war on two borders," Godric said.

"He might if he expects us to run to Tartalan's aid," Orion said. "We'd leave our own land undefended, and he'd have little opposition."

He was right. Nerves coalesced in Godric's stomach.

"We need to find Elder Phillipe," Shelton said. "One of his family can contact High Elder Lanley and my wife. They'll contact Madeleine and discover if she's seen any other signs of Molankan forces on her travels."

Orion gestured to one of his guards. "Go find the elder. We'll meet him on the docks."

Tremont couldn't have that many men. Only a desperate man would be so foolish. "What does he want?"

He hadn't realised he'd spoken aloud until his uncle responded, "Who?"

"Tremont. His people will be weak after the plague. Is he desperate for something—food, maybe?"

"He could have just asked for it," Orion stated. "We would have shared what we could."

Godric frowned. "What was the last communication we had from him?"

"That they weren't coming to your mother's birthday because Queen Emeline was ill."

"And before that?"

His father shrugged. "We don't communicate directly with each other regularly."

Not like they did with Tartalan, and that was because his mother liked to keep in touch with her family.

"Come, we must get down to the water." His father led the way out of the room so they could talk with the water fae.

Elder Phillipe was waiting when they got there. He bowed to the kings. "I am unable to contact High Elder

Lanley."

"Why not?" Jerek demanded.

"I don't know. She might be too deep in her caves, or too far away."

"What about Madeleine?" Godric asked. They all looked at him. "Is that how it works?" he asked. "You can contact any fae with royal blood?"

The elder shook his head. "They must be marked by the water fae. Whenever a new high elder comes to power, they meet with any fae royalty they can, but it is difficult to leave their land, so not everyone connects. The water fae travel the most because our water flows through the mountains, forests and valleys." He smiled. "My family have connections with High Elder Lanley and Elder Lorelei, but no one else."

"You should have marked Madeleine while she was here," Orion said.

Godric shuddered. No doubt the connection was useful, but she would constantly be contactable, practically on call at every minute of the day.

"Keep trying to contact High Elder Lanley," Orion said. "We need to know whether Madeleine has seen more Molankan."

"My father has sent scouts down the tributaries. I will tell you what he discovers."

"Send him my thanks," Orion said. "Come, we must finalise our preparations. Jerek must leave at once."

Godric followed them inside, his whole body tight with tension. Life was about to change forever.

Chapter 14

Madeleine's shoulders ached from the constant tension of expecting an attack. After exiting the marshland, they had travelled north-west rather than straight to the border. Her original plan was to hire a boat and sail upriver until they were close to the silk valley. But now, with the threat of invasion, she didn't want to get caught in any conflict. Instead, they would travel west to the launda forest in Sylta, where the launda fae could shelter them, and then cross the border and travel the short distance to the silk valley in Molanka. It would take longer, but if the men in the marshland were Molankan, then the conflict might be closer than she'd thought.

Before leaving the most recent inn, Madeleine spread the map in front of her. "We should reach the forest by nightfall." Her hand rested on the bag with the silkworm egg, caressing the fabric. The further they'd travelled from the silk valley, the fainter the worm's consciousness became. She prayed it would survive the journey.

Kiril nodded. "There's a crossing here." He pointed. "With the documents your grandmother gave us, we should have no issues, unless Molanka has officially declared war."

There'd been no news at any of the inns they'd stayed in.

Across on another table, a man spoke. "You're not heading into Molanka, are you?"

She glanced over. He had the look of a craftsman, muscled, and his leathery hands wrapped around a mug. "That was our plan."

He shook his head. "I wouldn't if I were you. Not without a full bodyguard and even then, I wouldn't risk it."

Concern filled her, and she moved over to his table. "Why not?"

"Haven't you heard? Highway robbers rule the roads in Molanka. No one can travel anywhere without being stripped of their possessions."

Kiril joined her. "When was the last time you were there?"

"Me? I'm one of the lucky ones. I left over a year ago." He sipped his drink. "I'm a stonemason and can get work all over the place, so I came here. Ain't no stone in Molanka anymore, anyway."

"Why not?"

He shrugged. "Rumours say the fae have forbidden it, but no one who goes into the mountains comes out."

Her skin prickled. She didn't want to hear that kind of news. "If you had to go into Molanka, how would you travel?"

The man pursed his lips. "I'd hire an entire contingent of soldiers if I could afford it, but why would you want to go there? There's no food, no resources, nothing but misery and disease."

How was it possible? No news had come to the manor house about it. "It's a family matter," Madeleine said.

He grunted. "Then hide any signs of wealth and travel fast. Sleep in inns, not in the countryside, even if you have to stop earlier than you want to. Be prepared to hand over anything of value. Most robbers are just trying to survive. They'll take your food before they take your gold because the money is worthless over there."

She exchanged a glance with Kiril. "Thank you for your advice."

"I'm just glad I got out before they closed the borders."

"Closed the borders?" the captain asked.

"Yeah. The king ordered them closed during the plague last year and has men patrolling the river. Only people with goods to trade are allowed in."

More obstacles. But his advice was invaluable, so perhaps she could return the favour. "There are rumours Molanka is planning to invade Sylta."

The man's eyes widened. "When?"

"Soon."

He got to his feet. "Thanks for the tip."

"Where are you going?"

"South, maybe west. Away from the border and the fighting." He hurried out of the room.

Kiril ran his hand through his hair. "We're still going, aren't we?"

Madeleine glanced at the bag with the egg. The baby was relying on her, and she wanted to meet it. "We have to." They would deal with any issues in Molanka as they came, but the fate of her people depended on her getting answers. She rolled up the map. "Let's go."

Mid-afternoon they entered the towering launda forest which stretched all the way to the Molankan River. The shade was welcome after spending so much time in the sun, and Kiril halted his horse. "Let's rest the horses and stop for lunch."

Madeleine dismounted, checking on the egg. She brushed a finger over the hard shell, and the vibrations inside increased as if it sensed her presence. Relief filled her. It was still there, even if its consciousness wasn't as strong. With a sigh, she closed the bag and unrolled her map. "We can water the horses at the crossing."

Madeleine went over to one of the huge launda trees, and placed her hand on the bark. She sent out her thoughts, like she did when she communicated with her mother, hoping to get some kind of tug back to show the launda fae were out there. They would know she was here, because the silk valley fae were aware the moment anyone non-fae stepped on their land.

She pressed the spiral mark on her palm to report back to her mother. *How goes things?* her mother asked, her voice fainter than it had been the day before.

Too slowly. We've reached the launda forest. Does Grandmother have any contacts here?

No. King Orion wishes to know if you've seen any more signs of Molankan men.

None. We've passed only a few travellers, all of them traders.

Travel swift and take care.

Madeleine rolled up the map, and they travelled in silence through the launda forest. The leaves whispered as the wind blew, and birds chirped to each other as they darted through the branches. Madeleine followed Kiril, who picked his way through the undergrowth. There would be no roads from this point.

"I feel as if I'm being watched," Kiril complained.

"The trees or birds might report back to the fae," Madeleine said. "The silkworms always report the movements of strangers through the valley." Or so Nadia had told her.

Suddenly a figure appeared before them. Kiril swore and reached for his sword, but Madeleine nudged her horse forward, and placed a hand on his arm. She inclined her head at the launda fae. His limbs were long and lean, and he scowled.

"I am Madeleine Hanretty, and I'm on a mission for High Elder Lanley of the Silk Valley." She handed him the message.

He read it and glanced at the soldiers with her. "You travel with the king's guard. Are they here in response to our call for help?"

She shook her head. "They are accompanying me. What help do you need?"

"We sent the king a message via pigeon. Molankan woodcutters are nearing the border, and we fear when they have chopped down all of their trees, they will come for ours." He grabbed her arm and shook it. "The Molankan fae have crossed the border to seek refuge as they are being killed if they try to defend their land."

Madeleine gaped at him, her heart pounding. "They're chopping down the forest? But that will kill the fae!"

"Exactly. We can't fight their new machinery and weapons."

The captain approached. "I've not heard of it, but the king doesn't confide in me."

"You acknowledge the king's men have a responsibility to defend the fae when requested?" the fae asked.

The captain gave Madeleine an apologetic glance and then nodded.

"Then you will come with us now. After you have seen the situation, you can report back."

Madeleine grimaced. "We have an urgent mission."

"I apologise, but my high elder has ordered me to take any king's men to her."

"Why hasn't she contacted the water fae? They can travel to the palace."

"They haven't come this way in months. The pollution from the Molanka River is shifting to the canals, and the high elder cannot get in touch with them."

That wasn't good news either. "Can she meet us at the border? I can contact my mother, who can contact water fae at the palace."

He studied her. "You are royalty?"

"Part-fae," she said. "My grandmother is High Elder Lanley."

"Very well. I shall tell High Elder Freya. Come with me."

They followed him through the forest, along a trail which almost seemed to appear before them as they walked. At the tributary, they crossed a bridge which was high enough to let canal boats underneath. It was getting dark by the time Madeleine heard the sounds of the river again.

A female fae appeared, her long, brown hair topped with a crown.

"High Elder Freya of the Syltan Launda Forest," the fae announced.

Madeleine curtsied. "My Sister. Thank you for meeting us here."

"It is your help I need. Georg tells me our message didn't reach the king."

"Not that we know of, my Sister, but I can send word."

"Leave your horses there and follow me. You should see what they are doing, so you can report the full horror."

Her skin prickled at the high elder's ominous words.

Madeleine followed with Kiril and the captain, leaving the soldiers to care for the horses. They travelled along the river, which was about ten metres wide there. The launda trees soared high above on both sides and where the high elder halted, two of their branches almost touched in the middle.

"You'll need to climb. I hope heights don't scare you." She pointed to the branch over the river above.

"The trees are as dense on the other side," the captain said. "We won't see anything."

The high elder smiled, and Madeleine understood. "You want us to cross the river using the branches."

She nodded.

The trunks stretched high and straight above them. No hand holds or branches. "How?"

"First you need to ask the tree's permission." Freya told them the words and after Madeleine had repeated them, notches appeared in the tree's wood.

The captain shook his head. "I'm not doing it."

It was a long way up. "There's no need for us all to go," she said. Kiril stared at the branches above, his jaw clenched. He'd fallen out of a tree when they'd been kids and broken his leg. She'd never seen him climb another one. "I'll go."

The high elder climbed, almost floating to the first branch, which was a good ten metres above the ground. Madeleine followed, glad she was wearing trousers. By the time she reached the cross branch, she was panting.

"The next part is tricky," Freya warned. "You must trust me. Your fae blood should help." She walked along the thick branch as if she was on solid ground.

Madeleine's stomach lurched as she spotted a leaf floating to the ground. It took a very long time to reach the bottom. Gritting her teeth, she took small steps, swaying from side to side. She desperately wanted to close her eyes so she couldn't see how far it was to fall. The high elder offered her hand, and Madeleine took it. Feeling more anchored, she followed Freya to the end of the branch.

The gap to reach the branch across the river was at least a metre.

"You need to jump," Freya said.

Madeleine almost laughed, but the queen wasn't smiling. "I won't make it."

"You will. The tree's essence will help you. You can hold my hand, but you *must* jump when I say so."

Her mother always told her she had to trust her instincts, feel her fae self. But she'd always doubted her abilities.

Be brave. The sooner she sent the message for Freya, the faster she could return to her own mission. She clenched her teeth. "All right."

"On the count of three."

At three, Madeleine leapt, keeping her eyes on the safety of the branch across from her. She fell like a nut, and she took a breath to scream when the high elder tugged her hand, and a force pushed her up and deposited her on to the branch.

Madeleine panted.

"That wasn't so bad, was it?" Freya chuckled.

Her legs shaky, Madeleine reached the trunk and hugged the rough bark, her heart pounding. She closed her eyes, wanting to stay there, but there wasn't much to hold on to.

"Come, it's not far now." Instead of climbing down, they went around the trunk to a branch on the other side.

Freya led her from tree to tree over a hundred metres from the river. Madeleine kept her gaze on the canopy and not the ground below. She rounded the thick trunk and though the sun was sinking, it was suddenly much brighter. She gasped. Tree stumps and broken branches to the horizon. Madeleine couldn't speak. Horror wasn't the right word. This was a massacre. The launda fae would die with so many trees gone. Nausea swirled, and she clapped a hand over her mouth to stop herself from vomiting.

The high elder spoke, her voice low. "They use coal-powered saws. This area was cleared in a week." She pointed to a metal carriage below them. Next to it two men stood, one dressed in trousers and tunic, and the other in the red uniform of the Molankan army. Their words carried. "You have two days to get the rest of these trees cleared," the soldier said. "Prince Baldrick is bringing his men here to cross."

"It's not enough time," the woodcutter complained.

"Work through the night. The barges are being launched tonight, and we need enough space for the army to gather."

Madeleine's hand shook and Freya's face paled. Madeleine pressed the mark on her palm. *Mother, the Molankan army is definitely invading. I've crossed the border with High Elder Freya and heard them say Prince Baldrick will arrive in two days. They've cut down most of the launda forest on the Molankan side. I think they're planning to use the canals to ship troops into Sylta.*

Are you all right?

Yes. We'll return to Sylta now. Can you send an urgent message to the king?

I'll do it immediately.

Madeleine whispered, "I've told my mother. She'll get word to the king."

"Good. Let's go."

Madeleine turned and her foot slipped on the branch. She shrieked as she fell, but Freya grabbed her flailing hand and pulled her back.

"Hey!" a cry from below.

Filthy bog marsh.

"Go!" the high elder pushed her towards the branch as an arrow thwacked into the trunk next to her.

Madeleine stumbled and found her footing again, moving as fast as she could along the branch. Freya brushed past her and grabbed her hand, pulling her. The air thickened and Madeleine's vision blurred, and in only a few steps she was back at the river.

"Jump!"

She had no chance to brace herself. She leapt and hit

the branch on the other side.

"Climb."

Madeleine acted on instinct, finding the notches where she needed them. When she reached the ground, Freya was already explaining the situation to Kiril and the captain. The high elder glanced across the river. "This way."

They followed her deeper into the forest and she led them back to where the other men waited.

"The king must send his men. My people are not trained to fight."

He wouldn't be able to get his men into position in time. Not unless men were already gathering to fight for Tartalan. "Captain, can your men sabotage the machinery?" Madeleine described the coal-fired saw.

"Anyone seen such a thing?" he asked.

They shook their heads.

Mother, we need to find someone who knows about the Molankan coal-powered machinery. Ask all our contacts. They had to protect Sylta, and the Molankan fae.

I will. Elder Phillipe is taking your message to the king.

"What would you do to stop the invasion?" Madeleine asked the captain.

He looked lost. "I don't know. Our role is to protect the palace. We've never fought in skirmishes."

Madeleine whirled to Kiril. "What would Brogan do?" He'd fought with her father in the civil skirmish fifteen years ago.

"They mentioned barges," Kiril said. "If we can find them, we could set them alight."

"No!" Freya yelled. "No fire. It's too risky."

"The only other way is to sink them, but we've got no catapults, and even if we could get some axes, the moment we attack, they'll defend."

Madeleine pressed her palm. *Ask Elder Phillipe if he can send scouts searching for the location of the barges.* She grabbed the map from her saddlebags. *Maybe in the tributary which runs to the silk valley.* It was the only place the river was surrounded by Molankan land. Everywhere else bordered Sylta.

Elder Phillipe is sending aid. Meet him at the canal-river intersection. And be careful.

Madeleine relayed the news.

Freya nodded as if satisfied. "Follow me."

If the Molankan had disregarded the treaty with the fae, what did it mean for her silk valley kin? Was the reason the Syltan babies were affected because something had happened to their Molankan kin?

She had to get to Molanka as quickly as possible. She hoped Elder Phillipe arrived soon.

Chapter 15

Godric was at the lake watching three ships being loaded with supplies. They would leave in the morning, under the leadership of King Jerek, travel down the canal where they would pick up more soldiers and then sail across to Tartalan to take Tremont by surprise. It was all Orion could offer with an attack on Sylta imminent.

He rolled his shoulders to release the tension and then caught himself, and straightened, wiping any sign of strain from his face and body. They were waiting to hear from both human and water fae scouts to discover if there were any further signs of the Molankan. The idea he could be soon forced to fight for his country and his life made it difficult to hold his royal persona in place.

Water splashed near him and Elder Phillipe launched onto the docks, his tail morphing into legs as he landed. Godric flinched. "My Brother."

"Urgent news from Elder Lorelei," he said. "I must speak to the king."

"This way." He led the elder along the docks to where his father had set up in a warehouse. Inside, Shelton and Brogan stood with the king around a table strewn with maps.

"Your Majesty," Phillipe said. "Elder Lorelei reports Molankan soldiers have been spotted along the Molankan River. They are in the launda forest preparing for Prince Baldrick and his army to arrive."

"How did she get the information?" Orion demanded.

"From Madeleine. High Elder Freya showed her where the Molankan have cut down much of the launda forest on the Molankan side, and they overheard soldiers speaking."

Godric's mouth dropped open and his father spoke. "Give me details."

"The Molankan have built barges to ferry the army across. Baldrick is to arrive in two days. My father has sent scouts along the river looking for the barges."

"Get me a map of the area," the king demanded. Shelton ran to obey.

When it was spread across the table, the king asked, "Where?"

The elder scanned it. "This area." He circled a section.

"Is Madeleine still there?" Godric asked.

Phillipe nodded.

"The canals will enable them to spread throughout Sylta," Orion said. "Is the captain still with Madeleine?"

"I'll ask." Phillipe was silent.

"Well?" Orion asked.

Godric clenched his hands, waiting for the answer.

"I've asked Lorelei, who must then ask Madeleine."

"Curse it. We need a mark directly on the girl," Orion said.

"Captain Sanders is with her," Phillipe told him. "Madeleine asks if anyone knows how to sabotage the Molankans' coal-powered wood cutting saws."

Godric exchanged a glance with Shelton, his heart racing. "Shelton and I spent time with the inventors when they came to town to sell them. They explained how they worked." In the end, the amount of coal needed versus the number of trees they had to cut down negated the benefits of the faster saw.

"Shelton, how many men do you need?" Orion asked.

"Depends on the number of saws. Half a dozen maybe."

"How quickly can we get troops to that area?"

Shelton responded. "It's normally a week, Your Majesty."

"If you used a lighter fishing boat, rather than a barge, the water fae could get them there in a day," Phillipe said. "The lighter the cargo, the faster we'll be."

"Shelton, gather your men. I want you on a boat within the hour."

"Yes, Your Majesty."

Phillipe held up a hand to stop Shelton from leaving and closed his eyes as if to concentrate. "Word from a scout, Your Majesty. The canal through the marshland has been cleared and there are several over-sized coal-powered fishing boats gathered at the ocean port."

Orion tapped his hand on the map in front of him. "We'll need another team to go through the marshland."

All at once the reality of the situation coalesced in Godric's mind. This was happening. Molanka would invade and they would be at war. The certainty and determination settled his nerves. "I'll go."

His father looked up, eyes wide, a little panicked. It was the first time Godric had seen his father drop his royal facade.

"I've trained under Shelton," he explained. "And I understand how the new technology works."

Orion hesitated.

"You need to stay central and manage the overall strategy. Shelton can go to the launda forest, I'll head through the marshland, and King Jerek will head out the final canal to the sea."

The king shook his head. "Tell Brogan how to disable the boats. He can monitor the marshland canal."

No. It wasn't right for others to fight for Sylta if he wasn't willing to. This was Godric's duty. "Then I'll accompany Shelton."

A long pause as Orion deliberated. Finally, he nodded. "All right. Gather your men. Phillipe, I want you to go with Godric. Ask your father to come to me."

"Yes, Your Majesty." Phillipe bowed and followed Godric out.

Within an hour, Godric was heading down the western canal on a fishing vessel. With him were Shelton, and half a dozen men, with Elder Phillipe and his guards scouting ahead in the water. King Jerek sailed eastward, and Brogan had already left on the marshland canal with a contingent of men. More soldiers would follow.

A sense of calm settled over him. Finally, he was away from the city, out from under his father's gaze, and helping his country. "Will we arrive in time?"

"I hope so," Shelton responded. "If we can destroy those saws, we'll prevent Molanka from spreading further into the forests, and protect the fae."

Each man was armed with swords, and bows and arrows. They moved too swiftly to be a normal fishing vessel, but speed was more important than stealth. Even if Molankan scouts saw them, they wouldn't get word back to their commanders in time to be of any use.

Phillipe leapt aboard, water dripping down him as he landed next to Godric.

Godric dropped his hand away from his sword pommel, his heart racing. "Some warning would be nice!"

Phillipe grinned. "That wouldn't be as much fun."

Shelton chuckled as Phillipe dressed in a pair of pants which he'd requested be left on deck for him, more to set the rest of the crew at ease than from modesty. "My men have set up a relay system," he said. "Each team will manipulate the water for several leagues before they'll change. If the wind picks up, we'll hoist the sail which will further increase our speed."

The canals had been built to transport goods and were used by horse-pulled barges and the occasional fishing boat.

"Any news from Madeleine?" Shelton asked.

Phillipe shook his head. "The last I heard, she and the captain were training the launda fae in defence."

She would be good at it. Even as a child, she understood how to use her smaller size to her advantage to best him. It had been confronting and had taken his ego down a notch or two. "What about the scouts in the Molankan River?"

"Nothing new."

"We need word as soon as they find the barges," Godric said.

Phillipe rolled his eyes. "I know."

Godric stared out at the green fields. Little daisies and pink sugar blossom flowers grew amongst the fields of grasses where sheep grazed. "Have you spoken to any of your Molankan kin?"

"We don't differentiate between ourselves," Phillipe said. "We travel the waterways no matter the country, but many people have moved away from the Molankan silk valley and Molankan harbour because of the pollution."

"So we don't need to worry about water fae attacking us?"

"I don't believe so. There's not much Tremont can offer the water fae. We don't want land, and he doesn't own the ocean."

Godric hoped Phillipe was right, but he kept his hand on the pommel of his sword just in case.

There was too much at stake.

Chapter 16

Madeleine gazed around the launda fae settlement in awe. The wooden buildings made from entwined branches merged with the trees both at the base of the trunks and high amongst the branches. They were at one with the surroundings, similar to the silk valley fae's burrows, but there was such artistry here. Freya led them into a central clearing where people gathered, some handing around plates of food, while other, paler fae lay on makeshift beds. Madeleine froze. This wasn't a settlement, it was a refugee camp, a hospital for the Molankan fae who were dying as their trees died. No fires were lit, despite the deepening dusk, but fireflies hovered in groups lighting the area.

Freya stepped onto a platform, and the fae gathered. "The Molankan soldiers plan to invade Sylta. They will cut the remaining launda trees near the river and then come for us."

A woman wailed. She sat on a bench, supported by two more fae. Her face was pale and her hand shook. "They can't," she gasped. "We'll die."

"Madeleine has contacted King Orion, and he is sending men to stop them," Freya said. "But they may not arrive in time. We must be prepared to fight."

Her announcement brought uproar in the community as people voiced their fears.

"He'll never get here in time," one cried.

"What if he agrees with Tremont? What if he cuts our own forest?"

Freya held up a hand, speaking in soothing tones, and order was restored. Running wasn't an option. "I need scouts along the river, searching for their barges. You may need to cross into Molanka." A couple of people raised their hands and departed. "We will attempt to destroy the saws," Freya continued.

The pale woman shook her head. "We tried. They're encased in metal. None of our tools will penetrate them."

Most fae used natural tools made from wood and stone rather than metal, though the marsh fae used metal and coal. "Do you use arrows?" Madeleine asked. They'd need weapons to fight.

"We have no need. We don't hunt, the forest provides our food."

Among the men Madeleine had with her they had maybe two hundred arrows. Not enough to stop an army, and they couldn't attack the woodcutters without it being an act of aggression from Sylta. That would justify Molanka invading. "We must prepare for the army to cross into Sylta." She thought about her training. "Set up traps and snares, and gather rocks we can drop on the soldiers."

"We don't know where they're going to land," one man said.

"No, so we'll need to use things we can easily move, or else we set them all along the border." It was leagues, and they had at best two days. "Kiril, you're good with traps, can you show them?"

He nodded and Freya directed some of her people to follow him and set others to work making arrows and teaching them to shoot. When everyone was at work, Madeleine approached the fae on the bench. "Are you from Molanka?"

"Yes, I am Dara."

"Have you had any contact with the Silk Valley fae?"

"Not for over a year. King Tremont ordered the forest to be cut down, and when our high elder protested, they killed her. We tried to stop the destruction for months, but their coal-powered saws and armed guards meant they slaughtered us. We withdrew to the Syltan side of the forest, but so many have died as the trees have died, and we all grow weak."

Anger sizzled in Madeleine's blood. Why had Tremont broken the treaty? "Is there anything you can do?"

"We took seedlings and nuts from the forest, and are nurturing them here, but they're too young to sustain our people, and even with the Syltan fae, they struggle to grow."

Could that be what was wrong with the silkworm babies? She shifted her backpack off and opened it, so she could touch the egg. It vibrated a little with a faint connection. If the Molankan silk valley had been similarly affected, the repercussions might reach Sylta. She would have to tell her mother and get all the fae to send letters of protest to Molanka.

Around her, the captain and his men helped the fae design ambush tactics, and Kiril worked with another group to create snares.

Madeleine, King Orion has sent men to sabotage the saws. The water fae are helping, and they should be there by morning.

Thank you, Mother. She shared what she'd learnt about the launda fae, and then passed on the news to High Elder Freya.

"Tell the men my people will meet them at the canal junction. We can take them faster overland to where they need to be."

Madeleine told her mother, and Freya sent fae to wait for the boat.

Around her, people worked together to prepare for the attack. With help on the way, perhaps Madeleine could continue her journey.

Her gaze caught on Dara, staring listlessly into the forest, hugging herself. No, she had to stay, do what she could until the king's men arrived. The launda fae needed her and her men.

She strode over to Kiril. "What do you need me to do?"

***

They worked through the night. Freya's scouts returned to say they had sighted barges in the silk valley tributary, and Madeleine passed the news to her mother. Those watching the woodcutters said they worked nonstop, and the distant hum of the saws carried across the border. It was early morning and Madeleine was speaking with Freya when the high elder straightened and looked in the direction of the capital. "They're here."

A few minutes later, eight men and eight fae appeared in the clearing. The men bent over, puffing, and Madeleine recognised the red hair of one. Her heart lurched. "Father!" She ran to him and hugged him, drawing comfort from his strong arms. He always knew what to do.

"Madeleine. I'm relieved you're safe."

Suddenly, she realised why he was here, and she tensed. "You're going to sabotage the saws?" That would put him in danger.

He nodded. "Prince Godric and I examined the new technology when a merchant came to the city to sell it." He gestured to the man next to him.

"Ric?" She bobbed into a curtsy. Why was the king

sending his heir to the frontline?

Godric scowled. "I ordered you to return to the palace."

She ignored him. "This is High Elder Freya." She motioned to the fae, and both men bowed.

"Thank you for coming. Do you need to rest before I show you the contraptions?"

"We slept on the boat, my Sister," Shelton said.

"Good. Madeleine, tell their men what we have done. You two, come with me."

Godric hesitated. "Shouldn't all the men see?"

Madeleine smiled. "Trust me, the fewer times you make the trip the better."

He frowned but followed the high elder out of the clearing.

The captain insisted he be the one to brief the soldiers Shelton had brought with him, and Madeleine was too tired to make a fuss. When the high elder arrived back with Godric, Shelton, and a water fae, the men were already hard at work, and the sun was rising.

"You must be Madeleine," the water fae said.

"Yes."

"I've heard about you," he continued. "I was hoping we would meet. I'm Phillipe."

She shook his hand and felt the tingle which signified she was meeting a royal fae. "Elder Phillipe?"

He nodded. "May I mark you so we can keep in touch?"

"She's not going anywhere now," Godric said. "It's too dangerous."

She glanced at her father, but he raised no objections. "I must get answers for the Silk Valley fae." She pointed to Dara. "See how weak she is? That's what might happen to all fae if I don't find a solution." She held out her hand to Phillipe, and he pressed a wavy mark onto it.

Godric gritted his teeth, but before he spoke, Phillipe

stiffened. He held up a hand as his eyes became vacant. Expression grim, he spoke. "My scouts report the Molankan are on the move. They will cross the river tonight."

No. They weren't ready.

"Tell Lorelei," her father said. "Tell me if they're ready." The love and concern on his face touched her heart.

Mother, the Molankan army is moving tonight.

Where are you?

At the border with Father. She felt her mother's spike of fear.

Why is he there?

He was going to sabotage the saws cutting down the launda trees. Was there any point now?

Tell him our men have joined the king's army and our women and children are sheltering in the caves in the silk valley.

Relief filled Madeleine, and she repeated the news.

Send my love to Shelton. Both of you be careful.

You too.

Shelton was already organising fae and men alike. They didn't need her here, and the more men her father had to help him fight, the safer he would be. It was likely Tremont had rounded up the brigands in the countryside and made them join the army. If she sneaked across the river and avoided his forces, she shouldn't have much trouble.

She played with the end of her braid. How could she get her horse across? Swimming would soak everything, but maybe one of the fae would carry her bags over the trees. She only needed Kiril to give her a second pair of eyes. Where was he?

"What are you planning, Madi?" Godric stepped in front of her.

She jumped and focused on the frown on his face. "I must continue." She stepped around him.

He grabbed her hand and drew himself upright and stiff, every molecule the prince he was. "You must go home."

She almost laughed. He never learnt his royal status didn't impress her. "No. I won't, so you can either help me, or get out of my way."

He swore.

"Your Highness, she's right," Shelton said. "Though I like the thought of it less than you do." He hugged her. "What do you need?"

"To get across the river." She visualised the map. "Up near the silk valley tributary."

"That's where all the barges are," Phillipe said.

"Then a little further west." The area wasn't as populated, so she shouldn't run into the army.

"We should focus our attack at the river junction," Shelton said. "Stop as many barges as possible so the army can't cross the river quickly." He turned to Phillipe. "What are the king's orders?"

"The water fae will do what they can to stop the barges, and Orion is sending his men to the border, but they'll be days behind."

High Elder Freya squared her shoulders. "Where do you need my people?"

Shelton rolled out a map and pointed to places on it. "Can you take one of my men to each of these spots? They can teach your people what to do."

In minutes Madeleine was left with Kiril, Godric, Shelton and the two royal fae.

"Can you transport horses as quickly?" Madeleine asked her.

"No."

"I've had our fishing boat brought around," Phillipe said. "It's through there."

Kiril had already saddled their horses, and they all headed down a path to the river where a fishing boat was anchored to the shore. A section of the bow folded down to form a gangplank, to help unload the catch, but it enabled them to lead the horses onto the deck. Her horse baulked at the boat until Kiril covered her eyes with cloth.

Across the river, Madeleine saw a flash of red. "We're being watched," she murmured. Louder, she said, "Thank you so much for taking me upriver. I never thought I'd reach my grandmother in time."

Godric hesitated and then called, "You're most welcome."

"We need to all get on board," Shelton whispered. "We'll disembark further upriver."

Freya disappeared as the rest boarded, and Godric cast off. Madeleine stayed with her horse, calming it as the boat rocked. Her shoulder blades itched, and she scanned the Molankan bank for movement. The red of their uniform was easy to pick even though they hid behind trees, and she noticed men along the bank. Curse it. Were they scouts, or did they have a force with them?

Godric and Shelton came over to her.

"We're going to have to go all the way up the river," Shelton said. "Or wait until dark and hope you can sneak through without being spotted."

"They attacked my kin," Phillipe said. "They attempted to get close to the barges to sink them, but the army was ready, and they had to withdraw."

They would have to sink the barges some other way.

"Is there a way of blocking the tributary which leads to the silk valley?" Shelton asked.

"The junction is wide," Phillipe said after a moment's pause. "They will investigate if there is somewhere further down river."

The day passed as they travelled up river. Now and then Phillipe gave updates from his kin or from High Elder Freya. They passed the Molankan barges, sailing down the river. There was nothing they could do. Though the men on the barges looked as if they were traders, Madeleine noticed how well armed they were. To attack was folly. Godric grew tense.

When they'd passed a half dozen, Shelton ordered them to stop. "We can't go on. I need to manage the defence of the launda canal. I suspect the soldiers will attack from there. They would be foolish to waste time fighting the launda fae, when they can use the canals to infiltrate Sylta."

"Of course." Madeleine couldn't keep them from their mission any more than they could keep her from hers. She studied the far bank and couldn't see any soldiers. "Let us off on the Molankan side. They shouldn't be concerned about two people travelling through the forest." She turned to Kiril. "We're brother and sister visiting our grandmother who lives in a village on the other side of the forest."

He nodded.

"May the Shelterer protect you, my daughter." Shelton hugged her.

"And you, Father." Godric looked distinctly unimpressed. "This is my duty, Ric. May you find Shelter."

He grunted and as she turned to go, he tugged her back and hugged her, the movement stiff, but warm. "You stubborn witch. Stay safe so I can berate you when you return."

She laughed. "I will."

"Send regular messages to Phillipe," Godric said. "I would like to know how you fare."

"I will, and if I can't reach him, I'll ask Mother to pass the message on." His concern reminded her of the teenaged Godric.

The boat bumped against the Molankan bank and Godric leapt ashore to hold it in place while Kiril unlatched the gate. Shelton joined them on the bank as Madeleine and Kiril mounted.

The day was still with only the trickle of water against the shore and the soft rustle of a breeze through the trees. Madeleine's skin prickled as she scanned the surroundings, looking for a hint of red. The sooner they left the better. She had only a vague idea where they were, but they would travel north to avoid any soldiers before turning west again.

A crunch in the bushes nearby made her hair stand on end. Probably a lizard, but standing around wasn't getting them any closer to their destination. "We must go," she said. "Stay safe."

"You as well," Godric answered.

A sharp whistle and then Kiril cried out in pain. Madeleine's heart pounded as he fell from his horse, an arrow in his chest. "Kiril!"

"Ride, Madi!" Godric yelled and slapped her horse. It skittered forward, and an arrow slammed into its rump. It bucked, and then took off through the bush.

No! She had to help Kiril. She jerked on the reins, but the horse paid no attention as it crashed through the undergrowth surrounding the river.

She pressed her palm. *Phillipe! What's happening?*

Soldiers, he said. *I'm taking Kiril to our healer.*

The fae would help him. *Father?*

He made it to the boat.

Godric?

She glanced behind to discover a rider chasing her. Curse it.

She sat low against her horse's neck, hoping to lose them amongst the trees. Then she galloped out of the canopy into the field of devastation. Tree stumps stretched in front of her, and a large group of men congregated in the distance. Filthy bog marsh.

Godric took Kiril's horse.

Was it him who followed? She heard her name being called. She pulled on the reins and used her legs to encourage her horse to slow. It did, slowing to a canter and then a trot. She whipped her bow off her back and readied an arrow in case it wasn't Godric.

"Madi, it's me." He held up a hand, and she lowered her bow and let out a breath. "What are you doing?"

He frowned, seemed a little uncertain. "I just reacted. You can't go on your own. We'll get back to the river and when Kiril is healed, you can continue."

She shook her head. "I can't, Godric. There's no time." Shouts in the distance made her heart race again. They'd been spotted and two men rode towards them. "You won't make it back either."

He stared at her, horrified, as if the implications of his decision were dawning on him. "I have to. My duty is to my people, to defend them."

Madeleine, the bank is swarming with soldiers. My kin have moved the boat away from the shore, so Godric will need to find another way back to us.

She glanced back to the river. "Phillipe's taken the boat away.

He swore.

"Come with me." She reached for him as the soldiers rode closer.

"I have a duty to my father."

"There's no safe way to get back." And she didn't want to go alone. "Godric, they're coming. We have to go."

He jolted as if only just noticing the Molankan soldiers. He swore again and kicked the horse into a canter. "I can't just take off on an irresponsible quest," he yelled.

She bristled. "The fae might not be your people, but my quest is not irresponsible." The soldiers were still following through the patchwork of tree stumps. She daren't shoot them in case it brought more soldiers after them.

Godric was silent, displeasure creasing his face.

She rode hard, glancing behind and finally the soldiers gave up and returned to their group. She exhaled. "They've stopped following." She slowed her horse and Godric followed suit.

He was still silent.

"We can report any movement of the Molankan army," she said, trying to make him feel better. "Any news we hear will be useful to the fight."

"My father will be furious."

There was no denying it. "The silk valley is only a few days' ride," she said. "We can get help from the fae and travel back. By then you'll have only missed the initial battle." She thanked the holy Trinity that he would miss it.

Finally, he sighed. "I have little choice." He gestured in front of them. "You'd better lead the way."

Part 3
Molanka

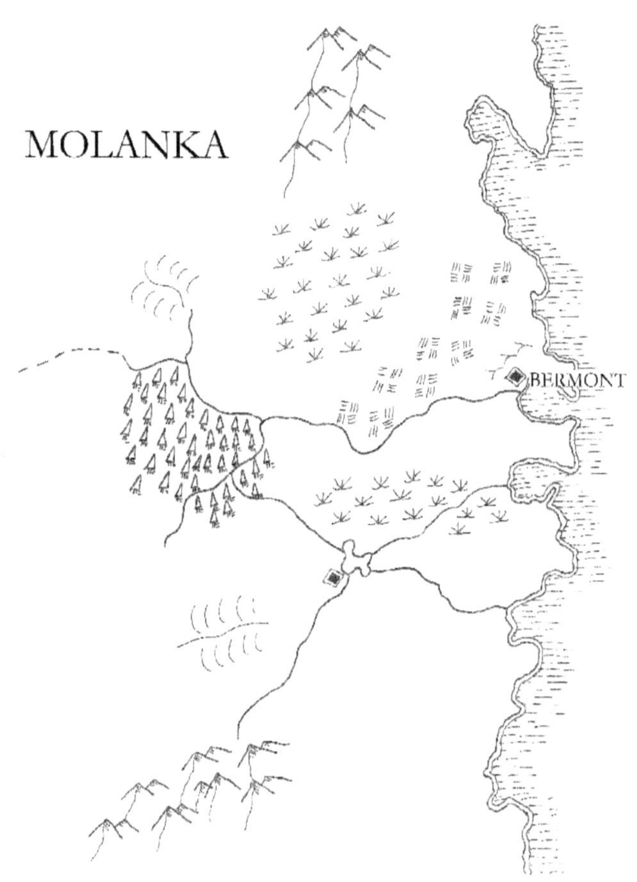

MOLANKA
BERMONT

Chapter 17

Her Royal Highness Princess Amber of Molanka used a silk fan to create some air movement in the stifling hot room. She was tempted to push open the window and let in some air, but she didn't dare disobey the doctor's orders. The outside air brought with it coal smoke from the city, and it could cause her mother's condition to worsen. So she dunked a cloth into the water by the side of the bed and squeezed it out, gently wiping the sweat from her mother's brow. The rich red silk of the covering turned darker where drops of water fell on it.

"Thank you, dear. I'm feeling much better." The smile Emeline gave her was weak, not at all like the normal vibrant grin she gave when no one was watching. "Any news from your father or brother?"

"Not yet." They'd only been gone a week on their search for a cure. The soothsayer had said the answer to Emeline's illness could be found in Tartalan and Sylta, but neither country responded to her father's requests for information. So he had gone in person, hoping his presence would force them to take his request seriously.

Amber couldn't believe neither country would help them. Where was their sense of loyalty? They had once been part of a single empire. Sylta had only been formed two hundred years ago after a king decided to leave part of the country to each of his twin sons. They seemed to have forgotten that kinship.

"Do we have any mountain berries?" Emeline asked.

Amber brightened. The fact her mother wanted to eat was a good sign. "I'm sure we do." Amber rang the bell and Daisy, her mother's maid, entered, curtsying. "The queen would like mountain berries."

The servant bit her lip. "I'll check with the kitchen."

"If they have none, send someone into the city," Amber ordered. Her mother had eaten very little over the past couple of months and it was showing in her sallow cheeks and lank hair. Perhaps it was time they washed her hair again. A bath always made Amber feel better. "Shall I send for some water so you can bathe?"

"No dear, but I would like to go into the garden." Her mother shifted, struggling to sit.

Amber helped her. "The doctor said you're not to go outside."

Emeline frowned. "The doctor doesn't know what's best for me."

Amber wanted to disagree, but she hadn't seen this spark of determination in her mother's eyes for almost a month. "Do you think you can walk?"

"No one is carrying me." She shoved the blankets down to reveal her red nightdress.

"I'll ring for your lady's maid."

"No. You can help me dress. Get my coat."

Too pleased by her mother's alertness to complain about being treated like a servant, Amber leapt to her feet to obey. It was a little tricky to do up the buttons with her mother unable to stand for very long, but she managed it. She then took out her winter coat.

"I don't need it. It's warm outside."

"The doctor said you mustn't get a chill."

The queen waved her hand. "Nonsense." She walked over to the door but was puffing by the time she reached it.

Unease filled Amber. "Mother, you will need help to get to the garden if you can barely reach the door." She folded the coat over her arm and hurried across.

"Anyone who helps will send word to Doctor Teregen, and he'll try to stop me. I don't have the strength to face him today."

"Doctor Teregen has business in the city this morning."

"I know." Her mother's smile was stronger this time.

Oh. So that was behind the sudden urge to get up. The doctor had insisted the queen stay in bed the entire six months since she'd taken ill, and Emeline hated being in bed.

"Which garden are we going to?" asked Amber.

"The rock garden."

Of course. Her mother's favourite place. She always said it reminded her of home because she came from the mountains. It was also the one closest to her chambers. Just two corridors and one flight of stairs to navigate. "Let's go."

Outside the bedchamber, two guards stood to attention. The older one, dark haired and with a strong nose, gaped at the appearance of the queen. "Your Majesty, we are under instructions not to let you out of your room."

"Well, I order you to let me," the queen said. "And my orders overrule those of the doctor."

The guard nodded. "But not those of the king."

Perhaps he was trying to protect his wife. "Father's first concern would be the health of my mother, and she wishes to spend time in the garden," Amber said. "Joseph, you may lend your arm to help her there," she ordered her personal guard, a man who hadn't left her side since her father left.

The stoic blond man glanced at his compatriot and a message passed between them. Amber braced herself for more argument, but it didn't come. "Yes, Your Highness."

Together Amber and Joseph helped the queen down the stairs and into the rock garden without seeing anyone. Emeline insisted on sitting on a large rock in the centre and sighed. "You may go."

The instruction was pointless as Joseph wouldn't leave them unprotected, but he moved out of the circle of rocks which enclosed the garden. Amber didn't know why her father had stepped up her protection over the past year. Joseph always accompanied her to events, but now he was on hand, waiting outside the room when she ordered privacy, but otherwise inside. Always ready to protect her. But the royal family were well loved, and they were on good terms with their neighbouring countries.

Still, Amber obeyed her father. She considered Joseph her shadow. He followed her everywhere and there was nothing she could do about it.

The queen placed both palms on the rock and closed her eyes, tilting her head up to the sun, which struggled to shine through the smog. For the first time in over a month, colour came to her cheeks.

Amber's heart lifted. She would make sure her mother came here as often as she liked. She rubbed her arms. Though Doctor Teregen scared the nourishment out of her.

She lay her mother's coat on the rock next to her and ran her fingers over the cool, pale surface, inhaling deeply. The air was a little fresher in this courtyard, as if the smog didn't dare cover the palace. She'd always loved this garden, perhaps because her mother told her stories about her home in the mountains, and it made her feel close to the kin she had never met. Aside from the large rock in the centre, smaller rocks formed a circle around the outside and mountain plants grew over and around them. The mountain berry bushes were clumped on one side, but the berries had barely formed, let alone ripened. Odd. She was sure they were normally full of fruit by now. The little succulents which grew out of the cracks in the rocks were paler than usual, as if they hadn't had enough sun. Maybe because the smog was thick today.

The pine tree's branches shaded the area, always out of place so close to the coast. It was the only one she'd ever seen.

Everything in the garden still felt foreign to her, and yet like her mother, she felt a sense of comfort here. She perched on one of the other rocks, mindful of the yellow dust she would have to brush off her clothing when she left. It didn't matter, as long as her mother was happy.

The birds fluttered through the pine tree and down to the berry bushes as if to check if the berries were ripe enough yet, before flying away disappointed. Even they looked scraggly, their feathers not as glossy as last summer. What was going on? Had Percy noticed the difference? Amber sighed.

No. Her brother wouldn't care, would tell her he had bigger things to worry about, like running the country in their father and older brother's absence. How much would Percy scold her when he discovered she'd helped her mother into the garden? If she was lucky, he wouldn't hear of it. He'd been too busy to visit their mother since Father and her older brother, Baldrick left for Tartalan and Sylta respectively to request help. She imagined he relished finally having some control. He'd always been bitter that he wasn't the eldest son and heir.

"What is the meaning of this?"

Amber jumped to her feet at the outraged bellow. She spun to see Doctor Teregen at the entrance of the garden, accompanied by the bulbous-nosed guard who had been outside her mother's door. Heart racing, Amber moved to stand in front of her mother, the doctor's dark gaze boring into her soul. He towered over her and often made her feel like an insect about to be squashed.

"Mother wanted fresh air," she whispered, hating her deference to him. She was a princess.

"Did I not say a chill could kill her? Do you want to murder your own mother?"

"That is enough, Teregen." Her mother's tone had its own chill. "I can come to the garden if I wish."

"The king ordered I heal you."

"How can you heal me when you do not know what is wrong?"

"The best research shows bed rest and warmth will help."

"And yet I feel more energised after a few minutes outside than I have for the whole six months I've been trapped indoors."

"The king gave me complete control over your health while he is gone. I must insist you return to your room."

Amber wanted to protest, but her father's orders were law, outranking them both.

"Very well. You can carry my coat." Emeline stood, brushing by the doctor with an imperious air, and Amber hurried behind her, leaving the doctor to carry the coat as requested. By the time they reached the top of the stairs, her mother was panting and leaning on Amber. On hearing footsteps coming towards them, she straightened and let out a breath before continuing to her room. Amber opened the door for her and when she tried to close it behind them, Teregen pushed past her.

"Your Majesty, you must stay in bed."

"Close the door, so I might change in privacy."

The man bristled at the order but did as she requested.

Emeline stood behind a privacy screen while Amber undid her buttons and helped her back into her night gown.

"What have you eaten today?" the doctor asked.

"I've requested mountain berries."

The doctor snorted. "You should drink broth. Berries will only upset your insides and make you weaker."

Nonsense. Mountain berries were the sweetest, juiciest berries, and she and her mother could eat them all day without getting a bellyache.

"Then you may send for some broth." Emeline climbed into bed.

"You should rest now." The doctor placed his hand on her forehead and tutted. "Definitely too much exertion." He glared at Amber. "You need to leave your mother in peace."

She stepped back, glanced at her mother. The king had ordered her to care for her mother and keep her company while she was bedridden.

"I will rest a short while," Emeline said. "Can you find Daisy?"

The mountain berries. She would find her mother some berries, even if she had to smuggle them in under her skirt. "Of course, Mother. Rest well."

Amber left the room. The guards were back in position, and she glared at them. Joseph didn't flinch.

She headed along the corridor towards the dining hall and her footsteps slowed. Where was the kitchen? She turned to Joseph, who had fallen in behind her and asked him.

"They're on the ground floor at the back of the castle."

"Show me the way."

"Your Highness, might I send someone to get what you need?" he suggested.

She frowned. He never spoke back to her. "I need

mountain berries for Mother and Daisy hasn't returned."

He inclined his head. "Very well." He led the way, weaving along corridors until the sharp scent of bellar spice bread reached her nose. He pushed open a door and a waft of heat and noise hit her. Inside people scurried back and forth, each with their own mission. Some sat at the table grinding flour, others prepared vegetables and meat. Chaos.

Amber stepped back. Who was she supposed to speak with?

Across the room, Daisy sat talking with another worker. What was she doing sitting there when the queen had asked for something? Amber strode towards her, ignoring everyone else.

Daisy looked up and panic crossed her face as she jumped to her feet and curtsied. "Your Highness."

Silence fell as around her everyone froze.

"Where are the queen's mountain berries?"

"We have none," the maid stammered. "We sent someone to the markets."

Amber frowned, looking around. "Why do we have no berries? They are the queen's favourite."

"I'm told there are none to be had," the maid said. "Honestly. It was a terrible season and the crops have failed."

How ridiculous. There were always mountain berries. The door across the room opened, and a boy entered. He stopped when he noticed the silence.

"He went into the city for them, Your Highness." Daisy pointed and the boy took a step back.

Amber strode over. "Where are the mountain berries?"

The boy curtsied, then bowed, his face red. "I'm sorry, Your Highness. I couldn't find any. The merchants all said they've had no deliveries."

It wasn't possible. Her father always complained

about the laziness of the palace servants. She bet the boy hadn't even left the palace grounds. "We'll see about that. Send someone for my carriage." If her mother wanted berries, she would get berries.

Amber swept out of the kitchen, Joseph right behind her.

***

Flynn Stonemason perched atop the steps of the town hall and looked down at the Bermont markets. Chaos. It was the only word to describe it. Sellers set up their stalls and lines snaked through every available space as people waited, desperately hoping they could buy a share of the meagre food available. The smell from the cobblestones covered in dirt and excrement was enough to turn his stomach. Even here, in the inner city where the upper class and nobility lived, there was little to be bought, though they had plenty of money to pay. Many women waiting in line had the tell-tale signs of hunger, gaunt cheeks, limp hair and their entire body slumped as if they didn't have the energy to stand upright. A year ago, maybe two and this market would have been full of pomp and ceremony, everyone there to be seen, dressed in their best shopping clothes. Now the clothes were worn, some even had patches, disguised as decorations, for cloth was scarce too.

Flynn might have given a damn if these weren't the people who turned their backs on his father after one mistake. They could rot for all he cared, and they deserved it for their lack of empathy. The wealthy quarter had shut themselves off when the plague hit, refused all cries for help, and now the country's lack of resources was hitting them as much as everyone else. They didn't even have their men to protect them anymore.

Flynn had watched from a perch in the harbour as the king and Prince Baldrick set sail with a flotilla of ships and promises of returning with food. The only place they could get it was from the neighbouring countries, and the soldiers on the ships said they would get it by any means necessary.

War.

He hoped it didn't come to that, but they had rounded up every able-bodied man to fight with the promise of two meals a day. And people were desperate enough to line up for the chance.

Not Flynn. There were too many children in the city relying on him to provide a bite to eat, a safe place to stay, or simply someone to talk to. The king had abandoned his people, but Flynn wouldn't. He couldn't. Hundreds of children were left without parents after the plague, and he kept thinking, if his sisters had been the only ones to survive, instead of him, he'd want someone to support them.

The king deserved to be on the streets, starving, with his family dead and no roof over his head. The most he'd done was allow the homeless to shelter in two warehouses on the docks which had been tagged for destruction.

Only a year before the plague, not long after he'd been crowned, he'd promised advancements, more stone, more silk, more bellar spice and other crops, when he'd touted the new coal-powered machinery. Instead, machines replaced many labourers and families lost their incomes, and the thick smog hung over the city like an evil ghost.

A shout nearby caught Flynn's attention as a figure darted away from a stall. A child no more than ten, holding an apple. The crowd surged around her, stopping her, and she struggled. "It's for my brother," she cried.

The watch strode over. One took the apple from her hand and returned it to the stall holder, and the other pushed the child towards the prison on the other side of the markets.

Flynn's blood boiled and his hand went to the chisel and hammer he kept on his tool belt. Anyone could see the child was starved, her bones visible in her stick-like arms. A good meal was the solution, not prison. He would have to bribe the soldiers to let her go. Though money had less and less value these days when there was nothing available to buy. A loaf of bread would have been better.

He sighed. No chance there'd be any spare food he could buy at the end of the day. He stood as a steam carriage pulled into the marketplace, causing people to scatter. He frowned. Only those fighting to hold on to their status used them anymore. It made them a target for desperate people. He almost turned away, but he registered the ruby red paintwork and the golden crest depicting mountains and boars on its door. Royalty. Anger surged. Had the king returned? No, it would be Prince Percy. The queen and princess never left the palace. And Flynn had a few words to say to the prince about the state of the city.

Two paces down the steps, his eyes glued to the carriage, and the door opened. He froze. The head poking out was framed by curly blonde hair, cheeks flushed with a healthy glow. As she stepped on to the cobblestones, the ruby red silk dress with matching slippers was a beacon, an announcement she differed from everyone else. Definitely not Prince Percy. She was a vision, almost like an angel, so out of place was her lustrous long hair and her unmarked clothing.

He drew in a breath. Princess Amber. But what was she doing in the central markets?

She glanced around as if uncertain, her eyes wide and her nose wrinkled at the smell. What had she expected when the people starved and had no energy to clean the streets? She was flanked by two personal guards, but several more worked to move people out of her path. One of her guards pointed towards a merchant selling fruit.

People around the princess curtsied as she passed, but their expressions couldn't hide their disdain. It was as if all the misery suddenly tightened to tension, and one wrong word would make the whole market explode. Flynn hesitated. Should he leave before things turned bad? Across the market, Flynn spotted his good friend, Roley, who had taken Flynn aside only yesterday and ranted about what he wanted to do to the king for the misery he'd caused. Roley grabbed a cactus fruit from his stall and strode towards the princess, determination on his face.

Flynn knew how Roley felt, but curse it, this wouldn't end well for anyone.

He continued to the ground, his heart racing, and weaved around people, the princess easy to spot as the brightest colour in the area.

She was a little ahead of him, but moved slowly, waiting for the crowds to shift to the side. Flynn had no compunction as he shoved his way through, calling out apologies.

"Oi, Your Highness!" yelled Roley. He ducked around an older woman and stopped. The princess was there, surrounded by her guards on three sides.

"Move, sir," the guard in front ordered.

"No. Not until I've had a word with the princess." Roley shook his cactus fruit as he spoke.

The guard placed a hand on his sword and a soft, refined voice spoke. "Let him speak, Joseph." Princess Amber moved forward to face Roley directly. Stupid, couldn't she see he was mad? "What did you wish to say?"

Some of the bluster left Roley, and he hesitated as if

unsure. Flynn moved closer, edging around the guards so he could defuse his friend's anger. "I want to know what you're doing about this here situation." He waved around at the crowd, and the cactus fruit slipped from his hand, heading straight for the princess. Flynn dived in front of her, taking the cactus fruit on his chest. The fruit, already overly soft, exploded in a shower of juice and pulp over Flynn's tunic. Roley stared in horror, and Flynn mouthed, *Run*. The guards would view the incident as an attack on the princess, not an accident of a clumsy, angry shopkeeper. Roley ran.

One guard shouted, as Flynn turned slowly, arms raised, not wanting to alarm anyone, and came face to face with the princess. Petite, fragile, her brown eyes wide and a little fearful.

He lost his breath.

"Get back." A guard shoved Flynn back a couple of steps and grimaced at the pulp that transferred to his hand.

The impact jarred Flynn from his daze and he bowed. "Your Highness," he said. "Please forgive the crudeness of your greeting. These are difficult times."

Her cheeks flushed a pretty pink. "Thank you for stepping in front of me." She glanced around and the guards made a circle around them, ever watchful. "What is going on?"

Flynn frowned. "I'm afraid I don't understand your question."

"Why are there so many lines? Where is the colour and vibrancy of the market?"

He gaped at her. "It's a little hard to be vibrant when you're starving." The words came out harshly and a guard growled, "Show the princess some respect."

Only when she earned it. The anger and frustration he'd been carrying about her father bubbled and hissed inside him. As he fought to control it, she said, "Why are they starving?"

She appeared completely baffled, and some of his anger cooled. "If I could hazard a guess, it's probably due to the devastating drought the country has been experiencing."

"Drought? My father spoke of no drought."

"Your Highness, there don't appear to be any mountain berries." Joseph took her arm. "You should return to the palace."

She turned to go, then shook off his arm. "No, Joseph. I will know what is happening in my country." The princess faced Flynn, and the determination in her expression gave Flynn a glimmer of hope. "How long has the drought lasted?"

He bowed his head in a token of respect. "Over a year, Your Highness. It started before the plague."

Her eyes grew even wider, and she stepped away from him. "What plague?"

She had no clue what happened outside the castle walls. "The plague which swept through the city last year, killing about twenty percent of the population."

She looked at Joseph and he nodded. "It was a serious business, Your Highness."

An understatement. "Is there anything the royal family can do to help the starving, homeless children?"

The princess blinked at him, and he added, "Many lost their homes when the plague killed their parents, and they have no one to help them."

Her mouth set in a firm line, and she held out her hand. "My purse."

Joseph handed it to her.

"What do the children need?" she asked Flynn.

"Food and shelter, Your Highness. Clean drinking water." The basics of the Trinity.

She nodded and moved to the nearest stall. "You've almost sold out of produce," she said to the gobsmacked stall holder. "Do you have a warehouse full of more fruit?"

Flynn laughed in disbelief. "Your Highness, these people are lining up because this is all the food in the city. I thought the palace might have its own warehouses."

Slowly, she scanned the people and stalls behind her. "That can't be true. Father wouldn't let our people starve."

Of course he would. He didn't care about his people.

She shook her head. "Did you know this was happening, Joseph?"

The guard pursed his lips. "My family mentioned food was scarce in their letters to me."

"But your family live in the country. They have a farm."

"The drought has been hard."

The princess's hand shook. "I must speak with Percy. Thank you for bringing this to my attention…"

"Flynn Stonemason." He bowed again.

"Flynn. How can I get word back to you?"

Would she bother? "I have a place in the tradesmen's quarter, Your Highness. Anyone can point you to it, and you can leave a message there. It will get to me."

She looked confused, so he added, "I have no fixed address. I gave up my rooms to some children who were homeless."

She opened her mouth and then closed it, shaking her head. "That is very kind of you. I shall send a message when I have answers," she said. "Good day."

He bowed again as she made her way back to her carriage. For the first time since his family died, he felt as if maybe there was someone who could help him. Though if there was no food, what could she do?

The carriage belched more smoke in the air as it left, and someone clapped him on the shoulder.

"Thanks for saving my skin," Roley said.

Flynn chuckled. "You can thank me by cleaning my shirt." The juice was sticky and uncomfortable.

Roley nodded. "Absolutely."

"What were you planning to say to the princess, anyway?"

"About what you said, but not as well." He laughed, and they walked back to his stall.

His apples caught Flynn's eye, reminding him of the child who had been arrested. "I'll see you later."

He pressed into the crowd, a few people whispering and staring at him. Few of them would have dared speak to the princess. Not when the king's anger with anyone he thought had slighted him was legendary. Flynn's father caught the brunt of it when a window frame they'd carved broke on the way to being installed in the palace. It left his father's reputation in tatters with no one willing to employ him, although he'd been working for the king. He blocked the memory.

Inside the prison, the man behind the desk grunted at him. "Should have known you'd be around soon."

"I'm beginning to think you arrest these poor kids just so you can see me and my coin," Flynn answered.

"She broke the law."

Flynn didn't bother arguing. "How much?"

"A quarter."

The price increased every time he came in, but there wasn't much else he could spend his money on. Flynn handed it over. "What's her name?"

"Didn't say." He stood and pulled open the door behind him. "Bring the kid out."

A few minutes later a small girl was dragged out. She took one look at Flynn and started struggling. "I'm not going with no whore master."

He blinked. That was a new one. "The name's Flynn," he said, hoping she might have heard of him. "I don't want you for anything. You're free to go. But in future when you're hungry, go to my friend Roley, across the markets, and tell him Flynn sent you. He'll charge what you take to me."

The suspicion on the girl's face didn't shift as she edged towards the door. He stepped away from it and she sprinted through, disappearing into the crowd.

"That's gratitude for you," the guard said.

Flynn didn't care. It was hard to trust in a world where you fought for every scrap of food. "Do you know anything about a whoremaster taking kids off the street?"

The guard shook his head. "But if it's true, I'd guess they'd be down at the docks."

Flynn stared at the man. "Don't you think you should investigate?"

The guard shrugged. "Got our hands full without looking for more work."

He clenched his fists and strode out the door before he did something stupid like punching the man. Outside, he exhaled and gave himself a moment to let his anger settle. His stomach rumbled, but he didn't have time to get in line for food today.

Instead, he headed to the docks to discover if there was any truth to the young girl's words.

Chapter 18

Flynn wandered down to the docks, keeping an eye out for children who might need his help. He spotted far too many begging on the street, and he gave coin to all he could, not that it helped with little food to buy. The smog blackened the walls, and the roads were covered in mud and manure. The docks had always been a rough neighbourhood, but when Flynn was a boy, the houses had clean walls and the streets were kept clear to make transport of goods to and from the docks easier.

He kept close to the edge of the road, hand in his pocket, firmly around his purse. The new coal-powered carriages made it too dangerous to walk down the middle of the road and thieves were light-fingered in this part of town.

He reached the first wharf and walked along the water's edge. The harbour was large, enclosed by headlands at each end, and stretched the length of the city. From here boats sailed across the bay or down the river to Sylta, and across the ocean to Tartalan.

Many of the warehouses at this end were empty, so he wandered further, searching for a couple of kids who lived down here. They regularly came to his home to leave news from the wharves. They seemed to believe because he helped to feed the homeless, he could fix all the problems in the city. But he was one person.

Princess Amber on the other hand... She had seemed genuinely concerned, but would she remember their problems by the time she returned to the palace? For her to know nothing about the starvation or plague in the city meant she was incredibly sheltered. Her biggest problem was getting mountain berries to eat. Showed her priorities.

A couple of ships were unloading coal to transport into the city. It seemed to be the only resource they weren't short of. The Marsh fae provided them as much as they needed, and unlike other fae who refused to leave their land, the Marsh fae travelled with the coal, taking it to whoever wanted it.

Flynn wasn't sure this progress was a good thing. The hills surrounding the city trapped the smoke in, making the light dim even in the middle of the day, and the thick, oily air was difficult to breathe. The dirty taste constantly coated his tongue, the only advantage being it made him less hungry.

Further down the docks he found the warehouses which had been abandoned by their owners and taken over by the homeless. During the plague, people had been ordered to stay confined to their homes and anyone who had no home had been crammed together in the warehouses. Flynn suspected the king had hoped they'd infect each other and die, so he didn't have to deal with them later. He must have been disappointed the disease had mostly killed adults. Those warehouses had become the children's homes, and the king had ordered they stay there, rather than roam the streets at night.

Something tugged on his pocket and Flynn caught a small hand holding a sharp knife. The child yelled and kicked at him.

"Settle down," Flynn said. "You're trying to steal from me."

"Don't turn me in," the child begged. "I'm so hungry."

He looked it too, with sunken eyes and a bulging belly. Flynn cringed, the familiar feeling of helplessness flooding him. Many times he'd wondered whether he would help more by leaving and going in search of food in Sylta, but he couldn't bear to leave the kids without someone to turn to, and he suspected Sylta might be in a similar situation if they wouldn't help. Nearby, a shop sold bread and the rich scents wafting out declared they'd just finished a fresh batch, ready to feed those folk brave enough to risk coming to the docks. "Come with me." He kept hold of the child's hand and dragged him into the bakery. "Half a dozen rolls," he said to the girl behind the counter.

The serving girl bagged them up, and he paid, letting go of the child as he did so. The child didn't run, instead stared with his mouth open as if the scent alone could feed him.

Taking the bag, Flynn withdrew a roll and handed it to the child. "Eat it slowly, or you'll make yourself sick. Make it last a day."

"Thank you, sir."

Flynn chuckled. "The name's Flynn, not sir." He walked outside. "Have you seen Nate around?"

The kid nodded. "He's usually at the harbour master's office."

To hear news from the ships coming in. Nate was filled with hope that one day he'd be able to sneak on board a ship going somewhere better than Molanka, but most captains knew to watch for him by now, and he was thrown back onto the jetty before they set sail. "Thanks."

Flynn made his way to the office central to the wharves. On his way, he handed out rolls to a couple of kids, and ate one himself. It was still warm from the oven and would have been perfect with a bit of butter, but that was a luxury only the super wealthy could afford.

He found Nate sitting on a retaining wall outside the harbour master's office. The fourteen-year-old's light brown hair dripped water and his skin was clean. The harbour provided plenty of water to wash with, but these days you needed to pick your spot and avoid the rubbish, before washing in it. Flynn handed Nate the last roll.

"Thanks, Flynn. What brings you down here?" Nate tore off a chunk of bread and chewed enthusiastically.

"Rumours." He used a nearby bucket to haul some water from the harbour and stripped off his tunic, washing the sticky cactus juice off it.

Nate grinned, his teeth crooked and one of his front teeth missing. "You've come to the right place. What have you got?"

Flynn squeezed the water from his shirt and laid it over the wall to dry, then lifted himself to sit next to the boy. "Something about whore masters taking kids from the streets to work for them."

Nate's smile vanished. "I've heard that too, but only in the past couple of days."

"Any truth to it?"

"I dunno. A few girls have gone missing, but no one knows for sure where they've gone."

"They got any family looking for them?"

Nate's laugh had a bitter edge. "Most families these days are happy to have one less mouth to feed. I know Ava's missing."

Shock made Flynn momentarily speechless. "She's ten." No one would force a ten-year-old into those kinds of services.

"Yeah. Last time she was seen was over by the clock tower four nights ago."

His youngest sister had been Ava's age. "The whore

houses are still at the south end of the wharves?"

"Yeah." Nate jumped off the wall and gestured for Flynn to follow him along one of the empty jetties. "There's something else you might find interesting."

Flynn grabbed his damp top and put it back on. "What's that?"

"A lot of soldiers have been seen at the north end," he said. "Rumour is they're guarding supplies. No one can get within a fae's splash of the warehouses up there."

"What supplies?"

"Everyone says it's food, but it can't be. It'll rot just lying there. There's been a lot of talk about storming the warehouses."

Which would get people killed. The soldiers were all armed and skilled fighters. It was something the king was proud of. "Stealth would be better. Find out for certain what's there, before risking people's lives."

"I agree. You volunteering?"

Flynn laughed. "Not right now."

"Crane is leading the calls to attack."

Flynn swore. He should have guessed. Crane had declared himself leader of the homeless kids, though he had already surpassed his twentieth year, and reacted without considering the consequences. He'd get everyone killed. "I'll go talk to him."

"Thanks, Flynn. I knew you'd help." Nate waved and wandered back to his wall.

How had he become someone the kids turned to? He hadn't meant to, but by doing the right thing, they came to him with their problems. And he didn't have the answers. The responsibility weighed on him, keeping him roaming the streets most days to find solutions, but there were none.

Crane's warehouse was on the way to the whorehouses, so he'd stop and talk to him. There'd be people there who would welcome him, even if Crane didn't.

He trudged back along the docks, which should be busier than they were. It was only mid-afternoon, but many of the jetties were empty, the ships taken into the service of the king.

Flynn arrived at a wooden warehouse which had panels missing from its walls, a slight lean to the north, and appeared as if a strong breeze would blow it down. That was probably another reason the king let them stay there. He didn't want to risk his valuable products being damaged if the warehouse collapsed. People were replaceable.

With those dark thoughts circling his mind, he pushed the main door open and walked inside. Children huddled in groups, but they all glanced over as he entered, the squeak of the door hinge enough to put anyone's teeth on edge.

"Flynn!" Cherie jumped up and ran to him, flinging her arms around him. He winced and extracted himself from the sixteen-year-old's embrace. She had hinted she wanted him to take her home, had suggested she could do things for him. Wouldn't happen. She was too young and too clingy.

"Hey, Cherie. How's things?" He walked further into the warehouse, waving a greeting at people he knew, all the while scanning for Crane.

"They've been better. Did you bring any food today?"

The guilt was hard. "I've already given it away." It wasn't his job to feed the kingdom—it was the king's.

Her face fell. "That's a shame."

His chest squeezed at his inability to help, making breathing difficult. "Is Crane here?"

"In his office."

Flynn's eyebrows raised. "Office?"

"Yeah, he put up some walls at the back." She pointed.

"Thanks. You take care." Two older teenagers stood outside the opening which led into the makeshift office. They scowled at him and stopped him from going further. "Name?"

"Flynn." He was certain both boys had come to him for food in the past.

"Let him in," Crane called.

They cleared the doorway. Crane sat behind a wooden desk, his feet on top of it, his hands behind his head. The soles of his shoes were in good repair and the clothes he wore, while not new, were in a lot better condition than the ones he'd been wearing the last time Flynn had seen him about a month ago. "What brings you to the docks?"

"Rumours," Flynn told him, brushing his fingers over the chisel. "Know anything about kids being forced to work in the whorehouses?"

Crane waved a hand, the strawberry birthmark on the back of it catching Flynn's gaze. "I'm sure they're just rumours. People go missing all the time. Sometimes they've left the city, and other times they die and their bodies are found later."

His lack of concern grated on Flynn's nerves. They were of similar age, but while Flynn tried to help others, Crane was creating his own office and gang of goons.

"So the rumours of a warehouse full of food at the north end are just rumours too?"

This time Crane's eyes narrowed, and he brought his feet to the ground. "What have you heard?"

"Only that people think it's true."

"It's for the war," Crane said. "The king will need to supply his army."

"If that was the case, couldn't he get supplies in the countries he's invaded?"

Crane shook his head. "He might need backup. A good king always has a plan B."

He would debate whether Tremont was a good king

some other time. "You're not planning on taking away his plan B?"

"You hear a lot up there in the city, don't you?"

"Bits and pieces." He placed his hands on the back of the chair in front of him.

"I'd suggest you ignore the rumours." The stare he gave Flynn was more of a warning.

Interesting. "All right. I'll see you around."

On his way out, he stopped to chat to a few people he knew, find out how they were doing, and to ask about Ava. They were even thinner than the last time he was here. If they didn't get food soon, they would starve. Again, the idea of crossing the border into Sylta entered his mind. It might only take a couple of days, if he found a place to sneak across. The king had closed the borders when the plague had started, and they hadn't been reopened.

No, that was an idea for another day. Right now, he needed to visit the whorehouses, because there was no way he believed Crane that they were rumours.

There were close to a dozen whorehouses arranged in rows near the wharves. Easy access for the sailors who were only in port for a few days. Though with fewer ships coming through, Flynn wondered whether the whorehouses were suffering as much as the rest of the city.

He walked down one row, smiling and greeting the callers out the front who attempted to entice him into their buildings. How could he discover if any of them forced children to work? The women and men in the windows were all adults, and he couldn't walk up and ask for a child. His skin crawled at the idea, but a few steps down the street he stopped. Maybe that's exactly what he could do.

He was in his twentieth year and so people might not

frown about him asking for a teen.

Still, surely not all the houses were taking in children to work.

"You going to come in and—" The low, enticing call cut off, but that wasn't why Flynn turned. He recognised the voice. The woman standing at the doorway paled, despite the layers of makeup on her face, but her shock of red hair helped him identify her.

"Jess?" She'd lived next door to him for years before her family had moved away. He'd always found an excuse to be outside whenever Jess was, had considered her the loveliest girl he'd ever seen. And she was still beautiful, though now he couldn't help comparing her to the princess's beauty.

She lifted her chin. "Flynn. It's been a while."

He nodded, coming closer. "How've you been?" Many people denigrated prostitutes but as far as he was concerned, they offered a service which was needed.

"I'm getting by," she said. "Wouldn't have thought to see you in this neighbourhood. Last I heard you were a successful stone mason."

"Stone's pretty scarce right now," he said. "No word has come from the quarries as to why, and the messengers don't return."

Jess nodded. "It's tough all 'round."

He lowered his voice. "Can I ask you something?"

She nodded and stepped away from the other caller at the door.

"There are rumours homeless girls are being made to work in this neighbourhood."

Jess scowled. "Not at my place."

"Any guesses whose place it might be?"

She frowned. "You want to buy?"

"No!" He grimaced. "A friend of mine is missing. She's only ten. I want to make sure she's not here."

"You always had a big heart, Flynn." She fluttered her

fingers in a wave at a marsh fae walking past. "If anyone was doing it, it would be The House of Pleasure or The House of Dreams. They're in the back row."

"Thanks, Jess. You take care of yourself." He went to walk away, and she held his arm.

"You not coming inside?" she asked. "I always had a crush on you. I can give you a discount."

The temptation was swift, and he took two steps with her before he stopped. "No, I can't. I need to find my friend, but ah, thank you for the offer."

She smiled. "It stands at any time." She kissed his cheek and heat flooded his face.

"See you around." He hurried down the street. He'd come back later, not to pay for her services, but to catch up and make sure she really was all right. Their childhoods had been prosperous times with the old king, and Jess's family had been well off.

A couple of streets away he found the two houses Jess named. They were the same as all the others in the neighbourhood, grey walls, large windows and bright colours to attract the eye, with callers out the front. Flynn found a seat near the canal which ran between the houses and sat, watching people in the street. Nothing marked the clientele who entered the houses as any different from those who entered the other buildings.

And there were a surprising amount of people entering considering the state of the city, but perhaps with nothing else to spend money on, pleasure was the best option.

What was the best way of approaching this? None of the women in the windows appeared to be underage.

He forced himself to stand and walk over to the House of Pleasure. The woman at the door greeted him with a smile. "I saw you over there," she said. "Wondered if you'd choose my place. I'm sure we have what you need." She took him by the arm and led him inside.

In the hall, stairs led to the first floor, but to the left was a large receiving room where several men waited. The decor was modern, with lush fabrics on the sofas and muted tones on the walls. Very classy. The woman stopped and said, "Why don't you tell me what you're after?"

Flynn cleared his throat. "Ah, I want a girl, around my age—maybe a little younger."

The woman raised her eyebrows and studied him. "You don't want a woman?"

Heat flooded his cheeks. "I, ah, don't know how comfortable I'd be."

"It's her job to make you comfortable, darling. Perhaps you'll find someone you like amongst these lovelies." She indicated the women walking down the stairs, all dressed in the latest fashion, and entering the receiving room.

Obviously, the whorehouses weren't having difficulty finding fabrics, or perhaps the clothes weren't used often.

Flynn scanned the women, but saw no one he recognised, nor anyone who looked as if she were underage. "I was hoping for someone a little younger," he repeated. "If you don't have anyone, I'll go elsewhere."

The woman placed a hand on his arm to stop him. "Wait there, darling. I'll be right back." She sashayed away.

In the receiving room, the men chose their women and were led upstairs. Flynn moved over to the corner and glanced out the window at people walking by. He spotted Crane coming down the street. What was he doing here? As far as Flynn was aware, he didn't have money to spend.

"Sir, this way, please." The caller was back and

gestured for him to follow her.

He glanced back at the street as Crane strolled towards the House of Pleasures. Quickly Flynn moved, following the woman down the hall and to a room at the back. Behind him, Crane's voice carried as he came inside. "I need to talk to Drury."

Flynn slipped into the office with a large desk and chair, and a filing cabinet in the corner.

"Wait here." The lady left.

No windows in the room, but a lamp hung from the roof, illuminating the space. Flynn's shoulder blades itched, which suggested he was being watched, but the room contained no other door. He wandered around, not having to fake his nerves as he read the titles of a couple of books and glanced at the paperwork on the table. The items and numbers on the paper made little sense to him. They weren't goods he'd ever heard of.

The door opened, and the woman returned with three girls, their faces covered in makeup. One was significantly shorter than the other two, who were about sixteen. All three of them had a glazed expression in their eyes.

Drugged.

Fury filled him.

"Will any of these suit you, sir?" the caller asked.

Flynn bit his tongue and made a show of examining all three. The first girl he'd seen hanging around the central market and was fairly sure he'd fed her before. The second girl was someone he didn't recognise, and the short one he almost didn't recognise until she lifted her gaze. Ava. Anger filled him as the girl blinked as if confused but didn't speak.

He faced the woman. "I'll take these girls," he growled. "And if I discover this or any other whorehouse is kidnapping children from the streets, I will ensure the city watch closes you down."

The woman stepped back, fear in her eyes. "I can't let you take them."

"You can't stop me. Ava's only ten for the Purifier's sake!" He placed his arm around the girl. "Come on, Ava. I'll take care of you. All of you. Come with me."

The girls turned as if they had no mind of their own, and he opened the door.

"Girls, stay here," the caller said.

The girls stopped moving.

Concern washed through him. "What have you given them?" No drug worked this way.

"None of your business. You're not taking them."

He stepped between the girls and the woman. "These girls aren't here willingly. I'll call the watch."

"And they'll be gone before you get back with them."

Frustration filled him. "I'll make a real ruckus and your clients would stop coming."

The woman laughed. "You'd be surprised how many extra clients we'd get if more knew these girls were on offer."

Nausea rose in his stomach. He couldn't leave them here. He shook Ava. "Ava, you need to come with me."

She blinked and took two steps forward.

"Girls, follow me, now."

The girls moved on his command until the caller said, "Stop."

The door was still open, and Crane walked past. Finally, someone who would assist. "Crane! I need your help."

Crane looked in and swore. He spoke to someone behind him in the corridor. "I told you he'd cause a problem."

Outrage took Flynn's breath away. "You're responsible for this." The new clothes, the denial he knew anything… Flynn surged forward, and his fist connected with a satisfying crunch to Crane's face. Crane yelled and staggered back, but before Flynn could follow up with another punch, he was grabbed from behind, both his arms twisted back. He grunted and shifted, but couldn't see who held him.

"Stop struggling or I'll make a new hole in your clothes," the man murmured. A sharp prick pierced Flynn's back, and he stilled.

"That's better. Now you're going to walk out of here and forget this ever happened."

Crane smirked at him as he wiped the blood from his nose.

"I'm not going without Ava."

"You're in no place to negotiate. I can make you disappear easily enough, but Crane tells me you might be missed if that happened."

What option did he have? Ava still stared blankly ahead, and the other girls hadn't moved. He'd never seen this kind of mind control before.

Helplessness washed over him. Even if he ran straight to the watch, and made them care, the girls would have been moved by the time he returned. "She's only ten."

"Some of my clients like them young."

Flynn clenched his teeth. Ava was a step inside the room, Crane stood between him and the door outside, and Flynn had a knife at his back. But a crazy grab at Ava wouldn't help anyone if he wound up dead. "I'll go."

"You tell anyone, and she'll end up floating in the harbour face down," the man said.

He swore and pulled away from the man. This time he was let go, but when he turned, the man strode back down the corridor, his face obscured, a slight limp on his right side. He could grab Ava now.

"Don't try it, Flynn." Crane had pulled a knife and pointed it at him.

He swore. He would make Crane pay for this, but right now he had to get backup. And there was one person who could help him.

He shoved past Crane and strode outside.

***

Amber barely felt the jostles of the carriage as she returned to the palace. She stared out at the grimy, filthy city she didn't recognise. She'd had to check with Joseph to ensure she'd been taken to the central markets as she'd requested. It didn't resemble the bustling, colourful square she remembered. It had always been a rare treat to be allowed to browse the wares, smell the delicious food cooking and watch the buskers performing.

Now it was a drab shell, like comparing a launda forest with a marshland. Women and children lined for food, misery on their faces.

What had happened? How long had this been going on?

She didn't notice the carriage had stopped until Joseph opened the door and offered his hand to help her out. She sneezed at the thick smoke from the carriage and hurried inside the castle to escape the polluted air. Something was very wrong here, and it wasn't possible it had only happened since her father had been gone. She stopped a guard in the hall. "You there, where is Prince Percy?"

The guard bowed. "I believe he's in the council room with the king's advisors, Your Highness."

She turned down the corridor, her footsteps slower. Did she want to burst in and speak with her brother while he was in meetings? She could imagine the outrage on both his and the advisors' faces. She had no business there.

Amber stopped, only half aware Joseph had stopped behind her. "Is everything all right, Your Highness?" he asked.

No, nothing was. She should know what was

happening in her own country, but her mother had been so sickly for the past six months that caring of her had taken all of Amber's time. She was loyal to her family, but how could things have become so bad? "I'm going to the library," she said. "Have someone tell me when my brother finishes his meetings. I need to speak with him as soon as he's done."

She didn't dare request he come to her. Percy hated being second born and therefore exerted his higher status over her at every opportunity. It didn't matter that she was female and not in line for the throne, he enjoyed bossing people around.

Amber changed directions, heading towards the large library on the second floor. Every report which had ever been filed ended up in the library, and she wanted to learn more about the drought and the plague.

Her father hadn't cared about educating her. He believed a lady's role was to be accomplished in the arts and beautiful to look at. Her mother had disagreed, but it was their secret. The king thought she was learning the proper way to manage a household—well, a country was like a large household.

The library was one of the largest rooms in the palace. Every wall was a bookshelf and there were several desks and lounges for the royal family to use. Emeline had taught her in here, because Amber's brothers had a school room of their own. No one was inside. Amber inhaled the new leather scent of the books, eager to get the stench of the streets out of her nose. She took a moment to let the tension fall from her shoulders and then went to the card index to find the items she wanted.

She'd begin chronologically—with reports about the drought. The pages crackled as she flipped through and her frown deepened. In the past year, the infrequent rain had a reverse effect on the plants, damaging them rather than nourishing them, and even in areas where crops grew, they were less productive. The suggested causes were equally alarming. One writer suggested the damaging rain had been caused by the water fae in retaliation for the increased pollution in the harbour. Another suggested the spice fae were to blame, and one report even said the fae had been moved away from the valley where the bellar spice was grown, but it hadn't helped matters.

That couldn't be right. Everyone understood the fae were linked to the land and couldn't be moved. Her father wouldn't have allowed it. She fetched another book from the shelf, one of her favourites which recorded the history of Molanka going back several hundred years. Flicking to the section which recorded the splitting of the kingdom into two, she found the paragraph which mentioned that some fae had moved from what became Sylta land, into Molankan land so both kingdoms had access to their resources. The transition was fraught with difficulty because Molankan land was less fertile and much of it was mountains, desert and marshland, but eventually the fae established a small silk valley, spice valley and launda forest. Many fae had died in the relocation and a caution was recorded in the stories that fae faded away if not connected to their element.

So where had the spice fae been moved to?

She returned to the reports but found no reference to where they had gone. Not good. Her mother had always told her the fae were the lifeblood of the land.

With a sigh, she moved to the next book, reports of the plague in the city. The numbers were horrific and her heart ached as she read details of the dead being thrown in a mass grave. The cause of the disease wasn't certain, but again there were many theories. One man blamed the coal smoke, but someone else had crossed out the suggestion and written the marsh fae were allies. Another believed the plague had come from the silk valley because people fell sick after a large shipment of silk had arrived in the city. There was a minor note that no one in the silk valley had been infected, so it was thought perhaps the fae weren't susceptible or it was some magic they had cast.

What nonsense. Perhaps they wrote what they believed her father wanted to hear, because he had ranted about the fae on occasion. He believed they limited the resources they gave to the kingdom and didn't believe they should have so much control. The marsh fae had been generous with their coal, and so the launda fae should be as generous with their wood. Amber didn't know enough to say who was right, but she'd read the peace treaty between Molanka and Tartalan, which granted the fae sovereign rights over their land, so her father could do nothing about it.

The door opened and Percy walked in, his blond curls bouncing. His always present scowl deepened when he saw her. He'd be an attractive man if only he smiled once in a while. "What are you doing here?"

Amber slammed the book shut, a slight tremor in her hand. "Reading." If he discovered what she was reading, she'd be in for a lecture. A princess should be seen and not heard. "I was hoping to speak with you."

"It's been a long day." His dismissive wave towards the door made her flinch.

"It has," she agreed. "Mother spent time in the garden…"

The outrage on her brother's face made her clench the book in front of her. "She's not allowed outside! She's ill."

Amber swallowed. "She wanted to go to the rock garden, and she looked much better afterwards." Before he commented further, she said, "She was hungry and wanted some mountain berries, but there aren't any."

"You should have sent someone into the markets," he said.

"I did," she said. "There are none to be had in the city. The crops never came in."

He grunted. "I'll get her some." He gestured to his guard and murmured something to him. The guard strode out of the room.

Amber frowned. "How can you get her some when there are none? Not even the bushes in the garden have fruit."

"We have supplies at the docks," Percy said.

It made no sense. "Then why aren't we feeding our people? They're starving."

His smile was patronising. "Don't listen to rumours. Our people are fine."

How dare he lie to her? "No, they're not! I saw the lines at the markets myself. People are hungry. Flynn said there are starving children on the streets."

"You saw them yourself?" Percy stood. "When? What were you doing out of the palace?" He glanced at Joseph. "Explain why you let the princess out."

She could still see all those people waiting in lines and the meagre produce available. "He didn't *let* me do anything," she said before Joseph spoke. "He is my guard, and he does what I say. Mother wanted mountain berries, so I went into the city to get her some. I didn't believe the servant who came back and said there were none."

"It's not safe for you in the city," Percy said. "You could have got yourself killed."

She shook her head. "Well, I didn't. You haven't explained why we have food stockpiled at the wharves."

"It's not your business."

Amber was sick of being treated as a child. "Yes, it is. Our people are starving. It's our job to help them."

Percy stalked over to her. "I said you don't need to

know. This is palace business and none of your concern. Father left me in charge while he is away."

Amber shrank back, recognising the stubborn tilt to his chin. He towered a foot taller than her and was far, far stronger.

"You will stay in the castle. I'll tell the guards on the gates not to let you out. Mother's health is your only concern, do you understand?" His glare could have melted the snow on top of the mountains.

"Yes, Percy."

He stared for a moment longer and then pointed to the door. "You'd better check on Mother now."

She longed to stand up to him and tell him no, but it had been several hours since she'd left her mother's side and she wouldn't win this battle with him now.

But that didn't mean she was giving up the fight.

With a regal tilt of her head, she gathered up the books she'd been reading and strode out of the room.

Chapter 19

The curtains were closed when Amber entered her mother's bedroom after her confrontation with Percy. She went straight across to the window and flung them wide. It wasn't as if they let a lot of light in with the smog hanging over the city these days.

Amber approached the bed and found her mother sleeping, the noise of the curtains opening not enough to wake her. Disappointment filled her. She'd hoped after their excursion to the garden her mother was improving, but maybe it had tired her more than she admitted.

She sat in a chair by the window and opened the book about the plague. Not light reading, but being in the city had opened Amber's eyes. She'd been so focused on her mother, she hadn't given a thought for anyone outside the palace walls, had assumed her father had everything under control.

Now she wasn't so sure.

How had things become so bad? When had they declined? She stared out the window, across to the hills which surrounded Bermont. When had she last been into the city?

Her mother had been sick for six months, and before

that, every moment of Amber's day had been spent learning how to be the perfect princess—etiquette classes, embroidery, learning various instruments and languages, and of course the secret classes with her mother so she understood politics. So perhaps it was about two years, back when they'd first got a steam carriage and the whole royal family had gone for a ride. When she'd questioned Baldrick about the smog, he had said there was nothing to worry about.

Amber sighed.

But her parents had argued fiercely about something, about twelve months ago. Her father had cancelled their visit to her mother's family, hadn't wanted them gone for so long. A queen's place was beside the king. Around then, her aunt Kleo had come to stay at the palace, just after her husband had died. She had brought news of the country with her, and Amber remembered the mention of little rain. But Kleo hadn't been to visit her mother since, and the king had said she was lost in her grief. Amber had been so caught up worrying about her mother, she'd forgotten about her aunt. She would have to check whether Kleo was still staying here.

Instead of picturing her aunt, the face of the man at the markets appeared in her mind. Flynn.

A little angry at first, but his brown eyes, the colour of launda bark, had softened when she'd insisted on hearing the truth. His long, almost shaggy brown hair had fallen in his face, and he'd pushed it back as he told her what was happening in the city. A stone mason who had given up his home so others could be safe and warm. A kind spirit.

And one who shouldn't have to do what he did. The royal family should help their people. She would have to go back to the library after Percy was gone and find more reports. She didn't dare send Joseph or Daisy in case they told Percy what she was looking for. He wouldn't approve.

But perhaps if she found no answers in the reports, she could ask Flynn. She sighed. If the guards let her out of the palace again, and she could convince Joseph to go with her. The man stood stiffly by the door, alert. It was difficult to break through his sense of duty, but now and then he would relent and converse with her. He was someone to talk to in the hours when her mother slept. Which of late had been most of the time.

"Joseph," she called.

He glanced at her. "Yes, Your Highness."

She waved him forward. "Come over here. I want to ask you about something."

"Yes, Your Highness." He opened the door and said something to the guards outside, probably telling them he was leaving his post, and then strode over. He stood to attention next to her.

"Please sit." She gestured to the seat across from her.

"It's not right for me to sit, Your Highness."

"Please." She smiled. "It will hurt my neck looking up at you."

His gaze flicked towards the door as if worried someone would come in and then sighed and sat.

Amber pressed her lips together, uncertain where to start. Would he know much more than her? He'd barely left her side since he became her guard. "What can you tell me about the situation in the city?"

Concern flashed over his face before he asked, "What situation?"

She raised her eyebrows. "The starving, homeless children, the dirty streets, the lack of food and the Nourisher knows what other resources."

He cleared his throat. "It's not my place to say, Your Highness. Perhaps Prince Percy will tell you."

"You saw him in the library just now. I'm not sure he'd tell me if the palace was on fire." She leaned forward. "I'm worried, Joseph. Bermont used to be a beautiful city full of light and colour. What happened?"

He hesitated. "I don't know how much of what I've heard is true," Joseph said. "People like to gossip and it's rarely accurate."

"I can figure out what's true," she said. "But I need somewhere to start. How long has food been scarce?"

"Over a year, Your Highness. My family wrote to say their past two harvests have failed, providing not much more than what they need to survive, and nothing to give to the kingdom."

"But how would they pay their taxes?"

"They can't, Your Highness. The last letter I received said they might get evicted from their farm."

She gasped. "Why didn't you say something? I can intervene."

He shook his head. "It's not my place to burden you."

She wasn't weak. "Nonsense. I'm able to help your family. They deserve something for your loyal service."

"Thank you, Your Highness." The gratitude and surprise in his eyes made her feel guilty. She'd been so caught up in her mother's illness, she hadn't considered others.

"I'll write a letter as soon as we're done here," she promised. "Now tell me about the plague and the dirty streets."

"The coal smoke dirties the streets, Your Highness. It's used in many new technologies like your carriage and is being burned far more regularly than in years gone by," Joseph said. "The smoke coats the buildings."

"Why is it so plentiful?" she asked. "Normally the fae are cautious with the amount of resources they sell."

"I don't know, Your Highness. Ask one of the marsh fae. They're regularly seen around the city."

She frowned. "They spend time outside the marshes?"

He nodded. "I'm told some have taken up residence here."

Strange. The books said they were linked to their land, so how could they be here? It was another thing she would have to research. "And the plague?"

"It began last winter and lasted almost until summer," he said. "No one knew what caused it, but many adults and elderly died."

"And so the children's parents died and they have no one to care for them?"

He nodded. "Families can barely feed their own, let alone other children."

"What has my father done about it?"

"I believe he contacted Sylta and Tartalan for help, but received no response, which is why he is going in person." He stared out the window as he spoke.

Suddenly she realised what had struck her as odd while she was in the city. "Where are all the men?" The people waiting in line were mostly women, and the men she'd seen were old or injured.

Joseph stood. "I must get back to my post, Your Highness."

Fear gripped her. "Answer the question, Joseph."

He turned with an apologetic expression. "I'm sorry, Your Highness. I'm forbidden to tell you."

"By Percy?"

He shook his head.

"My father."

He didn't respond.

What was so bad about the lack of men? "Did they die in the plague?"

He shook his head and headed for the door.

She jolted. He'd never turned his back on her before. What would require all the men to leave the city? It wasn't quite time for harvest. The only time she'd read about women outnumbering men was reading the tales of the war with Tartalan.

She gasped, her hand covering her mouth. "Have they gone to war?"

Joseph flinched but didn't answer. She gripped the arms of her chair, her mind whirling. Her father had said he was going to Tartalan to search for a cure for her mother's illness. He wasn't certain how long he'd be gone. Baldrick had likewise set sail for Sylta for the same reason. She hadn't been allowed down to the docks to wave them off.

How many ships had they taken?

The door opened and Percy strode in carrying a bowl of mountain berries. "How's Mother?"

"Are we at war?" she blurted.

Percy glanced at Joseph and then back at her. "What?"

"Have Father and Baldrick gone to wage war on our neighbours?"

"What would make you think that?" He walked over to their mother's bed.

He hadn't answered. She climbed to her feet, her limbs a little weak from the shock, and she prayed she was wrong, but Joseph's lack of answer spoke volumes. "The city is starving, and yet there are also few fit, young men in the streets," she said. "Father said he was finding a cure. Was he taking it by force?"

Percy whirled around and scowled. "If that's what it takes," he said. "They ignored our pleas for help, so they'll get what they deserve."

She clutched the post of her mother's bed frame. "But we've been at peace for centuries. Why would Father want to fight?"

"You saw what it's like out there. Do you want to leave our people to starve? We had little choice in the matter."

Her hand trembled. "When will we hear from them?

When will we know?"

"Who knows? Don't worry yourself about it. There's nothing you can do."

She wanted to yell at him, but he was right. It was too late to stop it. "So the warehouse of food is for the war effort?"

He nodded. "If they need it."

No, it wasn't right. "The people in the city need it now."

He scowled. "You know nothing of war."

She stepped back at his anger. "What about the fae? Surely the spice fae can provide more crops at least?"

"They've betrayed us. Refused to provide more." He clenched his fist. "Enough of this! How's Mother?"

The change of subject didn't surprise her. He'd dismissed her for as long as she'd been born. "She's been sleeping since I returned."

He placed the bowl of berries on the table next to the bed. "Tell her I've been by and brought her berries."

He strode out again.

She stared after him, her mind fighting to process the information. Why the secrecy? Had the king been planning to go to war from the beginning? They had no reason to believe Tartalan and Sylta wouldn't help after speaking directly with their kings. And what of the fae? The agreement went both ways, they provided resources and were allowed their autonomy. What had gone wrong?

Perhaps her father had mentioned nothing so as not to stress his wife.

Joseph shifted at his post, and she remembered her promise to help his family. She strode to the desk and grabbed a piece of parchment. She couldn't do anything about the war, but she would help him with this.

***

Flynn ran through the city streets, away from the whorehouse, dodging steam cars and people. At the corner of the central square, he spotted a teen with short spiky hair leaning against a lamp post. "Dietmar, can you do me a favour?"

Dietmar jolted. "Flynn! What's got you so worked up?"

He took a breath. "The House of Pleasures has been kidnapping homeless girls and forcing them to work there. Ava's one of them."

His friend's jaw dropped. "What do you need?"

"Get a couple of people and watch the house. The girls have been drugged and wouldn't come with me, and I reckon they'll move them. It's one of the whorehouses in the last row."

Dietmar nodded. "I'll go now. I'll find out where they're being taken."

"Thanks." It shouldn't be dangerous for Dietmar. No one paid the homeless kids much attention these days. There were too many of them.

Flynn dashed through the markets, briefly considering stopping at the Watch, but the guard's bored expression when he'd brought up the kidnappings made him believe he wouldn't get any help. The only one with any power was Princess Amber.

But could he get a message to her?

His steps slowed as he approached the closed palace gates. He'd been here twice with his father; once when he'd been commissioned to make a folly in the garden, and the other was the disastrous commission when his father had been fired. Resentment flared in his veins, and he took a moment to calm his breathing and study the guards. Would they even listen to him?

Only one way to find out. He straightened his jacket and walked across to them. They eyed him every step of the way. He cleared his throat. "I would like to speak with Her Royal Highness, Princess Amber of Molanka."

The taller guard laughed. "Sure you would."

"I met her this morning when she was in the markets, and she said she would get back to me about a situation. It's urgent."

"Go away, lad. You're not getting through."

Flynn bit down on his annoyance. He'd known it wouldn't be easy. "Please, I know it's a strange request, but could you tell her I'm waiting at the gate with news?"

"It's not worth our jobs to disturb the royal family for a commoner," the shorter guard said.

Behind them, a man strode out of the castle and across to the gates. He wore the red uniform of a Molankan soldier, but with gold trim which denoted he worked for the king himself. He glanced at Flynn but ignored him. "Orders from Prince Percy," he told the guards. "Princess Amber is not to be let out of the palace for any reason."

Flynn jolted. "Why not?"

The soldier raised his eyebrows. "It is none of your concern." To the guards he said, "If she tries to leave, Prince Percy is to be notified immediately." He turned to go.

"Wait!" Flynn called. "I have a message for the princess. I met her today at the markets."

The soldier scowled. "What is it?"

"There's a whorehouse on the docks kidnapping and drugging children to work for them."

The soldier's scowl deepened. "That's not information the princess should hear about."

Was he serious? "I hoped she could stop it."

"The princess doesn't need to be worried about such things. Go tell the Watch." He strode away.

"The Watch doesn't care!" Flynn yelled back. "One girl is only ten."

The man didn't even pause as he walked back into the

castle.

"And neither do you apparently." Flynn challenged the two guards, "Anything you can do about it?"

The taller one seemed a little more sympathetic now. "Afraid not."

What was the point of them then? Flynn stalked back down the road. The Watch was his last chance.

A few minutes later he strode into the building and the watchman looked up. "Back again? We've arrested no kids since the last time you were here."

"I found the whorehouse kidnapping kids," he said. "The House of Pleasures. They've drugged the girls."

The man blinked. "How do you know?"

"I saw them myself. You need to do something now, before they move them."

"I can't." He held up a hand. "All my men are out. I'll send someone when they get back."

Flynn huffed out a breath, trying to control his anger. It was the best he was going to get. "I'll send word if they change locations."

The man raised his eyebrows. "How would you know?"

Flynn pursed his lips. Best he didn't say. He didn't want the man to get defensive. "I have my sources."

He headed back to the whorehouse and searched for Dietmar but couldn't find him anywhere. Hopefully he was following Ava and not captured himself. Flynn would go past his usual sleeping place later.

He closed his eyes. Two years ago he never would have imagined this. There'd been rumours of a little unrest between the fae and the previous king, but nothing too serious. Then the king had been killed in a hunting accident in the launda forest, and Tremont had taken over. It was as if the entire land protested his succession, or mourned the king's passing, because nothing had been right since.

His steps carried him back to Nate on the wharf.

"Twice in a day, Flynn. This is a treat."

Flynn sat beside him. "Ava and the girls were at the House of Pleasures. They've been drugged by something which makes them do whatever anyone says."

"Fae juice," Nate said.

"What?"

"It's some new concoction rumoured to have been developed by the marsh fae." He shrugged. "Don't know if it's true." He turned to Flynn. "You able to get them out?"

He shook his head. "I went to the palace to get help, but they weren't interested. The Watch will go when they have men spare. Dietmar's watching the place, so hopefully he can tell me where they've gone."

"Thanks Flynn. We'll get them back."

Flynn wished he was so certain. "I think Crane's involved." The youth would spread word to be wary of him. "He was talking to the owner and did nothing to help me save the girls."

Nate frowned. "I'm not surprised. I steer clear of his warehouse. No one I've spoken to feels safe there."

Perhaps he could arrange another warehouse for the homeless to shelter in. The castle dominated its surroundings in the distance. The princess had said she would get word to him if she found more food. Flynn would leave a message at home to give to whoever Amber sent—if she sent anyone.

"You going to check out the warehouse to the north?" Nate asked.

He'd forgotten about it. "I might." It was another thing to tell the princess about if it existed. "Any chance you could borrow a telescope for me?" The harbour master occasionally loaned Nate one when he was feeling generous.

Nate brightened. "Let me go ask." He hurried into the

harbour master's office and returned a few minutes later with a telescope. "Got to have it back by the morning."

"Thanks." Flynn tucked it inside his shirt and hopped off the wall. "Contact me if you hear anything else."

"Will do."

Flynn wandered north along the docks. The sun was sinking below the hills which surrounded the city. Another couple of hours and it would be dark, but he wanted to look at the warehouses before he lost the light.

There were few ships at this end of the docks and fewer people. He nodded greetings to the couple of sailors who hurried past, but no one acknowledged him. Up ahead, Molankan soldiers guarded the entrance to the far end of the docks where three well maintained warehouses stood. Guards patrolled each building. It was easy to see how the rumour started. All those guards screamed something valuable was inside. He turned around before he got too close and aroused suspicion and backtracked to where a man hired fishing gear. There weren't many fish to be had in the harbour these days. Either they'd been over-fished by the nets or left to find cleaner waters. Still, he paid his coin and carried the rod and a small bit of bait back to one jetty close to the guarded docks. He sat, dangling his feet over the edge, and cast his line into the dark, oily water below, wrinkling his nose at the salty, algae stench coming from the water.

How could he get closer to the warehouse?

The water was deep here for the ships to dock, and Flynn had never learnt to swim. He doubted he would reach the dock without being spotted if he borrowed a dinghy. Coal-fired lamps ran the length of the jetties and come nightfall, it would be as light as day. He examined the water. Did water fae still live in this part of the harbour? He hadn't heard mention of them in over a year, so perhaps they'd moved upriver or along the coast. Still, he'd ask Nate whether he'd seen them lately. He might convince one to help him.

Behind the docks, the hills which encircled the city were steep. Even if he could push through the dense bush without being spotted, he would need a rope to lower himself down to the dock and that would leave evidence he'd been there.

He doubted he'd be able to sneak past the guards at this end. They were too alert, and their swords sharp.

He pulled in his line, surprised the bait was gone. He added more, wrapping it twice around the hook, and cast it back into the water. A fresh fish would be a treat. His mother used to cook fish in butter and spices. Flynn closed his eyes at the pain of the memory. Happy times when the house was full of light and laughter, scents of food cooking and sounds of his mother singing. Nothing would bring her back. His stomach rumbled, and he studied the warehouses again. The guards patrolled along the sides of the building, one on each side. It would be next to impossible to get inside. He hoped Crane wasn't filling those kids who stayed with him with foolish notions of storming the place. They would be no match for the guards.

The idea made his skin pimple. Crane didn't care about anyone but himself. All those kids would be a means to an end. Flynn had to reduce his influence.

He sat there, fishing and watching the warehouses until he ran out of bait. Either he was rubbish at baiting his hook, or there was life down there, but it was too crafty for him to feel it nibble.

After he returned the gear, he headed back into town to visit Roley. The markets were closed, but Roley had a small house in the merchant section of the city.

Roley's wife, Agnes opened the door when he knocked. "Flynn, how good to see you." She hugged him and he squeezed her back. She was thinner than she'd been the last time he'd visited.

"It's always a pleasure, Agnes. Is Roley in?"

"He just arrived back, telling me how you charmed the princess today. Was he telling tales?" She gestured for him to come inside.

He smiled, wondering if Roley had mentioned the cactus fruit. "I don't think charmed is the right word, but I spoke with Princess Amber."

Her mouth dropped open as she entered the kitchen. "The princess was really in the markets?"

"I told you she was, dear." Roley greeted Flynn, eyes beseeching as he limped over. "She won't believe her own husband."

Their two-year-old girl squealed and ran over to Flynn, throwing her arms around his legs. He grinned and picked her up, lifting her high in the air. "Hiya, Ilse."

"Flynn!" She wrapped her slim arms around his neck. As a baby she'd been a chubby thing, but with food so scarce she'd lost her baby fat. He settled her on his hip.

"Would you like to stay for dinner?" Agnes invited.

He shook his head, wishing for the day when he could without feeling guilty about eating their food. "I wanted to check how you all were." And also to ensure the palace guards hadn't tracked Roley down.

"We're all good," Roley said. "Never better."

Agnes rolled her eyes. "We *could all* be better."

"Yeah," Flynn agreed. "I discovered today the House of Pleasure has been taking girls off the street and putting them to work against their will." He sat at the table with Ilse on his lap.

Agnes scowled. "I wish we could take children in, but we just can't feed them."

"I know." They traded news for a few minutes and then Flynn kissed Ilse's cheek and stood, placing her back on the chair. "I'd better get going. You all have a good night." He saw himself out, relieved the family was all right. They were one of the lucky ones to survive the plague intact, and Roley hadn't been pressed into military service because of his club foot.

Night had fallen and the coal lamps on the buildings had been lit. He wove his way through the streets, past areas where the homeless slept to make sure they were all right. It was summer now and sleeping outside wasn't so bad if you could find somewhere safe to lay your head. He stopped in at his house and found every room full of children. "Flynn's here!" one of the little girls cried and ran over to hug him.

His heart swelled. This was why he did this. These kids deserved somewhere safe to live. Two of the eldest, Janice and Charmaine, who were both sixteen, took care of them. Janice greeted him. "How was your day?"

"Eventful." He smiled. The kids would love his story. "I met the princess today."

The kids jostled around him, begging him to tell his story. He laughed and sat, and told them about what had happened.

"So a messenger from the palace might come *here*?" Janice asked, brushing down her dirty dress. She'd been a maid for a wealthy merchant before the plague.

"Yeah. If they do, can you give them a message?"

She nodded and handed him some parchment.

When he'd written about the warehouse and the whorehouse, he folded it and gave it to Janice for safe-keeping. "I'll be spending time down by the docks," he said. "If you need to get urgent word to me."

"I hope a messenger comes," Janice said as she walked him out. "You do a lot for this city."

He waved away the compliment. He didn't do as much as was required. Besides, he couldn't spend his days doing nothing, it would drive him insane. "See you tomorrow."

Visiting his house inspired and depressed him. It reminded him what he was fighting for, but made him feel as if he was getting nowhere. The number of children staying there had grown until the neighbours had complained to the Watch, and he'd been told to limit who stayed and keep the noise down. As if that was the biggest problem the city faced.

He headed out the northern gates, greeting Tomas, one of the guards.

"How are you, Flynn?" Tomas asked.

"I was hoping to slip out of the city for a stroll."

The man squinted at him. "What are you up to?"

"Trying to stop people doing rash things." He and his father had repaired the guardhouse a couple of years ago and had been friendly with Tomas.

Tomas sighed. "All right." He opened the gates. "Give me a hoy when you want back in."

"Thanks." He slapped the man on the back and slipped along the outside of the city walls towards the docks. He'd get a better view of the warehouses from the hill behind them and might overhear the guards talking.

He had nothing better to do.

A narrow path ran along the base of the wall, but he still had to push his way through shrubs and branches. When he smelled the stale harbour water, he slowed, hoping the strong sea breeze would hide the rustle and snap of leaves and twigs from the guards. He headed up the hill, so as not to draw any of the soldiers' attention. He was unused to pushing through bushes and after a year of no stone to work, he'd lost much of his fitness. He was puffing by the time the trees parted and the harbour stretched out before him, a black mass, glistening occasionally when the moon broke through the smog. Across in Sylta, the lights in a couple of villages glowed.

Behind him the city was alight with lamps in the richer areas and dark in the poorer ones. The castle glowed like a signal of hope not too far away from where he stood.

People moved inside, too far away to make out faces, but at one window someone stared out at the night. Flynn withdrew the telescope and focused on the figure.

Princess Amber. She'd tucked her hair up off her neck and she still wore the red dress he'd seen her in that morning.

Behind her was a lushly decorated room. Was it her bedroom? He lowered the scope. It was too far away to throw a note tied to a rock, and he didn't have the slightest idea how to shoot an arrow, even if he sourced one. He counted seven windows from the front edge of the castle to her room.

The wind carried voices up to him from the docks below. Remembering why he was here, he tucked away the telescope and moved down, slowly making his way closer to the water's edge.

He eased the branches aside to peer below. A ship was tied to the last jetty and people moved along it carrying goods. The warehouse doors closest to it were wide open and there were boxes and bags inside. Flynn put the telescope to his eye and examined the writing on the goods. Bellar spice, oats and sugar.

Enough food to feed the city for weeks. He scanned the rest of the warehouse spotting fruit and vegetables being dried.

The rumours were true. The king had food here while his people starved.

Anger filled him as he thought about all the children huddled in warehouses, skin and bones, and crying from hunger. The urge to storm the warehouse and grab armfuls of food was so strong he caught himself leaning forward. His death wouldn't help anyone. He sighed and sat back.

The warehouse guards and the sailors all wore red uniforms. In his patchy clothing, he'd stand out.

Who was he kidding? Even if he got inside the

warehouse, what he could carry out wouldn't be enough to feed the kids in his house for more than a day.

He sat back, wishing he could capture an image of the warehouse to show the princess. So much food, so close and he was helpless to get it.

He turned his attention to the ship. Where was it heading after it had been loaded? Could he intercept it somehow?

Flynn shook his head. He'd read too many pirate tales when he was a kid. The boat was full of soldiers, and he had no way of accessing it. A shout below captured his attention, and he noticed a few newcomers arrive and stride along the wharf. He used the telescope and recognised the man in front as the one who'd ordered Princess Amber not to be allowed to leave the grounds.

She was to be a prisoner inside, but at least she wasn't starving.

The palace guard said something to the sailors, and they increased their pace. The tides would go out soon, and they would want to set sail before it did.

The man scanned the area and his gaze rose so he looked directly at Flynn. Flynn froze, not daring to move in case he drew attention.

"You there!" The palace guard pointed directly at him. "Get the spy!"

Curse it! He shoved the telescope into his jacket and scrambled back from the edge of the trees.

"Get me a bow," the man bellowed.

Fear spiked and Flynn ran, not caring how much noise he made as he took the easiest path through the bushes, heading down but away from the docks. He didn't dare yell to tell Tomas he was coming. He had to lose the guards first.

Trees scratched his face as he pushed his way through, and he ignored the pain. He shouldn't have run. It made him look guilty. Too late now. He doubted anyone would believe his story, particularly with them at war with their neighbours.

Something crashed into him from the side. He hit the ground hard and twisted to fight the body above him.

Then something connected with his head, and he remembered nothing else.

Chapter 20

Queen Emeline revived after she ate the mountain berries, and the next day stayed awake chatting to Amber about palace life. Any other time, Amber would share her concerns about the city with her mother, but she didn't dare burden her with the knowledge. Instead, she asked her mother to tell her stories of the fae. It had always been a favourite topic, and her mother's knowledge was more than could be found in books.

"Mother, what was Molanka like before the fae came?" she asked. "Why was Captain Farlon sent to find new lands?"

Her mother smiled. "Molanka encompassed Sylta, and the capital was in Lanta. This section of the country was quite barren with marshes and deserts. Few people lived here, and those who did were nomadic, moving from place to place to find food. The king wanted more for his people, and so sent Captain Farlon out to discover new plants which would grow in the inhospitable places."

"And he discovered Tartalan?"

Her mother nodded. "He was gone a year and when he returned, he told the king he had found nothing. But one of his sailors told of the magical land they had found full of lush forests, plentiful food and strange creatures called fae and Tarta."

Amber remembered this part. "The captain lied because he'd promised the Tarta and fae he would keep their secret."

"Yes. He and most of the men who travelled with him fought to protect the land and took up arms against the king." Her mother smiled but Amber frowned.

"Surely fighting the king was bad."

"They were doing what they promised, what they thought was right. They'd spent much time with the fae and the Tarta while they repaired their ship and realised the king would not like the agreement Farlon had reached with these people. It was honourable."

"There was much bloodshed during the war."

"Yes, many died, but the outcome was an understanding between the two countries. Some fae longed to leave the island and explore the world, but their connection to the land was too strong. Now they knew another land existed, they could work together, and discover a way to leave."

"So how did they?" If the Tartalan fae had found a way, then perhaps the spice fae had used the same method.

Her mother pursed her lips. "They had to take the land with them," she said. "The launda fae took seeds and seedlings of the launda tree, the spice fae took spice plants, the marsh fae took coal and marshland, the mountain fae took stone and rock, and the silk fae took worms and their food. But still many died when plants died, or the distance became too much."

So if the fae had been moved on as the reports suggested, they must have taken some of the land with them.

Her mother yawned. "I will rest now. Will you tell

Percy I want to see him this evening? It has been days since he visited."

"Of course, Mother." Amber helped her to lie down and when her breathing indicated she was asleep, Amber retrieved the book she'd finished, and walked to the library. She'd read report after report, but the more she read, the less she liked. Her research took her back several years to when her father had become king. That's when all the problems started.

Perhaps Aunt Kleo could offer her some insight. It was time Amber visited her. The king and Baldrick had been gone for almost two weeks. Surely there must be some communication from them. But any message would go straight to Percy, and she doubted he would share it with her.

Perhaps he'd notify the council of advisers and there would be reference to it in their meeting minutes. She sighed. If she was caught around the council rooms, people would notice. She had to find out when it was unoccupied.

If her father or Baldrick had been successful in getting supplies, then the stockpile at the docks could be shared with the city.

In the library, she returned the book to the shelf, and found one which discussed the rules of the council. It would be useful to learn more about its powers. She hated Doctor Teregen lauding his authority over her. As a princess surely she had some rights.

She tucked it into a bag and wandered down the hall towards the council rooms. Two guards stood outside the room, and they bowed to Amber.

"Is the prince inside?" she asked.

"Yes, Your Highness," one answered.

"Then I would like to enter."

The guards glanced at each other, but didn't move aside. "Your Highness, they are questioning a prisoner.

It's not appropriate."

She frowned. "Prisoners fall under the purview of the Watch."

"I gather it's an exceptional case."

Very unusual and concerning as well. Percy didn't normally pay any attention to the abidance of laws in the country, as long as those who broke them were punished. Perhaps it had something to do with the war, in which case she wanted to know. "Open the doors," she ordered.

"Your Highness, perhaps you should come back another time," Joseph said.

She didn't look at him and instead stared at the guards waiting for them to obey her. A princess didn't ask twice. The one who had spoken grimaced and did as she asked, opening the doors to the large room. Amber braced herself and entered. Seated around the long wooden table were three of her father's advisors, including his steward, and at the head of the table sat Percy. They all turned at the interruption and her pulse rate spiked, but she kept her steps measured as she spotted a man held between two guards, his head hanging. She gasped.

"What are you doing here?" Percy demanded. "This is no place for you. Leave at once."

She faced her brother. "I have a message from Mother. She wishes for you to visit today after she has woken from her rest."

"Fine. Now leave."

She clasped her hands in front of her to stop them shaking. "I would like to stay and observe. With the king and crown prince gone, I feel it is my duty to help our country."

"Your help isn't needed." Percy's disdain was clear.

Two of the advisors shook their head in disapproval.

Heat rose in her cheeks, and she pivoted to go.

"Princess Amber." The voice was barely a whisper

and came from the prisoner.

She glanced over. The man raised his head and his launda brown eyes pierced her, his face a canvas of bruises from black to purple to yellow. Recognition made her step back and place a hand to her chest. "Flynn?" What was he doing here? Why was he so injured?

"You know this man?" the steward demanded.

"Yes. I met him in the markets a few days ago." Had she been in danger then? "He raised concerns about the children starving on the streets." Uncertainty prickled her skin, and she asked Percy, "What are the charges against him?"

"Espionage."

She frowned. "Who was he spying for?"

"He will not say."

"Your Highness…" Flynn wheezed and a coughing fit overcame him.

She moved closer, so he didn't need to speak so loudly, and Joseph stepped in front of her. She brushed him aside. "Flynn is being held by two guards. In his state, he won't hurt me." He looked like he had no energy to squash a bed bug.

"Joseph, take her out of here," Percy ordered.

This time she wouldn't be swayed. "No, brother. I will hear what this man has to say." A chair squeaked along the paved floor, but she didn't turn. "Are you a spy?"

"No, Your Highness." He cleared his throat and continued, his voice pained. "There were rumours of a warehouse full of food on the docks," he said. "People spoke about storming it, so I went to confirm whether the rumours were true. I didn't want anyone to get hurt."

He stared into her eyes, begging her to believe him.

She didn't know this man, not really. Was she naïve to believe him?

"And after you confirmed the rumour was true,

would you have led the attack?" Percy demanded.

"No. It would have been suicide."

"What would you do?" Amber asked.

"I tried to get word to you, Your Highness, though I failed to convince the palace guards we were known to one another."

"When did you try?"

"The day we met, Your Highness. I discovered children are being forced to work in whorehouses against their will. They're being drugged, and I hoped there might be something you could do to stop it."

She had read with the rapid increase in technology children had been put to work in factories, but it should never be against their will. "And what work do they do in these whorehouses?" How dangerous was it for the children?

Flynn's eyes widened and beside her Percy laughed. "It is far too delicate a subject for your ears, sister."

Her cheeks flushed. She hated being ignorant of anything. "I assure you I can handle the truth." She nodded to Flynn. "Tell me."

Flynn glanced at Percy as if unsure. Now wasn't the time for him to look to her brother for guidance.

"Tell me," she insisted.

He looked at the ground. "Whorehouses deal with matters of the flesh, Your Highness. What happens between men and women in the privacy of the bedroom."

Her mouth dropped open and her cheeks heated to such a temperature she could have heated the entire room. "I see." She swallowed. "Then children definitely should not be involved in such places. Who would do such a thing?"

"Drury owns the House of Pleasures," Flynn said. "I confronted him, but the girls wouldn't come with me, because they were being influenced by a drug—fae juice." He panted as if talking was taxing. "One girl is only ten."

Horror filled her. She spun to her brother. "We must stop this."

"It may not be true, sister. This man has not proven to be trustworthy."

"Then send people immediately to validate his claims."

"Your Highness, the girls may have been moved," Flynn interrupted. "I confronted Drury, but he didn't care. When I came to the palace to get help, I asked a friend to watch the house."

"And did your friend witness anything?"

"I haven't spoken with him, Your Highness. I was arrested that night."

"Typical," Percy growled. "Another thing which cannot be confirmed. See, sister, he makes things up to suit him."

She pressed her lips together. "He didn't lie about the starving children in the streets," she said. "I've read the reports of the plague and the families destroyed by it." She lifted her chin. "It seems our family has failed our people."

Percy raised his hand as if to hit her and then lowered it. "Why do you think the king and Baldrick left? We are trying to provide for our people."

"By raiding other countries rather than investigating the true cause of our crops failing?"

"The fae have turned against us, sister," Percy yelled. "They did so when they killed our grandfather, and they continue to control our land by withholding their help."

His certainty and anger weaved some doubt into her. She hadn't seen the rest of the country. All she had were second-hand accounts.

But no, she wouldn't believe the fae had betrayed them. Not when her mother spoke so highly of them.

"We must talk to them."

"They have disappeared. Only the marsh fae are our allies now."

"It's best if you leave the running of the country to the educated, Your Highness," the steward said from behind her.

She clenched her teeth at his dismissal. She wouldn't, not if this was the mess they made of it. "I want Flynn's accusations thoroughly investigated."

"You have no authority to demand such a thing, Your Highness," the steward said. "Your father left Prince Percy in charge."

There had to be something she could do. As soon as she returned to her room, she'd read the book she'd got from the library. She beseeched her brother. "Please, Percy. I don't ask for much."

He glared at her.

"They're children." She clasped his hand. "We need to protect them from such things."

"I will send some men," he finally promised. "Now you must return to Mother."

"What will happen to Flynn?"

Percy hissed out an exasperated breath. "I will keep him in the cells until we hear from my men."

"And then?"

"And then he will get whatever punishment he deserves."

She opened her mouth to protest.

"Leave, sister. You have interfered enough for one day."

She met Flynn's eyes, nodded at him, trying to communicate she would do what she could to help him. Then she curtsied to her brother. "Thank you, Percy."

At the door she turned to see Percy speaking with Joseph. Her guard pressed his lips together as if unhappy by whatever he was being told. She left the room, hurrying down the corridor towards the wing of the castle where her aunt resided. Heavy footsteps pounded behind her as Joseph caught up. "What did my brother ask of you?"

"It is not my place to say, Your Highness."

"Did he order you not to tell me?"

He winced. "No, Your Highness."

"Then what did he say?"

"He asked me to keep you from the library and away from matters of the state."

She scowled and clutched her bag tighter. She needed to find out what rights she had. "Come along."

She continued along the corridor, twisting and turning until she reached the south wing. She stopped a servant in the corridor. "Where is Princess Kleo?"

The servant curtsied. "In her sitting room, Your Highness."

Nerves filled Amber. Her last memory of Kleo was when she'd first arrived and had visited Emeline in her bedroom. The two women had spent a few lovely hours reminiscing about earlier times. Amber had learned a lot about them during those talks. Kleo was a strong woman who had loved her husband. If she'd been lost in her grief for a year, what would she be like now? Amber knocked on the door to her aunt's sitting room.

"Come in."

Joseph pushed the door open, and Amber found her aunt sitting on a chaise lounge having tea. Kleo's eyes widened, and she stood, bobbing in a curtsy. "Your Highness."

"Aunt, please sit. There is no need to curtsy." At Kleo's gesture, she sat in the chair opposite. Her aunt dressed in all black as was fitting for a widow, but her face was unlined, and she showed no outwards signs of grief or fatigue. Amber relaxed. "Joseph, you may leave us."

He scowled, but after surveying the room, he did as she ordered.

"What brings you here? It's been months since I've seen you."

"My apologies, aunt. Caring for Mother has occupied my time, and I find I've lost all concept of what is happening outside her bedroom walls. How are you? I miss your visits."

Kleo raised an eyebrow. "My brother said it was unbecoming for a widow to be heard laughing during the first year of her loss."

Amber gasped. "Father said that? Has he forced you to stay here?"

"Forced is a strong word, Your Highness. He simply said I could continue living here under his protection or find my own way in the world."

Which would leave her penniless. Amber gritted her teeth. She had been ignorant of events for far too long. No more. "Father is with Baldrick waging war on Tartalan and Sylta. I doubt he has left orders to watch whether you laugh."

Kleo gaped at her. "We're at war?"

"Apparently, though I only just learned about it." It was a relief to speak openly. "There has been much I have been ignorant about."

"Tremont always thought it best women weren't informed about such things," Kleo agreed. She called for another cup of tea. "How is your mother?"

"I thought she was improving," Amber said. "We sat in the rock garden last week and her health improved, but the doctor has forbidden her to leave her room and the past couple of days she's slept more than anything."

"My suggestion is you ignore the doctor," Kleo said.

Amber shook her head. "Father left orders he is to be obeyed and Percy supports him."

"You are a princess. You have as many rights as your

brother."

Amber frowned. "He outranks me."

"No, he doesn't. Only the heir outranks the rest of his siblings. You and Percy are equals. It's written in law." She tapped her finger on the side of her cup. "And while the country is at war, princes and princesses have more rights, so they can command troops."

"How do you know?"

Kleo smiled, a wicked glint in her eye. "Your father used to drive me crazy with his orders, so I educated myself. The library is a trove of information."

"I've discovered that," Amber agreed. This was her way to change things. "Can you show me where it's written, Aunt?"

"Of course."

The tea arrived and when the server left, Amber told her aunt about the situation in the city and about Flynn.

"My husband worried about Tremont's methods," Kleo said. "He disagreed about the way the fae were being treated and believed the rapid advancement of technology would do more harm than good. Tremont didn't like to hear it. He always blamed the launda fae for Father's death."

"Wasn't Grandfather killed in a hunting accident?"

"Yes, he was shot by a stray arrow, and the launda fae tried to heal him. They failed and your father believed they hastened his death, because the king had asked to clear more forest to make way for a mill."

Amber pressed her lips together. "I've read reports which say the fae have disappeared."

Kleo's mouth dropped open. "No wonder the crops are failing. Without the fae, Molankan land will revert to the barren wasteland it was before they came."

Amber stared at her. This was far, far worse than she'd realised.

But what could she do to save it?

Chapter 21

Flynn had lost count of the number of days he'd been in the dungeon. With no windows, he tracked the time by the frequency of his meals, and they weren't frequent at all. He'd hoped after seeing Princess Amber in the council rooms he would at least be moved to one of the gaol cells on the ground floor, but no, they'd taken him several levels below to where torches flickered on the walls, throwing barely enough light to see. Not that he saw much through his puffy eyes. His whole body ached, and the guards had given him no water with which to clean the blood from him, so the rats and mice were becoming more and more bold in their attempts to taste. He'd realised the king didn't care for his people, but he had hoped Amber did.

He would rot in this cell before she would come to his aid.

All because of his pride. He thought he could solve some of the city's problems, had wanted to be the hero by proving there was no reason to attack the warehouses, and therefore stop a riot. His optimism needed to be crushed. He swatted away a rat, which sniffed at his pants. The ground was hard and cold, and the stench of his own waste soured his stomach. The guards didn't even have the decency to change the bucket, and it was almost full. Another thing which drew out creatures who lived in the dark.

Voices echoed down the stairs, but he lacked the energy to climb to his feet as he would have at the start. It would just be the guard with his bowl of watered-down soup, half of which would end up on the floor when the guard thrust it at him.

One voice rose and though he couldn't make out the words, he heard the panic in its tone. He stiffened. That wasn't normal. He pushed to his feet, leaning against the stone wall to get his balance and work past the agony of the pins and needles.

The cell grew lighter as the light neared and the voices rose.

"Your Highness, I must insist you go back. This is no place for a lady."

Hope filled his chest at the next words. "This is no place for anyone." Amber's disgust was clear as her voice carried to him. "How can you justify locking someone away in this dark, dank place?"

"Prince Percy ordered it, Your Highness. The prisoner is dangerous."

She snorted. "Nonsense. Percy simply wants to forget he exists, so he doesn't have to deal with the problem."

Flynn straightened, brushing down his clothes, wanting to appear presentable to the princess. The footsteps stopped outside his cell and the glare of the torchlight stung his eyes, forcing him to look away. A gagging sound and then Amber's voice was full of revulsion. "Have you not cleaned his cell since he's been down here?"

"No, Your Highness."

"I have a mind to lock you in here for days and see how you like the stench."

The guard stammered and Flynn shaded his eyes to protect them from the light and bowed as low as he was able. He hissed at the pain in his ribs. "Your Highness, I am humbled by your visit."

"My apologies, Flynn. If I'd known the condition in which you were being kept, I would have come sooner. Unlock his cell."

A different voice this time. "Your Highness, he's a dangerous criminal."

"I will not question him here in this stench, Joseph," Amber said. "Bring him upstairs to the regular cells and give him water to wash, and clean clothes."

"Yes, Your Highness," Joseph said. "Why don't you wait for us above?"

She frowned. "No, I don't think so. Work quickly now." She clapped her hands together.

Keys jangled as the guard opened the cell and gestured Flynn to follow. Flynn took a step forward and winced at the pain. He breathed deeply and stepped again.

A sound of distress came from Amber. "As soon as we get to the regular cells, you will fetch the doctor. How many other prisoners are down here?"

"A few."

"I want a list of their crimes brought to me immediately, and I want all the cells cleaned. No one should have to live like this."

"They're prisoners, Your Highness," Joseph said.

"They're people first, Joseph. I don't know what circumstances brought them to commit the crimes they did, but they deserve some level of decency."

Somewhere along the corridor a voice called, "Thank you, Your Highness."

She turned to it as Flynn reached the doorway. Her nose wrinkled. "Guard, take him up." She walked down the corridor towards the other prisoner, Joseph following.

Flynn smiled, watching her walk away, her stride determined and her chin up. He hadn't imagined her strength when he'd first seen her in the markets.

"Come on." The guard prodded him, hitting one of his many bruises.

He gritted his teeth and headed up the stairs. Prince Percy was sure to be informed, and he wanted to wash before they forced him back into his cell.

Half an hour later he was clean and wearing a fresh pair of pants and a shirt. While he'd washed, he heard voices arguing and he made out Amber's voice, but not the words. Percy must have arrived. No one else would dare to speak to the princess that way. The door opened and the prison guard gestured to him. "Follow me."

He walked down the stone corridor into a room where both Princess Amber and Prince Percy stood with their guards. Percy glared at him. He had the same colouring as Amber, but his permanent sneer and hard eyes dissolved any comparisons to angels his blond curls might have evoked. He was the dangerous one. Amber's chest heaved as if she'd been running, and a defiant determination filled her eyes.

Being the cause of conflict between two royals who wanted different things would not end well for Flynn. He bowed.

"The doctor should be here soon, Flynn," Amber said. "Please, sit." She gestured to the chair in the room.

"Doctor!" Percy exclaimed.

"Hush, Percy. Look how he's walking. He's clearly injured, and since you haven't proven the charges against him, he deserves assistance."

Flynn jolted. Did that mean he was free?

"We can't prove the truth of his claims of kidnapping either," Percy said.

"Perhaps Flynn will get us more evidence when he returns to the city."

"Sister, you don't have the authority to free him."

"Actually, I do." She was very solemn. "Section thirty-two of the Law of the Land states any royal person can pardon a criminal." She turned to Flynn. "I pardon you for the crimes you've been accused of."

Hope and gratitude washed away his fatigue and Flynn bowed again, pushing past the pain. "Thank you, Your Highness."

"Nonsense! Show me where it is written," the prince demanded.

"The books are in the library, Percy. You'll have to fetch them yourself as I'm not permitted in there." She raised her eyebrows.

Percy glowered. "He is not to leave until I return," he told Joseph, and stormed out of the room.

The moment he left, Amber's eyes lit up, and she smiled. "I do like it when the law is on my side." She dragged another chair closer to Flynn and sat. "Joseph, go check what's taking the doctor so long."

"Your Highness, I'm not leaving you alone with the criminal."

"He's not likely to hurt me since I just pardoned him," Amber said.

"You know nothing about him," Joseph protested. "This might all be an act."

She pursed her lips, studied Flynn.

He shook his head. "I would protect you with my life for your kindness, Your Highness." He smiled, hoping to seem less threatening. "I already took a cactus fruit for you."

She chuckled and waved her hand for Joseph to follow her orders. "Fetch Flynn's things."

Joseph moved towards the door but kept his eye on Flynn. Flynn didn't blame him. If Amber was his charge, he wouldn't trust an accused criminal.

"Flynn, I have a job for you," Amber whispered.

Suspicion pushed aside his hope. Of course she wouldn't free him without something in return. "What is it?"

"I need you to tell me what is happening in the city. I daren't leave myself—Percy will take only so much of my defiance at a time—and people might not talk to me. I believe I know why the crops are failing, but I need proof to take to Percy."

His skin tingled in anticipation. "What is it?"

"Why was I called down here?" A man strode in carrying a black bag.

"Doctor Teregen, I want you to examine Flynn, and do what you can about his wounds."

The doctor curled his lips. "He's a prisoner."

"Not anymore," she responded. "I will wait outside. Joseph, please stay here to ensure the doctor takes good care of Flynn."

"Your Highness—" the frustration in Joseph's voice made Flynn smile.

Amber waved him away. "I know, you can't leave my side. I'll leave the door open and stand to the side so Flynn has privacy, and you can watch us both." She strode out of the room, far more confident than she'd been during his mockery of a trial. Something had happened in the past couple of days to change her.

Flynn wanted to kiss her. She was marvellous. The doctor poked his arm, bringing him back to reality. "Take off your shirt, man."

Flynn did as he asked, and the doctor examined the cuts which had become infected. He smeared some sweet-smelling ointment on them and then prodded his ribs. Flynn grunted as pain pierced him, stealing his breath.

Teregen grunted. "May be broken. Nothing we can

do about that."

By the time he'd finished his examination, Percy was back, the dark expression on his face revealing Amber had been correct. The prince waved the doctor and Joseph out of the room. "You've got away this time," he growled at Flynn. "Next time I'll make sure Amber never finds out you've been arrested."

Great. He'd made an enemy of the most powerful man in the city. "Your Highness, I assure you, I'm innocent."

Percy rolled his eyes and stormed out.

Flynn reached for his shirt when he heard a gasp. Amber stood in the doorway, her eyes wide, staring at his black and blue chest. She hurried over. "I'm so sorry they hurt you." Gently, she brushed one of his bruises, her touch so light it warmed his body. He resisted the urge to hold her hand there, ask her to examine all his injuries. He was a fool. She was an innocent and a princess. It was unlikely she realised what her touch did to him.

Joseph cleared his throat. "Your Highness, perhaps Flynn might be cold." He held Flynn's possessions including the telescope he'd borrowed from Nate.

She snatched her hand away, and he missed her touch. "Yes, of course. My apologies." She gestured for him to dress and turned her back while he did so.

Sweet that she would give him a measure of privacy, even though she'd seen him shirtless. He threw his shirt back on. He wanted her theory behind the drought, but she didn't seem to trust her guard. "Am I free to go?"

She pursed her lips, glancing at Joseph. "Yes. I'll walk you to the gate."

"Lead the way." He winced at the ache in his chest, and pushed through it.

She led him out of the prison cells, and Joseph handed him the telescope and Flynn's tool belt with his chisel and hammer. When they reached a wider corridor, she gestured for her guard to stay back. "I have been reading reports from the past few years," she said. "There appears to be a link between the fae leaving their lands and the crops failing."

He blinked. "The fae have left?"

"Or been forced out, but I can't find any evidence of where they've gone. Do you have any contacts who might help?"

He hadn't seen his stone supplier in over a year, but he would know the fate of the mountain fae as he quarried the stone from them. "Perhaps." Roley would know people as well.

"Good. I'm working to get the food in the warehouse distributed throughout the city, but it will take me more time. We need to figure out a way for you to get messages to me."

He glanced behind. "You don't trust your guard?"

She sighed. "I'm not sure. Percy can order Joseph to tell him everything I'm doing, and Joseph can't disobey him."

The options weren't great. "I could send a couple of homeless kids with messages, but are they likely to be passed on to you?"

She shook her head. "Percy won't let anything get through to me."

"It's a pity I can't shoot an arrow," Flynn murmured.

"What?"

He flushed, not realising he'd spoken aloud. Would she throw him back in prison if he mentioned he'd seen her in her bedroom?

"Flynn, if you have an idea, please tell me." She placed a hand on his and it was impossible to fight the earnestness in her warm brown eyes.

"The night they arrested me I saw you standing at a window in the castle. If I knew someone who could shoot an arrow accurately, I could send a message that way."

Amber frowned. "My room faces the hill."

He nodded. "I was in the trees there, getting closer to the warehouses to investigate what was inside."

She was silent a moment. "Perhaps it would be better if we found someone we can trust who can travel between the palace and the city. Do you know of any girls who need a job?"

He laughed. "Only about a hundred."

"My personal maid was called home to care for her sick mother," Amber said. "I never replaced her because I've spent my days with the Queen and used her maid when I need something."

Janice would be perfect. "My friend, Janice, has worked as a maid."

"Wonderful." She hesitated and glanced at her guard. "Joseph, I'm hiring a maid. Where should I send her?"

Joseph's eyebrows raised. "A maid, Your Highness?"

"Yes."

Flynn was impressed Amber didn't explain herself.

"She would need a permission pass to enter the castle, and then she would report to the kitchens."

"Where do I get a permission pass?"

"You can write one, Your Highness."

"Lovely." They headed up some stairs and into a sitting room far more lavish than anything Flynn had ever seen. The rich red satin brocade covering the settee had no signs of ageing, and the desk had to be made of launda wood, which was far more valuable than any other type of wood. At the desk, she pulled out a sheet of parchment and dipped her quill into ink.

"Does the pass need to say anything in particular?"

"No, it simply needs to have your seal on it." Joseph glanced at Flynn. "Your Highness, it isn't appropriate for you to be alone with a young man."

She didn't look up. "We're not alone. You're here."

Flynn kept his distance to appease the guard. A curl fell loose around Amber's face and she pushed it back impatiently as she wrote, her strokes confident and fast. His admiration for her grew. When she was done, she scattered sand across the document. "Flynn, come here."

Joseph moved with him, and Amber shooed him back. "Stay there, Joseph."

"Your Highness, he could still be a threat to you."

She pressed her lips together. "Have you heard from your family, Joseph?"

He blinked at the change in topic. "Yes, Your Highness. I received a letter yesterday."

"Are they still in danger of eviction?"

"No, Your Highness. They asked me to thank you profusely for interceding."

Flynn was missing something here.

"Will you tell my brother what I did?" she asked.

"I doubt he would be interested, Your Highness."

"And if he asks?" Amber pressed.

"Then I will tell him."

"What if I asked you not to say anything?"

Joseph shifted. "I cannot disobey an order from the man your father left in charge."

She nodded. "And that is why you're staying over there while I speak with Flynn."

Joseph opened and closed his mouth twice, and then gave a small nod. "Wise, Your Highness."

Amber patted the chair next to her and Flynn sat. "Will it be safe for Janice to go into the markets by herself?"

He shrugged. "I don't know, Your Highness. If she's dressed in the royal livery she might be safe, or it might make her a target."

She sighed. "I'd prefer fewer people involved, and a guard is likely to report her movements to my brother."

Now she was aware of what was occurring in

Bermont, she was quick to understand the situation. He was impressed. "You give her leave to visit her friends once a week on the Shelterer's Day," he suggested. "She could wear normal clothes and take your messages to my house." And he'd get Dietmar or Nate to make sure Percy's men didn't follow her.

"A good idea." She tipped the sand from the document and folded it before heating some wax. "What do we do if you need to speak to me urgently?"

"I can send a message via your window," Flynn said. "At night, I'll get someone to flash a light three times in the woods behind the hill if I need to contact you. You or Janice just need to go to the window at sunset and before you retire for the night."

She sealed the document and handed it to him. "All right, however, if the matter is urgent, then you can use this to get into the palace." She wrote another permission pass.

He smiled. "I suspect your brother would arrest me on sight."

"Then you can send one of your friends in your stead." She sealed the other document and gave it to him. "I didn't ask you whether you can write."

"I'm literate, Your Highness. Though some messages may be best committed to memory."

She gave him a piece of parchment. "Write something for me so I recognise your handwriting. I would hate to be duped by someone pretending to be you."

Duped. Utterly charmed by her, he did as she asked.

"Is there anything I have missed?" she asked.

"No, Your Highness. I will investigate what has happened to the fae and will send word about city events. I suspect it won't be long before Crane disrupts things."

"Keep me advised and be careful. My brother might order someone to follow you when you leave."

She was right. And he would disappear if they caught

him again. "I'll send a weekly report to you via Janice," he said. "If you don't receive it, you may like to search your dungeons for me again."

Her smile was radiant. "I will. Thank you, Flynn, for bringing this to my attention."

"Thank you for caring, Your Highness."

She stood and accompanied him to the palace gates. He bowed to her again, hoping it wasn't the last time he would see her face.

Chapter 22

Flynn moved as fast as his injured ribs would allow him after he left the palace, heading for the markets where he could get lost in the crowds. He spotted the guards following him almost immediately. They hadn't even changed out of their palace uniform, so they were easy to track. But Flynn wouldn't underestimate Percy. Perhaps those men were supposed to keep his attention while others followed him.

He couldn't outrun them, so he used his knowledge of the city to evade them. At the markets, he didn't dare acknowledge Roley, though their eyes met. Flynn recognised the concern in them, shook his head, and moved in the opposite direction. He would get word to Roley later.

Weaving through the queues of people, he used them to block his passage from his pursuers. He ducked down an alley which led to a five-way road junction, and broke into a run, holding his ribs and gritting his teeth at the pain. At the junction he checked behind him, saw the guards coming and ducked down the road with the most branches. He chose paths at random and finally lost the guards.

Moving quickly, he went to Dietmar's usual haunt. The youth was hanging out at the corner and his eyes widened in concern. "Where have you been?"

"I was arrested," Flynn said. "Walk with me."

"You look like bog marsh." The youth followed him towards the docks. "I've been trying to find you for days."

"How long since I asked you to watch the House of Pleasures?"

"A week. You were right, they moved the girls, but only to another house a block away. The House of Delights."

At least they were still in the city. "I'll do what I can to help them. I have another job if you want it."

"Does it pay?" Dietmar asked.

"Yes. A copper a day."

"What is it?"

He checked behind them to ensure they weren't being followed. "I've got Janice a job at the palace. She has time on Shelterer's Day to return to my house and I need you to go with her, make sure she isn't followed, and protect her if she gets attacked."

Dietmar frowned. "Who would attack her?"

"Anyone desperate enough. I'll ask Nate to join you."

"All right. The whole day?"

"Yes, until she returns to the palace."

"What's going on, Flynn?"

He pursed his lips. He didn't enjoy asking Dietmar to do something without explanation, but the fewer people who knew, the safer everyone would be. "I can't say right now. Do you trust me?"

The youth nodded. "You've been good to us."

They found Nate sitting outside the harbour master's office. Nate rushed to him. "Where have you been? Do you have the telescope?"

Flynn pulled it out of his jacket pocket and handed it

to him. "I'm sorry about the delay. They arrested me."

"The warehouse was full?"

He didn't want to lie to the boy. "I was spotted, and they thought I was a spy."

"I want to hear everything, but let me return this to the harbour master. He was furious." Nate ran off and a few minutes later returned.

"Can I drag you away from the docks one day a week?" Flynn asked him. "I've got a job."

"Does it pay?"

"Yeah. You'll be working with Dietmar."

"All right."

Together they walked back into the city towards Flynn's house, and he explained what was required of them.

"How'd you get Janice a job in the palace if you were a prisoner?" Nate asked.

"Princess Amber interceded on my behalf. We met when she was in the markets last week."

"Lucky," Nate said.

He entered the house and was surrounded by cries of welcome. He winced as the hugs pressed on bruises and cuts. Eventually, he found Janice in the kitchen.

"Flynn! Where have you been?"

"In the palace dungeons," he replied, hugging her. "Has everything been all right, here?"

"Yes. We were all worried when we hadn't seen you in days."

"I have a job for you," he said. "Lady's maid at the palace."

She gaped at him. "What?"

"For Princess Amber."

Janice laughed. "Only you could get arrested and come out of it with a job with one of the most important people in the country."

He smiled. "It's a live-in position if you want it." He

wrote a note on a piece of paper and folded it in half.

"Of course I want it. I might get better food." She glanced around. "But what about the kids?"

He hadn't considered that. "Charmaine's still here…" Who else could take care of the younger ones?

"If there's a bed spare, I'll take it," Dietmar said. "I can watch the kids."

Nate pouted in disappointment.

"Is their room for them both?" he asked Janice.

"If they don't mind sharing a single bed." She grinned.

Nate raised his eyebrows at Dietmar. "I don't care if it's a roof over my head."

"Yeah, we can deal."

Great. The two of them would be good with the younger kids. "Get your things," Flynn told Janice. "I'll take you to the palace."

In no time, they were on their way back to the palace, Flynn scanning the surroundings for guards. "The princess has asked me to find some information for her," he said. "I'm to report to her once a week and you'll pick up the report when you visit the house."

"Why don't you send it to her?" Janice asked.

"Prince Percy will intercept anything I give to the guards, and she won't get it." He gestured to Nate and Dietmar. "These two will follow you when you leave the palace to ensure you're safe and not followed. Though the princess pardoned me, I'm still on the prince's bog marsh list." He handed her the note and the permission pass. "This is the first report for the princess. Ava is being held at the House of Delights. The sealed message is to get you into the palace. You'll go around the back to the kitchens when you arrive."

"What's the princess like?"

Amber's image floated in his mind, making him smile. "Innocent, but determined to do what's right by her people now she knows something is wrong."

Janice grinned. "She sounds like my kind of woman."

"She's interesting," he agreed. "I have more people I need to visit." And he didn't want to get too close to the palace. "I wish you well."

"May you find shelter, Flynn."

He nodded. "You too." The pain in his ribs was inconsequential. With the princess's help, he'd improved the lives of three people today. That was worth any pain. Flynn headed back to the tradesmen's quarter to find out more about the fae.

***

By the end of the day Flynn had put together a startling picture which made him feel ill. Every tradesperson he spoke to said the same thing. The fae had cut off contact and supplies were non-existent. One man, a carpenter who specialised in launda wood, had travelled to the launda wood forest and been horrified to discover much of the land by the river had been cleared to set up sawmills. That had been six months ago.

Around the same time, the silk merchants had received their last bolts of silk, but there'd been no indication the fae wouldn't continue to supply the fabric. Those trading in bellar spice had said the crops had failed and there was little seed to try again, and from the mountain fae there'd simply been no word.

He walked back towards the docks to find out whether his message to Amber had received any response yet. The street was full of onlookers and he shifted through them so he could see what was happening. Ava stood in front of the whorehouse with several other young girls, their expressions as blank as they had been when he'd seen them a week ago.

One watchman stood with them, and another two guarded the door into the building. Just inside, Drury spoke with Prince Percy. Flynn frowned.

"What happened?" a woman next to him asked.

The man beside her answered. "They've been forcing underaged children to work there."

She huffed in outrage. "Those poor girls. Someone should fetch their parents."

"They're orphans," Flynn said.

The woman turned to him. "Have they no one to take care of them?"

He shook his head. They were going to need support, the type he couldn't provide, when they came off the drug. He hoped they wouldn't remember much about their time there. Percy came out of the whorehouse, but there was no sign of Drury. Percy said something to the Watch commander, and the man called, "Go about your business, folks. Show's over."

"Aren't they going to arrest someone?" Flynn demanded, outrage filling him. He hadn't meant to yell it, but Percy spotted him. Their eyes met and Percy's gaze shifted to hatred. Curse it. Percy lifted his arm to point.

"Demand they arrest Drury," he whispered to the woman.

"Stop that man!" Percy's command rang out through the still air.

Flynn ran, but behind him he heard the woman cry, "How will you punish the man who did this to the poor girls?" The crowd murmured in agreement.

He checked over his shoulder, as the crowd moved forward, blocking the Watch's attempts to get through.

He smiled and disappeared into the dusk.

***

Janice was a competent lady's maid and an excellent conversationalist. Amber was thrilled when she arrived and told her Flynn had discovered where they were keeping the children. She'd interrupted another council meeting to demand action, and Percy had no choice but to do something.

The first Shelterer's Day, Janice returned with news the Watch had arrested the culprit and he was now in the city gaol. Amber was tempted to throw him into the dungeons, but she'd been so vocal about moving the remaining prisoners out of them that it would be hypocritical to send him there.

Amber had been sickened to find several marsh fae in the dungeons as well, pale and weak. As soon as they'd been transferred to the ground floor, the greyish colour came back to their skin. But she hadn't had a chance to speak to them about why they had been arrested.

Her mother had deteriorated again, and Amber had spent most of her day by her bed, trying to make her comfortable. She feared leaving her bedside for even a moment and sent Janice to the library to get the books she needed. So far she hadn't been stopped and Amber had learnt some very interesting things about the law.

Amber wiped the perspiration from her mother's brow, but her mother didn't wake. There was a knock on the door and at Amber's call, her aunt Kleo walked in. Amber smiled. "What are you doing here? I thought you weren't to leave your rooms."

"It has been twelve months since my husband died." Sorrow crossed Kleo's face, but it meant she was officially out of mourning.

"It is good to see you."

"How is Emeline?"

"Not good. She's barely woken all week. Perhaps the trip to the rock garden wasn't as good for her as I thought."

"You look tired, dear. Why don't I sit with her, and you can take some air?"

The air wasn't revitalising, but it would be nice to see something other than these four walls, and Amber still wanted to question the fae prisoners. "Will you fetch me if anything changes?"

"Immediately."

Amber stood and washed her hands, then headed outside. Joseph fell in behind her. She wished she could trust him not to inform Percy of her actions. It would make her life far easier.

Still, she walked down to the gaol cells, brushing by the guards who stood at the doors. Three cells in and she stopped. The marsh fae both sat on a bed, not speaking, not doing anything except staring at the wall.

"I wish to speak with them," she told the guard who was spluttering behind her. "Bring them into the interrogation room."

The fae glanced up and the older one frowned.

The guard protested. "Your Highness—"

"Do as she commands," Joseph interrupted him.

She peered at her guard, surprised, and he smirked. "They need to learn to obey you."

Amber appreciated him standing up for her, though she wished it wasn't necessary. She stood aside while the guards transferred the fae and chained them to a ring on the floor so they couldn't move far. That was wise. "Leave us."

She shooed the guards out the door. "You too," she told Joseph.

He nodded, though he seemed unhappy about the request.

Amber estimated the length of chain and then moved her chair, so she was outside its range. "May I have your names?"

The older fae hesitated. "Is it not recorded, Your Highness?"

"No."

"I told you we would disappear from history, Father," the younger fae said.

His father shushed him. "I am Luka, and my son is Eban."

"Tell me, what are the charges against you?"

Luka grimaced. "We were arrested for disagreeing with the marsh fae high elder."

She frowned. "Isn't that a matter for the fae to deal with?"

"Not when there are other marsh fae who agree with us," Eban said. "Better we get forgotten."

Amber knew nothing of fae politics, had thought disagreements were few because they were forced to live in such close proximity. "What did you disagree about?"

"The use of coal, the advancement of technology," Luka told her. "Though it has allowed us to explore more of the country, it comes at a cost. The smog is killing people, and the technology pollutes the river. The country is out of balance, and we must set it right."

She frowned. "Is that why you can leave the marshland—because of the smog?"

Luka nodded. "It contains coal particles which come from the marshes, so it is like being surrounded by our land."

Interesting. "Why doesn't your high elder agree that the country is out of balance? Surely he can see the damage being caused?"

"The high elder is selfish and resentful. For decades he's felt stifled by the agreement between fae and man and has wanted to travel. King Tremont agreed to do away with the agreement, and the result is what you see from your window."

"And not all marsh fae agree with him?"

"He has a group of core followers, but many of us disagree, and many more are too afraid to speak up," Eban answered.

"Is there anything you can do to stop him?"

"Can you stop your father, Your Highness?" Luka

countered.

She sat back as the magnitude of the situation washed over her. Her father knew what he was doing, even if perhaps he didn't believe there was a connection. Would she stand up to him? Could she do anything to stop him?

There was one thing. It would allow her to change things, at least while her father was away at war. Perhaps it would be enough to make a difference. But if she went through with it, it would mean leaving her mother alone.

Could she ask Kleo to take over her duty? "Perhaps," she said. "Do you know where the other fae have gone?"

The fae exchanged glances. They weren't sure whether they could trust her.

"I'm tempted to lock you in here since you seem to enjoy the ambiance so much," Percy growled.

Amber flinched and shifted to the door where he stood. "I'm merely seeing to the welfare of my people."

"The fae aren't your people."

She shrugged. "They live in Molanka. Can I help you with anything?"

"You can stop interfering in politics. This is no concern of yours. Why aren't you with Mother?"

"Aunt Kleo is visiting. Her mourning period is at an end, and she is keen to catch up with what has been happening in the palace."

He grunted. "I don't have time to keep coming down here when you decide you want to talk with the unwashed."

"I didn't ask you to, brother. I'm capable of visiting prisoners with Joseph by my side. Besides, I'm almost finished. Shall I stop by the council rooms when I'm done?"

He glanced at the fae and then back at her. "Do that." He strode away.

Something had happened since she'd seen him last, something that made him not so angry at her. Had realising Flynn had told the truth softened him towards her?

Amber turned back to the fae. "I understand you don't know who you can trust," she said. "My goal is to find the fae, correct the wrongs my father has done to them, and heal Molanka."

The son opened his mouth to speak, and the father elbowed him. "It is a worthy goal, Your Highness. One I hope you will succeed in."

The son pressed his lips together. She wouldn't get anything more from him. "I pardon you both," she said. "You may return home or wherever you need to go to help your people." She asked the guards to unchain them. Then she said, "If there is anything I can do to help you, send word to Flynn Stonemason. I gather he is rather well known in the city." Janice had told her so.

The son nodded, and she said to the guards, "See them safely out of the castle."

She returned upstairs, her thoughts on what the fae had said. She would be going against her father. There was no telling how long the war would last and whether it would succeed.

She pushed open the door to her mother's room. Kleo looked up, her expression worried. "I was just about to send for you."

"What's happened?" Amber's heart raced, and she hurried over to her mother's bedside.

"I can't wake her. Her meal arrived, but she won't stir."

"Have you sent for the doctor?"

"Yes."

Her mother was milky pale, and she didn't move as Amber shook her. "Mother, wake up."

No response.

Amber gently lifted her eyelids and her mother stared unseeingly at her.

The doctor strode into the room. "What now?"

"She won't wake," Amber said.

He pushed her out of the way and examined the queen. After a few minutes, he sighed. "There's nothing I can do, I'm afraid. If she doesn't wake, she won't last more than a few days without food or water."

No. There had to be a cure. She refused to believe her mother would die.

She ran from the room and flew down the stairs, bursting into the council rooms.

Percy glared at her. "What now?"

"Mother won't wake," she said, panting. "Father or Baldrick must have sent word by now. Doctor Teregen says she has only days."

Grief crossed his face. "They sent a ship full of food, but no word on a cure."

It wasn't good enough. Tartalan was supposed to be a land of magic and healing. Their nastin plant healed many common ailments. She glanced out the window and spotted the rock garden. The last time they were there, her mother had revived. Amber hurried back, her breath coming in gasps. Kleo still sat by the queen. "Joseph, I need you to carry Mother to the rock garden."

Joseph hesitated. "Should she be moved?"

"You heard what the doctor said. She's likely going to die in a few days. Carrying her to the garden will not hurt her." Amber prayed it was true.

He did as she asked and Amber, Janice and Kleo followed him down into the garden. He sat on the largest rock where Emeline had sat the last time she was there and held her on his lap.

Amber hovered, waiting, watching.

Did her skin have a little more colour to it, or was that wishful thinking?

Amber checked her mother's eyes, and they focused on Amber for a split second before darting away. "It's helping."

"But what is it about the garden that helps her?" Kleo asked.

Could it be the scent of a flower? Nothing had bloomed yet. It certainly wasn't the smoggy air, only marsh fae enjoyed it.

"Your Highness, if I may ask?" Janice ventured.

"Yes?"

"Is your mother part fae?"

Amber frowned. "No." She glanced at her aunt for confirmation, and she shook her head. "Why do you ask?"

Janice peered at her feet. "I've heard stories about the mountain fae. A quarry man once found a mountain fae on the shores of a river. She'd been washed down by a storm and was weak like your mother. He carried her to his wagon and put her amongst the rocks, planning to take her to the nearest village and find her transport home. Within only a few minutes she was alert and chatting to him. She asked for a piece of rock when they arrived in the village and travelled home. The next time he went to the quarry he found her healthy and happy."

Her mother came from a manor house close to the mountains. Perhaps there could be fae in her heritage somewhere, but she thought fae blood had to be activated. If the king knew his wife was part fae, he'd be horrified.

"Please don't mention this to anyone, Janice. The king would not be happy." She glanced at the others. "That goes for you both as well. Not a word, and that's a royal order."

Both nodded.

Her mother's cheeks had the pale blush of a pink rose to them. Whatever it was, it was helping her. But they couldn't shift the rocks inside. "We must set up a bedroom here," she said. "We'll run some covers across the courtyard to protect it from the elements and erect walls for privacy."

"Your Highness, the doctor and the prince will never approve," Joseph said.

"Look at my mother," she ordered. "Tell me she doesn't seem healthier than she did ten minutes ago."

Joseph sighed. "She does."

"They can't argue with that, and I can make it law." She turned to her aunt. "Kleo, get the servants to source the equipment we need. Joseph, you stay here with Mother. Janice, fetch more blankets from Mother's room."

"Where are you going?" Joseph called.

"To take control." She strode back to the council room, her heart beating in time with her stride. This time the guards opened the doors for her before she arrived.

Percy groaned.

"Section 17 of the Law of the Lands states at a time of war, the royal family may divide the management of the country amongst themselves," she announced and took a moment to calm her breathing. "As such, I submit my petition for control over palace affairs, Bermont city, and to be liaison to the fae and all management regarding them."

Percy glared at the steward, who opened a book and read a few pages before nodding. "She has the right."

"Don't be ridiculous," Percy said. "The fae are gone, and the palace has always been your domain. There's no need to be so official."

Amber fought not to show her eagerness. "Then you have no issues with my request?"

"I deny your request, because it is stupid."

She raised her eyebrows at the steward and he sighed. "The remaining family members may disagree on which section of the country each other manages, but they cannot deny the request outright. If you refuse her the fae, the city and the palace, she may choose another area of the country."

"I could add the lands along the river to my request and leave you with the surrounding country," Amber said.

He swore. "So be it. You can liaise with the fae and have control of the palace, but not the city. It's mine."

Amber hesitated. She couldn't distribute the warehouse food to the city if she didn't have control of Bermont. "The city isn't much extra, brother."

"No," he growled.

She closed her eyes. If she could protect her mother and reach the fae, perhaps it would solve the city's problems. She inclined her head. "All right." At the door, she turned. "Just so you know, brother. I have moved Mother's bedroom into the rock garden should you wish to visit her."

He spluttered, but she didn't allow him time to answer. She swept out of the room and grinned.

She would save their dying land.

Thank you for reading!

I hope you enjoyed Kingdom of Secrets. If you did like it, and want to show your support, there are a couple of things you could do. The first is to leave a review wherever you bought it. I love reading my reviews and it gives me a real boost when I'm having a difficult writing day.

If you're not comfortable with that, you could always recommend the book to friends, add it to lists over on GoodReads, or ask your library to buy a copy. Every little bit helps more people discover my books so I can keep writing them.

Acknowledgements

Kingdom of Secrets has been a long time coming. It started out as a single book, but the story grew so it was not able to be contained by so few pages. The storyline also jumped from country to country to see what everyone was up to, but some beta readers felt it to confusing which is how it ended up in three parts. Rest assured their stories will merge as the novels progress.

I want to thank my critique group and beta readers for all their feedback and I want to thank my editors, Ann Harth and Teena Raffa-Mulligan for their work.

Realm of Lies

Fae Touched #2

Book 2 is coming soon. To be notified when it's released, make sure you sign up to my New Release newsletter. This newsletter only sends notification when a book goes up for pre-order and when it is released, so you'll only get a couple of emails a year. Sign up on my website https://claireleggett.com/new-release-sign-up/

www.ingramcontent.com/pod-product-compliance
Lightning Source LLC
Chambersburg PA
CBHW060754190726
48285CB00002B/431